JONATHAN PINNOCK ha~~~~~~~~~ ~~ories and poems published in place~ ~oth exalted and downright insalubrious. He has even won a prize or two and had work broadcast on BBC Radio 4. He is married with two slightly grown-up children.

JONATHAN PINNOCK

Mrs Darcy
versus the
Aliens

LONDON

PUBLISHED BY PROXIMA AN IMPRINT OF SALT PUBLISHING
Acre House, 11–15 William Road, London NW1 3ER
United Kingdom

© Jonathan Pinnock, 2011

Printed in the UK by CPI Cox & Wyman

Typeset in Bembo 12 / 13.5

ISBN 978-1-907773-13-6 paperback

1 3 5 7 9 8 6 4 2

Mrs Darcy

versus the

Aliens

Prologue

E LIZABETH DARCY STIRRED in her sleep and felt the soft breeze on the back of her neck. She was awake in an instant. The curtains were wafting backwards and forwards in an elegant moonlit dance. How long had the window been open? She sat up in bed, her heart beating a furious tattoo, and her eyes scanned the gloomy room to see if there was anything out of place. Once she had established that there appeared to be no intruder compromising the security of her chamber, her breathing began to settle down to a more regular pace.

Mrs Darcy swung her legs out of bed and stood up. She lit a candle, and it was at that point that she noticed the letter.

It was on the floor underneath the window. Putting down the candle, she rushed over and picked the letter up, tearing at the seal.

Mrs D, it said. *Come at once to Macfadyen's quarry. This time I have irrefutable evidence. Yours ever, W.*

Her hand shot to her mouth to prevent herself from crying out. She ran to the window and peered out into the night. For a moment, she was convinced she could hear hoofbeats, but if there were any, they were soon swallowed up in the wind.

Mrs Darcy threw on a coat over her nightclothes, grabbed her riding boots and eased open her bedroom door. She paused outside the door to Mr Darcy's bedroom, and her hand moved towards his door. Then she shook her head. This was something she had to do by herself.

She crept down the grand staircase, and headed out into the night through the kitchen, pausing only to don her riding boots.

Glancing around to be sure she wasn't being observed, she made her way to the stables and found her favourite mount, Keira.

Speaking softly to Kiera to calm her down, she led the dappled grey out and away from Pemberley, until she was far enough from the house to mount in safety. Then she leapt up into the saddle, kicked away with the stirrups and urging Keira on towards Macfadyen's quarry at as fast a pace as she dared in the half-light.

Mrs Darcy reached the quarry within half an hour and dismounted a little way before she reached it, next to a small clump of trees. There, she tied the horse up and continued on towards the quarry on foot. She was a hundred yards from its rim when she caught sight of a man lurking beside a tree in the middle distance, his face darkened by a cloud passing over the moon.

She immediately crouched down behind a bush, but it was too late. He had seen her.

The man motioned to her to stay still and be quiet. Then she saw something begin to emerge over the lip of the quarry. In the dim light, she couldn't make out what it was, but it was heading towards the stranger.

She saw him draw his sword. A gust of wind caught her off guard, and whilst Mrs Darcy was struggling to keep hold of her bonnet, she missed the start of the confrontation. An unearthly roar merged with the sound of the gale as the mysterious swordsman hacked away at whatever was attacking him.

Something flew up in the air and landed at her feet. It

seemed part of some kind of tentacle. It hissed as it landed, spurting out a bubbling yellow liquid. Up ahead, the man continued to hack away with his sword, and another revolting body part spun off and caught Mrs Darcy full in the face. It smelt foul. She wiped it away and spat on the ground in an unladylike manner. It was probably a good thing that Mr Darcy had not accompanied her, since he tended to disapprove of that kind of behaviour.

The fight ended as abruptly as it had begun

The victor sheathed his sword and came over towards her. She struggled to her feet, attempting to brush the dirt and slime off her clothing.

'Good evening, Mrs Darcy,' said the man. 'I take it you received my note?'

'Good evening, Mr Wickham.' she replied, looking down at the tentacle still wriggling at her feet. 'Once again, sir, I find myself showered with the debris of your encounters.'

Mr Wickham gave a slight bow. 'I most humbly apologise, ma'am. I had not expected to be attacked on this occasion. Thankfully, I did at least succeed in dispatching the fiend.'

'Would that the aim of your affection were as clean and as true as that of your sword, Mr Wickham.'

'Mrs Darcy, as I have tried to explain on several occasions, my intentions towards your family have always been entirely honourable.'

'Indeed, sir? Then you have certainly kept your honour well hidden.' She softened slightly. 'So, to what do I owe the pleasure of our encounter on this windy night? I trust you are not leading me on yet another merry dance.'

'No indeed, Mrs Darcy,' said Mr Wickham, 'I hope you know me well enough by now to trust that I shall do no such thing. No, come this way towards the quarry. I

3

have something to show you. This time I really do believe I know what has happened to poor Lydia.'

For a moment, Elizabeth was lost for words. 'Pray do not trifle with me, Mr Wickham,' she managed at last.

'Believe me, Mrs Darcy,' replied Wickham, 'I would never trifle with you on the subject of your sister. Remember she was—is—also my wife.'

He paused, then looked her full in the eye.

'The truth is out there,' he added significantly. 'Though it is not yet universally acknowledged.'

Chapter One

A problem of succession — Mr Bingley's big opportunity — Mystery at the quarry — Mr Wickham is patched up — Much misunderstanding in Whitechapel

T HE SOFT MORNING sun cast a soothing glow over the Pemberley breakfast table. Elizabeth stifled a yawn and helped herself to another slice of pound cake. Her head was less sore than it had been when she awoke, but it was still throbbing regularly in time with the clock on the mantelpiece. On mornings like these, she was grateful for her husband's habitual taciturnity. However, at that point, Fitzwilliam Darcy gave a little cough, and her ears pricked up in response.

'Are you quite well, my dear?' he asked. 'You seem a little distracted this morning.'

'I am perfectly well, my beloved,' she reassured him. 'However, I fear I did not sleep at all well last night.'

'Ah,' said her husband, satisfied with her reply. She could tell that he hadn't quite finished, and a few moments later, there was another discreet cough.

'I have to go to London for a few days today,' he remarked.

'So soon after your last visit?'

'Yes, my dear. Business.'

'Really? You gentlemen certainly know how to enjoy yourselves.'

As usual, she could tell from his face that he wasn't entirely certain as to whether he should treat this comment at face value or as a joke.

'Indeed,' he concluded after some thought. 'We do. However, I am sure you do not wish our breakfast to be sullied with tiresome talk about investments and suchlike.'

'I most certainly do not,' agreed Elizabeth, with some feeling. Silence hung in the air for a few moments longer, and then her husband coughed again. She almost made some comment about getting the physician in to see if there was anything that could be done for him, but thought better of it.

'I . . . I have been giving some thought to another pressing matter,' said Mr Darcy. He seemed reluctant to elucidate.

'Go on,' Elizabeth urged him.

'As you will be aware,' he continued, 'my estate is worth in excess of ten thousand pounds a year,. It is therefore incumbent on me, now that I have a wife, to consider . . . to consider . . . the question of succession.'

'Meaning?' said Elizabeth, raising one eyebrow.

'Meaning I wish to . . . I wish to . . . re-open the question of an heir.'

Elizabeth considered this for a moment or two. 'My dear Fitzy, I would be very happy to assist in this. Although, from what I understand, the procedure would of necessity require both of us to be involved—indeed, that both of us should be in considerable proximity to each other for the duration of the procedure. And if you intend to be in London for the foreseeable future, this would seem to pose an insurmountable barrier to such a conception.'

Mr Darcy came close to smiling at this. 'My dear Elizabeth, you tease me,' he said. 'It can wait until my return.' He gave her a meaningful look. 'And when we . . . would you . . . would you mind . . . wearing that—?'

'The one with the—?'

'Yes, yes, that one. That one. Yes, that's the one.' He was deep in thought again. 'And would you like me to—?'

'No, no, it's quite all right,' she replied, and then instantly regretted her hasty negative. Though even in the summer months, the wet shirt was becoming a bit of a dampener on proceedings.

Following Mr Darcy's departure for London, Elizabeth strolled out into the gardens and settled beneath a canopy to read the letter from Jane.

My Dearest Lizzy,

I hope this finds you well and happy. We feel truly blessed here at Netherfield. Little Lydia grows bigger every day and we surely expect her to walk soon. She misses her favourite Auntie very much and is looking forward to seeing her again soon. (By the by, I have to add that Mother is continually asking when you and Mr D are going to bring her a grandchild as well, so be warned.)

As it happens, Charlie and I may well be coming up to your part of the world in the next few weeks, so you may indeed get to see Little L soon. The reason is terribly complicated and all to do with the business of men—but I have been trying to take an interest for Charlie's sake. I wonder sometimes if he is as naïve as I am in the ways of the world, and perhaps we both need to look out for each other. He can be so easily influenced.

Anyway, it seems a Mr Bradford, whose acquaintance

we made at a dinner party recently, has taken quite a shine to my Charlie, and as you know, he finds it difficult to make friends, so this pleases me greatly. This Mr Bradford has a significant number of mining interests in Derbyshire, but the problem is, although he possesses much skill as a prospector (indeed, he has apparently found a major untapped gold seam just south of Ashbourne), he lacks the necessary capital for investing in new equipment. And this is where Charlie comes in.

It's all terribly exciting. Bradford and Charlie are forming a company together to exploit this mine, and we had a long conversation over supper the other evening about what the company should be called. My suggestion was 'Northern Rock', because after all, it's rock that they're mining and it's in the North. I was a little disappointed that Charlie laughed at this, but Mr Bradford thought it was a capital suggestion, as a result of which Charlie sulked for the rest of the evening.

But I don't suppose it really matters whether the company is called 'Northern Rock' or even just 'Bradford and Bingley', because with those two involved, it's bound to be a raging success.

Anyway, I must finish now. Little Lydia joins us in sending our love to you and Mr D, and I'll let you know when we are coming North to join the Derbyshire gold rush!

Elizabeth smiled. It would indeed be lovely to see Jane and Mr Bingley again, although Little Lydia could be somewhat wearisome. Every time she saw her niece, Elizabeth wondered if she would ever be cut out for motherhood and, truth be told, she had found the conversation at breakfast a little worrisome.

Sitting back in her chair, she began to wonder again

about everything she had seen last night. Or had it been some ghastly nightmare? How on earth had Wickham become involved in it too? What he had said about her sister had been truly disturbing—not to say grotesque and unbelievable.

No alternative lay before her. She would have to return to Macfadyen's quarry and investigate for herself. Only in broad daylight this time.

Elizabeth dismounted and tethered Keira to a convenient tree. The quarry looked very different in daylight. For one thing, there were teams of men at work, hewing whatever it was that they hewed out of the rock and then hauling it up the slope. For another, all traces of whatever she and Wickham had encountered last night had completely vanished. There was nothing left to see.

Elizabeth took her whip and thrashed about at the undergrowth, but there was not the slightest sign of anything untoward there—least of all a severed tentacle.

After a short while, she realised that she was being watched. Sitting on a log at the edge of the quarry was a man, puffing away at a pipe. Perhaps he might be able to help. She began to approach him, and then with a sinking feeling realised it was old Mr Firth, the local mentalist. She gave a deep sigh and turned away.

'Mis' Darcy!'

Don't waste your time, Lizzy, she told herself. Just don't. Walk away now. Forget last night. Admit that you imagined everything.

'Mis' Darcy! I seen you there!'

Oh, where was the harm in it?

Drawing closer to the old man, she caught a whiff of his revolting pipe. It smelt strongly of badger.

'Ha-har, Mis' Darcy!' said old Mr Firth.

'Hello, Mr Firth—' Mrs Darcy began, but the old man ignored her and continued with his speech.

'Reckon you'll be'm after the confabulation 'ere yon nether watch . . .'im a–lolloping like a good 'un, you'll see.' He nodded sagely. ''E were wearing them big breeches . . . I dun seen 'im . . . I dun seen 'im, y'know . . .'

Yes, conversations with old Mr Firth were very rarely fruitful.

'Mr Firth, I appreciate the good sense of much of what you say, and your speech as always demonstrates your supreme erudition. But I really would like to know if you've—'

'Blether, blether . . . rat–pack and fungible . . . todger, grommet and wallop . . . thrust upwards . . . yea, upwards . . .' (Here he gestured with his right hand.)

'Thrust?' said Elizabeth, hopeful.

Old Mr Firth nodded. 'Like a herring. A big round herring.'

'Oh.'

'And then he comes back into town. Walks right up the street . . . stark bollock naked.'

The latter part of this was delivered in a conspiratorial whisper. Elizabeth felt the old man's pungent breath waft into her face as he leant in close, and she recoiled.

She decided to adopt a firmer approach.

'Mr Firth, can you please tell me if you saw anything unusual hereabouts either last night or first thing this morning?'

The old man looked hard at her, then shook his head.

'Nope,' he admitted. 'But I were pissed as a fart last night,' he added.

Oh, this was hopeless. Back to Plan A, she thought. Go home, put feet up, and ignore any more cryptic messages from bloody Wickham. Have lots of babies and live happily ever after with Fitzy.

She turned to go. But as she did so, old Mr Firth suddenly leapt up off his log and grabbed her roughly by the shoulders.

'Unhand me, you filthy man!' she exclaimed, astonished.

But old Mr Firth held on, and in a strange, unearthly voice intoned: 'SHE IS RISEN! THE DARK WITCH IS COMING! SHE COMES TO CONQUER ALL!'

Elizabeth stared at him. 'I'm sorry?'

'Sorry what?' asked old Mr Firth, releasing his grip. 'Bugger me, I think I've done me back in.'

Then he slumped back on his log and began puffing at his pipe again.

The nurse dabbed away with the sponge at Wickham's shoulder. He winced in pain, but did not flinch.

'You have a gentle touch, nurse,' he remarked. 'What is your name?'

There was the slightest hesitation, which Wickham found rather fetching. 'I am Nurse Hathaway,' she conceded.

'Ah, Hathaway! Such a pretty name,' said Wickham. 'Do you have a Christian name as well?'

The girl gave a tinkling little laugh. 'Why yes, sir, of course I do. My name is Jane.'

'Another pretty name. Two pretty names, in fact, for the price of one. Come here: let me see you again, and verify that the person is indeed as pretty as her label.'

The girl stepped obediently in front of Wickham. 'I fear that I do not look very becoming in this uniform.'

'Oh, no, I assure you that you are most becoming,

Jane,' said Wickham. 'Most becoming. In fact, I shall call you Becoming Jane.'

'I am finished, sir. How are you feeling now?'

'To tell the truth, I feel a little stiffness coming on.'

The nurse rolled her eyes and shook her head. 'You know something?' she commented. 'You were doing so well up until then. But that line was as cheesy as Mrs Steadman's Stinking Bishop. Get your shirt back on, the Colonel'll be here any minute. I'll be seeing you.'

Wickham tried to think of something witty to say, but all he could come up with was 'Er—'

'ER?'

'Er . . . I'll be seeing you too, then, Nurse Hathaway,' he said.

As Wickham was pulling on his shirt, Colonel Sutherland stepped into the room.

'Ah, Wickham, my man!' he exclaimed. 'How are you, old thing? You took a bit of a risk last night.'

'Sir? This is a mere scratch. And I assure you that old Squiddy is no match for Wickham's flashing blade.'

'That wasn't what I meant and you know it. I was talking about the Darcy woman.'

'You know my views on this, sir. Mrs Elizabeth Darcy is central to our future strategy. Without her, yes, we may ultimately prevail. But many lives will be lost, and many great families corrupted and destroyed. With her working alongside us, we shall surely defeat this scourge before the year is out.'

'I understand. But are you sure your judgement is not clouded by past fancies?'

Wickham sighed and shook his head. 'No sir. Elizabeth is married now.'

'To a man you hate!'

'I do not hate Darcy, sir. Darcy hates me, it is true, for

what happened to his sister. But perhaps one day he will learn what I did.'

'What you did to save her? She was still probed, Wickham, and for that we can never forgive ourselves.'

'I know, sir. I know.'

'So did you tell her about Lydia?'

'I told her as much as I felt able.'

'Well, I hope you didn't go raising her hopes too much.' He was silent for a moment. 'This is a damnable business, it really is.'

'But with Elizabeth helping us . . .'

'No, not yet.' Colonel Sutherland held up his hand. 'We have other fish to fry. We have picked up some intelligence about unusual goings-on in the East End of London. Women disappearing, reports of apparitions, that sort of thing. Now of course, that probably goes on all of the time there, but something tells me there's more to this than meets the eye. I want you to go there under cover and see what you can find out. When you get back, we can resume the search for Agent Lydia. With or without her big sister.'

Later that night, in the labyrinthine streets around Whitechapel, Mary Ann Nichols leant against a wall and took a swig of cheap gin from her hip flask. Trade was poor tonight. Perhaps her clientele had been put off by the rumours that were circulating. Not that she believed in any of that rot. If you started to give credence to that kind of fancy, Gawd alone knew where it would end.

Then she heard the footsteps. They were somewhere between a fast walk and a slow run. More of a scurry, she thought.

You're wasting your time with this one, she thought, but nonetheless, she called out as the man came close.

''Ere! You! Fancy a good time?'

The man stopped and looked at her. He was of medium height, but held himself in a kind of upright crouching position. His hair was greasy and unkempt.

'I beg your pardon?'

'I said do you fancy a good time? We all need a good time every now and then, don't we,luv?'

'I'm not sure I catch your drift, young lady.'

'All right, I'll tell you what I do. I do *sous-pelisse*, I do straight French, red hot Dutch, Wellington's fancy—that's with or without the boots—but I don't do no Prussian.'

The man gaped at her.

'No, sorry, luv. Prussian's right out. Ever since the wimmin's sexual health team came round.'

'Madam, I am not at all interested in your offer. I am a missionary.'

Mary Ann laughed. 'Funny, we don't get much call for that these days. Still, takes all sorts, and at least I get to lie down. OK, this way, and I'll throw in a Belgian for free.' She made to take hold of the man's hand.

'No, madam. I have no intention of partaking of your sordid trade. My esteemed patroness would cast me to the four winds if I were to indulge in the pleasures of the flesh.' There was a particular relish in the way that the man pronounced the word 'flesh'.

'Oh, Gawd. I get it. You just want to talk. I get a few of those. So what's the problem? Wife don't understand you?'

The man bridled at this. 'The impertinence! Madam, I can assure you that my dear wife . . . is very . . . dear to me.'

'Then what is it you want? I 'aven't got all night, you know,' said Mary Ann. The man was getting on her nerves. At least two more potential punters had passed by on the other side of the street while they had been chatting. She was losing money, and if she didn't get in a few more jobs before the night was up, she wouldn't have enough to pay for a bed for the night.

'Young lady,' said the man, with an air of triumph in his voice, 'I have come to save you!'

'Save me from what?'

'Not save *from*, my dear, save *for*. Save you for the Lord! My patroness has charged me with establishing a mission for fallen women such as yourself.' He leant in closer. 'And I see that you have fallen a very long way indeed. I have found you not a moment too soon.'

And with this, he grabbed her by the arm and began to march her away.

'Oi, Mister,' said Mary Ann, digging her heels in. 'Wait a mo'. If I come with you, do I or do I not get a bed for the night?'

'The Lord will provide,' he insisted.

She weighed up the pros and cons. 'All right, you're on,' she said. 'Just this once. As long as there's not too much Jesus. And what did you say your name was, luv?'

'My name? You may call me Mr Collins.'

Chapter Two

Dastardly deeds on the moor — Company at last — Mrs Collins' predicament — Mr Wickham's discovery — Trouble at the Mission

THE CARRIAGE RUMBLED through the mist towards London. The man inside leant out of the window and called up to the driver.

'Can't you go any faster? We need to get to Watford Gap by nightfall. The little chef will have my special waiting in the oven.'

'Aye, sir,' said the coachman. 'But we don't want to lose a wheel and get stuck on the moor.'Appen there's mischief afoot. They say the Dandy 'ighwayman is abroad.'

'The Dandy Highwayman?'

'Aye, sir. So if you don't mind, I'll take it carefully until we reach the Gap.'

The passenger sighed and sat down again. He took out some papers to read through.

There was a sudden flash of light and a dull explosion. The carriage jolted and then came to a shuddering halt. He leant out of the window again.

'What the h——?' he cried.

In front of the carriage, just visible in the mist, was a man astride a black horse. He wore vaguely military uniform, topped off with an extravagant tricorn hat, and his face was daubed with white stripes. He was waving a pistol in the air.

'Stand and deliver!' he cried, and his horse whinnied by way of accompaniment. 'I'm the Dandy High—'

'Yeah, we know,' said the coachman.

The highwayman levelled his pistol at him. 'Watch it, you. None of your cheek.' He brought his horse nearer to the carriage and peered in, his pistol still pointing at the driver on the roof.

'Good afternoon, sir,' he smiled.

The occupant of the carriage glared back at him.

'This is quite intolerable,' he exclaimed. 'Will you please let us go?'

'I don't think so,' said the highwayman. 'Seeing as you have something that we have need of.'

'I carry very little money with me, if that's what you're thinking.'

'It's not your money we're after. C'mon. Out you get.'

He re-trained his weapon on the man inside. The coachman seized this opportunity to dismount and attempt a hasty retreat. But before he had gone but a few feet, a long tentacle snaked out of the gloom. It wrapped itself around him and dragged the unfortunate man off, screaming. The screams intensified for a moment and then stopped altogether.

'Now, mister, where were we?' demanded the highwayman, his pistol still pointing at the passenger. 'Are we getting out or not?'

Shaking, the man opened the door of the carriage and stepped out onto the moor. Then another, female, figure emerged from out of the mist.

'Good lord, it's—' said the man.

'Indeed it is. Surprised, are we? Well, these are strange times we live in, are they not?' She turned to the highwayman. 'Tie him up. Make sure that he can't escape. And be careful—I don't want him injured.'

The highwayman dismounted and reached into his saddlebag for a length of rope. He bound the man hand and foot, humming to himself as he did so. When he had finished, the highwayman picked him up and leant him against the side of the carriage, face down.

The woman approached, and the two of them stood behind their prisoner.

'Right,' said the woman. 'Pull his breeches down. Then—' she paused for dramatic effect, 'fetch my reticule—'

Their prisoner relaxed slightly at this command. 'A reticule is nothing to be scared of.'

'—and then open it and take out the probe,' finished the woman.

'Ah,' said the man.

Elizabeth was seated at her escritoire next to the upstairs bay window. From here she could observe the whole vista of Pemberley spread out before her, from the ornamental lake of delicious memory to the strange tower known as Blethyn's Folly in the far distance. Sometimes she needed to pinch herself to remember she was mistress of all she could see.

She was trying to compose a reply to Jane, wondering whether she should mention anything about her two curious encounters at the quarry.

Out of the corner of her eye she caught sight of a carriage commencing the long journey up the drive to the house. Company at last, she thought to herself. She still had a few minutes, so made one last effort to begin the letter.

Dear Jane,
You'll never believe

No, that would never do. She scrunched it up and tossed it away.

Dear Jane,
Guess what happened to me . . .

She shook her head and threw that one in the bin as well.

Dear Jane,
Remember Mr Wick

Elizabeth didn't even complete the name before crossing everything out several times, tearing the letter up into small pieces, shredding it into even tinier ones, and finally discarding the remnants.

No, it was best not to say anything at all quite yet. Whatever was she thinking? Poor Jane would worry herself sick.

The carriage was by this time almost at the house and Elizabeth rushed downstairs to greet the new arrival. Hollander and Dench were already in place, and as soon as the carriage came to a halt, Hollander stepped forward to open the door.

No one emerged.

Hollander stood to attention, holding the door back, whilst Dench gave Elizabeth a quizzical look.

Still no one emerged.

Dench looked at Elizabeth again, and this time she motioned to him to look inside. He peered into the carriage, retreated and held a brief, whispered consultation with Hollander. The latter shook his head fiercely while Dench nodded back at him with a similar degree of fervour. The two continued this silent pantomime for a minute or so, until eventually Hollander acquiesced and the pair of them clambered into the carriage.

They emerged a moment later, bearing a comatose woman awkwardly between them. Elizabeth took one look at their burden and sighed.

'The blue room, I think,' she said.

'Yes, Ma'am,' replied Dench.

'And Dench?'

'Yes, Ma'am?'

'When you take her luggage up, make sure that any medication you find is stored safely. Somewhere else, perhaps?'

'I understand, Ma'am.' Dench lifted one finger up to tap his nose, letting one of the woman's legs dangle loose as he did so. Clumsily, he picked it up again, and the two footmen carried their burden into the house.

Poor Charlotte, thought Elizabeth. Still on the laudanum.

Charlotte Collins appeared ill at ease. She seemed to be finding it difficult to sit still, and the drumming of her fingers on the dining table was beginning to annoy Elizabeth.

'Are you all right, my dear?' she said.

'I am quite well. The journey from Rosings was taxing, and I did not sleep well last night.'

'Indeed. You must be exhausted. And here I am bothering you with tiresome enquiries about your health.' She paused. 'Is the venison to your satisfaction?'

'It is very satisfactory,' said Charlotte, with a slight twitch.

Silence descended. Elizabeth surmised that Charlotte's present disposition was connected to the fact that Dench had indeed managed to intercept her supply of laudanum and secrete it in a safe place. She had little experience of these matters, beyond the content of Mr Coleridge's famous pamphlet, 'Just Say No, Quoth the Albatross', and the message contained therein was ambiguous to say the very least.

'Charlotte—' she began.

Charlotte threw down her cutlery and stood up,. She drooled slightly and her eyes were as wide as the Darcys' best dinner plates. 'What NOW?!' she screamed.

Elizabeth was taken aback, but held her ground. Asking the servants to leave them for a moment, she said, 'Dearest Charlotte, whatever is the matter with you?'

Charlotte advanced around the end of the table and loomed over Elizabeth. 'What have you done with it?' she demanded.

'What?'

'You know full well. I cannot live without—'

'Without what?'

Charlotte's voice dropped to a whisper as she sank into the chair next to Elizabeth. 'My little bottle,' she muttered.

'Ah,' said Elizabeth, trying hard to disguise the triumph in her voice. 'Good, good. I'm glad you're facing up—'

'You have no idea—'

'—to your problems—'

'—what it's like living with him—'

'—because I feel I can really help you here—'

'—can you imagine what it's like when he creeps into bed with you—'

'—I want to help, Charlotte, I really do, but you need to accept—'

'—when that greasy little body slides up behind you—'

'—that it's just a crutch and it's not addressing the underlying problem, is it?'

'—and he goes finger, thumb, finger, thumb, finger, thumb all the way down your spine until he grasps hold of your—'

'Charlotte? Were you listening to a word I was saying?'

There was a moment's silence, broken only by soft whimpering from Charlotte. 'I can stop whenever I want, you know, Lizzy,' she said. 'I really can.'

'I know,' agreed Elizabeth, embracing Charlotte and rocking her gently to and fro. 'I know.'

'And I hate Rosings, too,' said Charlotte. 'That horrible de Bourgh woman—'

'Yes, well—'

'And the noises and lights in the sky that keep me awake—'

'Sorry?'

'And the tentacles—'

Elizabeth disengaged from Charlotte and sat bolt upright.

'Charlotte, did you say tentacles?'

Charlotte suddenly looked bemused. 'I don't think so. Why would I say tentacles?' Her eyes were wandering all over the room. 'I can't think of any reason why I should say tentacles. Did I really say tentacles? Sorry. Sometimes I get a little confused.' She gave a sad little smile. 'I think I should retire.'

Elizabeth helped her friend up to her chamber and made sure she was comfortable.

Poor, poor Charlotte. But what on earth had she been babbling about? There was only one man alive who could help her find an answer, and, unfortunately, she had no idea how to get hold of him.

George Wickham took the hunk of mutton out of his pocket and tore off a mouthful. Then he reached for his hipflask and took a swig of gin. He grimaced at the rough taste and made a mental note to ask Provisions to fill it up with Plymouth next time.

Still no sign of any movement from the house opposite. Footsteps approached, and he melted back into the shadows of the alleyway.

The footsteps stopped and someone peered in his direction.

'Anybody there?' asked a female voice.

In one swift, practised movement, Wickham grabbed hold of the woman and pulled her into the alleyway, clamping one hand firmly over her mouth.

'Apologies for the rough handling, my dear,' he hissed, dragging her further into the alley, 'but I haven't been on the Chivalry Refresher Course this year and my manners are a bit rusty.'

Once they were safely away from the street, Wickham released her. He took out one of the Professor's Chancel matches and lit it by dipping it into a bottle of acid. 'Well, my dear, and who are you?' he demanded, holding the match up to her face.

The woman was a rough sort, evidently ravaged by laudanum, gin and bad sex—known to the medical profession as Harker's Triple Whammy.

'I'm a simple 'ore, sir,' she stammered, backing away from the flame. 'A simple 'ore, a-going about me honest trade of a night. You after a good time?'

'At this precise moment, my dear, no. But circumstances may change, so give me your card anyway.'

The woman passed him her card, and he examined it by the light of the match.

ANNIE CHAPMAN
'Ore
Testimonials available on request
'The customer always comes first'

'Glad to hear it,' muttered Wickham, pocketing the card. The match fizzled and went out. 'Bloody French technology. Listen, my dear, I work for some important people—'

'Ha. Don't talk to me about important people. D'yer know what I said to the Prince Regent the other—'

'Yes, I'm sure that's terribly interesting,' said Wickham. 'But I'm more interested in reports of unusual things going on around here?'

'Not sure I catch your meaning, sir.'

'Disappearances, perhaps? Anyone you know on the street suddenly *not* on the street, as it were?'

The woman's face lit up. 'Ooh, funny you should say that, but I was just thinking about old Mary Ann Nichols. We usually meet up for half a dozen gins on a Tuesday and she ain't been around for a few days.'

'Interesting. Do you know anything about the Mission for Fallen Women over there?' He jerked his head in the direction of the street.

Annie Chapman laughed. 'You're not suggesting Mary Ann's found Jesus, are you? That'd be the day.'

'I'm not suggesting anything. But I'm wondering if anyone you know has ever been there?'

'Ha, no. Once they go in there, you never see them again. It's like they're too good for the likes of us any more.'

'Really?'

'Yes, it's as if there was something wrong with being an 'ore. And I don't know what they get up to in there, I really don't. You should hear some of the noises.'

'Hymns?'

'Nah. Wailing, more like.'

'Fascinating. Well, I tell you what. Here's my card. If you come across anything else unusual, drop me a line, eh?'

'That'll be tricky. I'm illiterate.'

'Dear me. Have you an amanuensis?'

'Not last time I was checked out, no. Listen, I'll get word to you somehow. Nice meeting you, sir. I like a man in uniform.' She winked at him in what she evidently hoped was a coquettish manner.

'Mmm,' said Wickham, eyeing her. 'I don't suppose you do Prussian, do you?'

Annie slapped him hard. 'Filthy bugger,' she exclaimed, and strode off into the night. Wickham followed her to the end of the alley, still rubbing his cheek. As he reached the quiet thoroughfare, he noticed a figure glancing from left to right before entering the Mission.

'Good Lord,' he said to himself. 'Surely not?'

Mary Ann Nicholls paced up and down her cell. She glanced up at the figurine on the wall cross. 'Listen,' she said bluntly. 'I think you need to have words with some of the people what run this establishment of yours. The food's shite, the service is terrible and the furnishings could do with a once over. And I really don't know where the probes fit in, either.' She paused and adjusted her undergarments. 'Actually, I know exactly where they fit in, come to think of it.'

There was a rap on the cell door.

'Surrogate Nicholls! Prepare for inspection!' came a voice from the corridor. The door opened and a large woman in her late forties marched in.

'Look, can I just say,' said Mary Ann. 'If it's the probe again, could you perhaps warm it up this time?'

'Silence, Surrogate Nicholls. Come with me.'

The woman seized hold of Mary Ann and frog-marched her out of the cell, down the corridor and into an office at the end. She recognised the man at the desk as Mr Collins. At last. A chance to speak with the management.

'Ah, Mr Collins. I've been wanting to have a word with you.'

'Silence!' shouted the woman again.

Mr Collins looked up at her and winced. He shook his head slightly. 'It's all right, Mrs Pike, I'll deal with this now.'

Mrs Pike muttered something under her breath and then let go of Mary Ann. Then she turned around and marched out of the room.

'So, Mary Ann Nicholls,' said Mr Collins. 'How are we settling in at the Mission?'

'Well, as I was saying—'

'Good, good,' interrupted Mr Collins, waving his hand. He put the tips of his fingers together and then brought both hands up to his lips. For a moment, he appeared to be in a trance, and then just as quickly snapped out of it. 'Miss Nicholls, as you will be aware from the bible study in which you have been engaged, the Lord moves in mysterious ways. And it would seem that you have been Chosen.'

'Chosen?'

'Yes, Chosen. In fact, I had you brought here this evening to meet a very special person.'

'Father Christmas?' asked Mary Ann, hopefully. That was usually what they meant when they talked about a very special person. Although it usually turned out to be some old tramp with bad breath.

'No, not Father Christmas, Mary Ann. But he is very special indeed. And he is very keen to meet you.'

'Hang on a minute,' said Mary Ann. 'I think I know where this is leading. And if you think anyone's going to get any without paying for it.'

Mr Collins looked aghast. 'Oh, good Lord, no. Good Lord, no. I mean to say . . . no, no, no. The very sugges-tion—'

'Perhaps I can explain,' a new voice interrupted him. A proud, arrogant voice. Mary Ann turned and watched the newcomer enter the room behind her. He was dressed in the finest clothing, the hair was perfectly coiffeured and he held the bearing of true aristocracy. She stared at him, open-mouthed. She'd seen a few nobs in her time, but this man was something else.

'S-sir?' was all she managed to say.

'But first, let me introduce myself. My name is Darcy. Fitzwilliam Darcy.'

Chapter Three

Worms, spiders and albatrosses—Naked and ashamed—A change of plan—Accoutrements—In Whitechapel, no one can hear you scream

E LIZABETH JERKED AWAKE from a surprising dream involving a lot of tentacles, and for a moment wasn't quite sure where she was. Then the rocking motion of the carriage brought it back to her. She was accompanying Charlotte on her journey back to Rosings, partly because the poor woman wasn't safe to be let out on her own, but mainly to have a proper look at the place again. There was clearly something odd going on there and, in the continuing absence of Wickham, she felt duty-bound to investigate it. She hardly dared hope it might lead her to Lydia.

Charlotte dozed in the opposite seat, snoring loudly and occasionally muttering odd comments about albatrosses. Poor thing, thought Elizabeth. She used to be such a nice, dull person, and now she was full of raving madness. It was almost time for luncheon, so she reached into the hamper next to her and looked to see what Cook had prepared for them. There were several cuts of cold meat, along with some of Farmer Olivier's notorious pork pies—which were mainly there in order to ward off attacks by highwaymen. There were also some of those new-fangled bread creations made popular by their use in Italian gambling parlours, invented by the Duce di Ciabatta.

Charlotte stirred and opened her eyes. For several seconds they were completely vacant, and then a sheen of pain descended over them.

'Are you recovered yet, my dear?' Elizabeth enquired.

'I feel a bit poorly,' said Charlotte. 'My humours are out of balance and I am in need of the fur of the spaniel.'

'I understand.' Elizabeth nodded, not following a word of what her friend was saying. 'You must eat, though.'

'I cannot. See—it crawls with worms! The evil stench of corruption!'

'Are you sure?' Elizabeth took another look in the hamper. 'I think you may perhaps be mistaken, for I perceive no worms therein,'

'There!' screamed Charlotte, pointing at Elizabeth. 'The spiders are coming for me! The spiders! Five-foot high, sixteen-legged spiders!'

Elizabeth held up her hand. 'One moment, please: you confuse me. Could we first decide whether your problem is related to worms or spiders?'

'Albatross! Get this albatross off me!'

'Ah. We seem to be back to albatrosses. Perhaps I should begin again. I've got some exceptionally diverting Italian bread here, some perfectly fine pork pies—'

'They're crawling over me!'

Charlotte grabbed hold of the carriage door. Before Elizabeth could do anything, she opened it and leant out.

'Argh! The ground moves!' she screamed, looking down. 'It's alive! The wildebeests are upon us!'

Elizabeth hauled Charlotte back into the carriage and closed the door again. Charlotte sagged down into her seat. Elizabeth took hold of her hands and looked her firmly in the eye.

'Charlotte,' she instructed her. 'Take a few deep breaths. Count to ten with me. All right? One . . . two . . . three . . . four . . .'

Charlotte joined in, silently mouthing the words and nodding with intense concentration every time.

'Thank you,' she whispered. 'Thank you.'

'It will get easier,' said Elizabeth, more out of hope than any real knowledge. 'It will.'

'I know,' said Charlotte. 'Especially when the spiders leave me alone.'

Elizabeth sighed deeply, and rummaged in the hamper for something to give to her. She hoped that the poor woman might feel better on a full stomach. Yes, that was what she needed.

'Cold turkey?' she asked.

The prisoner lay curled up on the damp stone.

'Hey!' he cried out. 'Somebody help me! I'm cold, ashamed and naked upon this floor.'

No one replied. He felt torn. How had he got into this imbroglio? There had been a mist. A highwayman. Tentacles. A probe.

Oh God. The probe.

He tried to stand up, and then quickly sat back down again.

Oh God. The probe.

'Hey!' he called out. 'Somebody—'

'Yeah?' came a voice from the other side of the bars. 'What's the problem?'

'Ah, yes. Good. Well, I've got a number of complaints about the way I'm being treated here. For one thing—'

''Ere, Tom. Prisoner says he's got some complaints.'

'Really?' said another voice. 'Well, he'll have to fill in a form, then, won't he?'

'Yeah. Have we got one handy, Tom?'

'Nah, we're right out of forms, Bob.'

'Look,' said the prisoner. 'Do you know who I am?' He felt confident that this usually had the desired effect.

'Yeah,' said the one called Tom. ''Course we do. But do *you* know who you are?'

The prisoner considered this in silence. 'Ah,' he said. 'Now you come to mention it, I have no idea who I am. No idea whatsoever.'

'Well, that'll make filling in a form difficult, won't it?' Bob pointed out with an unnecessary air of triumph.

'Blast,' muttered the prisoner. Then he had a thought. 'But you know what my name is, don't you?' he asked, in a slightly more conciliatory tone.

'Yeah,' Tom agreed. 'Nice name it is, too. Dead genteel.'

'So then . . . does it begin with, say, J?'

'No clues,' Bob insisted.

'But this is preposterous! I really must protest about this!'

There was a silence for a moment.

'We could make your life miserable,' said Bob.

'It's already pretty miserable.'

Tom laughed. 'You don't know you're born. We haven't even started.'

'So if I were you,' said Bob, 'I'd think about adopting a slightly more respectful attitude towards us.'

'Yeah,' agreed Tom. 'What Bob said.'

'Oh, very well, then,' said the prisoner.

There was silence again.

'I'm still waiting for a special word,' Bob prompted him. 'Have you heard it, Tom? 'Cos I haven't.'

'Nope,' said Tom. 'Such a small word, too. Wouldn't take much.'

'Oh, all right. Sorry,' said the prisoner. 'Sorry.'

'Now that's better, isn't it, Tom?' said Bob. 'So nice to deal with a man who understands his position in society.'

'Well, now that we have an understanding,' said the prisoner, 'would it be possible for me to perhaps have my clothes back? And maybe you could possibly tell me when the next meal is? It's just that the thin gruel I had a few hours ago—nutritious though it was, and I did like the ant garnish, that was a lovely touch—didn't really fill me up quite as much as I'd expected. In fact if I'd known, I might have gone for the—'

'Shut it,' said Tom brutally. 'You'll get clothed and fed when we decide and no sooner.'

There was a sound of footsteps approaching.

'No time for food now,' commented Bob. 'Lucky boy's got a visitor.'

The prisoner looked up as the door swung open.

'Oh, it's you,' he muttered.

'Indeed it is,' she said. 'It's time for your therapy.'

'Will this involve a probe?'

'Therapy always involves probes. But in your mouth this time.'

'Ah.' He considered this. 'You have washed it, haven't you?'

Colonel Sutherland studied the report in front of him and frowned. 'Are you sure that it was him?' he said. 'Can you be absolutely certain that your own feelings ?'

'I'd recognise that haughty demeanour anywhere, sir,' said Wickham. 'There was no one else it could possibly have been.'

The colonel sighed. 'In that case, Wickham. I have no

alternative. I'm taking you off the investigation. You're far too emotionally involved. And we need to keep our senses in control of our sensibilities, if you see what I mean.'

'But sir—'

'God knows, it's difficult enough with you being involved with a member of the Bennet family.'

'That was just a job.'

'I know.'

'And I made a dashed right royal mess of it.' With that, Wickham thumped the desk, stood up and walked away.

'Miss Bennet may yet be alive ,' said Sutherland.

'She was only a child,' Wickham remarked, almost to himself. 'I mean, obviously not in the sense of anything dodgy, but—'

'I know.' Sutherland himself stood up and went over to Wickham. He placed a hand on his shoulder. 'Come on, old man, it wasn't your fault. You didn't know then half of what we know now.'

'But half of that is speculation, and a whole third of *that* is incomplete conjecture, and nine-tenths of the rest is probably the rabid fantasy of a deranged imagination.'

'And yet, that still leaves . . .' The colonel paused for a moment, making the necessary mental calculations. 'One sixtieth that may yet be of use to us.'

They both looked at each other for a few seconds.

'Are you sure?' queried Wickham. 'Look, if you take a half of a half .'

'It matters not,' Colonel Sutherland interrupted. 'All that is important is that Lydia may still be alive and unharmed. And it is our duty to find her.' He paused. 'Come here. I've got something new I want you to look into.'

He went back to his desk, and Wickham followed.

'We've had another sighting. From one of our operatives in Kent. Take a look at this sketch.'

He handed a piece of paper to Wickham.

'Nice work,' said Wickham, admiring the sketch. 'I like the way he's depicted the thrusters particularly. But just one moment, sir. This house . . . I recognise that glazing.'

'I thought you might.'

'My God. It's Rosings.'

'Indeed it is, Wickham.' The colonel took back the operative's sketch and locked it in his desk drawer. 'I want you to go there and find out what's going on. You must infiltrate the establishment and see what Lady Catherine de Bourgh is up to.'

'Lady Catherine? Surely not. I really can't believe that old bat—'

'Assume nothing, Wickham. These are strange times.'

'But how am I going to get anywhere near Rosings Park? Lady Catherine knows me. She hates me. I seduced her niece, remember? And she's Darcy's aunt.'

'So you're going to need a disguise.' Colonel Sutherland handed him a calling card. 'We tend to use these chaps. Theatrical types. Know their disguises inside out.'

Wickham took the card and raised an eyebrow. 'Old Compton Street, eh? Can we trust them? Are they straight?'

'Straight?' repeated Sutherland. 'Not sure what you mean, old chap.'

The sign over the door said 'Whiteside and Malone: Disguises, Theatrical Novelties and Accoutrements. All Pride, No Prejudice. We Serve Everyone.' Wickham pushed the door open and a bell rang.

'Hello?'

Whilst he waited to be served, he began to browse. The shop had a musty atmosphere and was filled with mannequins clothed in an extraordinary range of outfits. Wickham recognised uniforms from some of the most flamboyant regiments in the British army, such as the Queen's own Polari and the Jolly Hussars. There was also one of Aunt Fanny's bodices from a production of Sheridan's early play 'Camping in Scarborough,' and a complete set of moustaches from an obscure Italian opera about snuff-taking in the Venetian gondolier community.

'Has Sir found anything to his liking?' asked a voice by his right ear. Wickham whirled round. He found himself face to face with an immaculately coiffed gentleman who was regarding him through an elaborately engraved lorgnette. There was a strong scent of pomade wafting around him.

'Or is Sir still open to suggestions?' asked another voice behind him. Wickham stepped back slightly and was now able to observe both sales assistants. They were dressed in identical tailored suits with cravats in complementary colours.

'Well, Mr Whiteside,' said the one on the left. 'What do you think?'

'What do I think, Mr Malone?' said the one on the right, cupping his chin with his hand. 'Could be a bit of a challenge.'

Mr Whiteside advanced on Wickham and gave him a thorough examination, head to toe.

'Does Sir wish to make himself more appealing to the ladies?'

'Well—' began Wickham.

'Would Sir like to have the ladies falling all over him? Would you? I bet you would, Sir. I bet you would.'

'Actually—'

35

'If I were a lady, would you like to have me all over you, Sir? Would you, Sir?'

Wickham frowned and backed away again. 'That's rather a queer thing to say.'

'Is it, Sir? I bet you do want the ladies though, don't you, Sir?'

'Well, that wasn't what—'

Mr Malone had joined them now and was busy measuring Wickham's inside leg.

'Which side does Sir dress on?' Malone asked.

Wickham hesitated. 'I'm not sure.'

Whiteside and Malone exchanged knowing glances.

'Not sure?' said Whiteside. 'So Sir is not sure which side he dresses on?'

'N-no,' said Wickham. 'Look, I haven't actually come here for an outfit. I've come here for a disguise.'

Both assistants stepped back.

'Ah!' said Malone. 'Is Sir a military man, then?'

'Well, yes I am.'

'I bet the ladies love Sir in his regimentals,' commented Whiteside. 'I bet they do.'

'I—well, that's as maybe.' Wickham was anxious that the conversation was drifting away from him once again. 'But it's a disguise I need now.'

'Well,' said Malone. 'Sir definitely needs a beard, for starters.'

'Definitely,' agreed Whiteside. 'And perhaps a scar.'

'Oh yes.' Malone nodded. 'Sir most definitely needs a scar.'

'But is Sir looking to be a high and mighty lord or a rough cottager?' asked Whiteside.

'I bet Sir would make a wonderful rough cottager,' said Malone.

'Oh yes, Sir.' Whiteside nodded. 'I can just see Sir in a

rough cottage. What do you think, Sir? Would you like it, Sir?'

'I hadn't really thought—' said Wickham.

'Done, then,' said Malone. 'Rough cottager for Sir. With a scar.'

'And a beard,' Whiteside added. 'Don't forget Sir needs a beard.'

Two hours later, Wickham re-emerged onto Old Compton Street, unrecognisable and slightly flushed. Right, he thought. Now to see what the old cow's up to.

It was suppertime in the Mission for Fallen Women, although Mary Ann Nicholls was unsure if it was day or night. She had spent the last twenty-four hours drifting in and out of consciousness whilst all manner of peculiar things were done to her. Or had she just been dreaming?

''Ere,' said one of the others at the table, a large, dark-skinned girl who always wore a bandana around her head. 'What was he like, then?'

'Who?' asked Mary Ann.

'That posh bloke,' said another girl with rippley hair. 'You was with him for ages. Mind you, I wouldn't have kicked him out.' She gave a raucous laugh, and the girl in the bandana joined in.

So it *had* happened.

'I don't know,' she managed. 'It was like a really bad dream. Like I was being smothered.' By something slimy, she thought. 'Tell you what though,' she said out loud, 'I'm starving.'

'Well, get stuck in then, girl,' said the one in the bandana, indicating the plate of stodge in front of her.

'Yeah,' said Mary Ann, picking up a spoon. But as soon as she took the first mouthful, she felt odd. Something inside her wasn't quite right. She tried to swallow, but it seemed to be stuck in her throat. 'Ouch,' she said, as a spasm of pain shot through her guts. Then she felt it move. She shuddered. Something inside her had definitely moved. Something with teeth and tentacles.

'What's wrong?' asked the rippley-haired girl.

'Ggggaahhhh,' gurgled Mary Ann. 'Cramps . . .'

Mary Ann grasped the table and began lurching around. 'The pain!' she screamed.

She stared down at the front of her dress, which had turned a bright crimson. Mary Ann writhed in agony, held down by the other two girls.

There was another intense spasm of pain. Something pushed hard at her from the inside.

The tip of a tentacle poked through her dress.

'Fetch a nurse,' shouted bandana girl. 'Quick!'

But no one left the room. Instead, a crowd gathered around Mary Ann's twisting, bloody body. Another tentacle forced its way out and joined the other one in a crazed, wriggling duet.

'God help me!' Mary Ann screamed as whatever it was finally burst out of her in a tangled bloody mess of intestines and tentacles.

Mary Ann screamed again as the thing pulled itself free, spraying blood and viscera around the room.

'Please . . .'

But no one came to help her. Everyone was transfixed by the creature sitting on what was left of Mary Ann.

It waved its tentacles around in an experimental flourish and then gave out a malevolent squawk. One or two of the girls screamed. Its purulent leathery face swivelled round to take one last look at Mary Ann. To her weakening eyes it seemed as if the creature was grinning at her. Then it slithered off towards the door.

The other girls saw it coming towards them and screamed, scattering in all directions.

As Mary Ann began to slip into oblivion, she became faintly aware of newcomers in the room.

'We've had a rejection,' said Mrs Pike, leaning over her.

'Damn,' said a male voice: a cold male voice. 'She seemed so promising.'

His voice grew louder. 'All right, everybody out,' he insisted. The man clapped his hands, and the room slowly emptied. 'Everybody out! Nothing to see here.'

'She's still alive,' remarked Mrs Pike, when everyone had gone.

'Not for long.'

'What do you want me to do?'

'Dispose of her,' he told her. 'Wipe the minds of all the witnesses. And catch that bloody thing before it escapes. Doubt if it's house-trained.'

'Dispose of her? The poor girl—'

'No one must know of this. Eliminate her entirely.' The man produced something that appeared to be a kind of weapon and gave it to Mrs Pike.

'But I haven't been trained.'

'Just aim the thing at her and squeeze the trigger.'

'Is it reliable? It's just I've heard tell that it some-times—'

'Of course it's reliable!'

'I don't want to get blown into next week, you know.'

'Cease your tiresome objections, woman! Just use it. And when you have got rid of this one, find me another surrogate. The programme must continue.'

'Yes, Mr Darcy,' she said. 'As you command.'

Chapter Four

*Dissected alive — The good ghost — Jennifer is
upgraded — The rough cottager arrives —
An unexpected guest*

T HE WOMAN WAS in a terrible state. He'd seen
corpses in the dissecting room that were in a better
condition than this one.

'What in God's name happened to you?' Chambers
demanded to know.

'Ripped apart I was, ripped . . .'

'I can see that, Miss . . . Sorry, what was your name?'

'Mary . . . Ann . . . Nicholls. Mary . . . Ann . . .'

'Who did it, Mary Ann?'

A look of horror passed across the woman's face. 'It
was a thing that burst out of me.'

'Like some sort of abscess?' he queried.

'With tentacles,' said the woman, shaking her head.

Chambers looked at her in pity. She was clearly deliri-
ous. 'Don't say another word, Mary Ann,' he murmured,
covering her with his cloak. 'Just try to relax. I'll look after
you as best I can. My name's Chambers: I'm a medical
student.'

Though he'd never encountered anything quite like
this, he had to admit to himself. There was nothing he
could do for her other than make her comfortable and

wait for nature to take its course. It was like something from hell.

That was it.

From hell.

The woman started to babble again, talking about aliens with tentacles and how she'd tried to be an honest girl and hadn't told anyone about the Prince Regent.

'The Prince Regent?' repeated Chambers. 'There is no Prince Regent, Mary Ann. Do you mean Prince Albert, the Duke of Clarence? What has the Duke done to you?'

'Prince Regent . . . ripped apart . . . Mary Ann Nicholls.' Then she gave a violent cough and was silent.

Chambers felt for her pulse, but the woman was dead.

'You there!' came a voice from behind him. He froze. It was Gull. Of all the people that he should come across this night and in these circumstances, Sir William Gull, physician to the Royal Family and frequent lecturer at the College of Physicians, was probably the one he would have picked last.

'Sir?' he said, turning round to face his interlocutor. As he did so, he dropped his copy of Gray's 'Anatomy in a Country Churchyard'. Gull picked it up and handed it back to him with a precise, deliberate movement.

'Who is this woman, laddie?' demanded Gull. 'And what is a medical student like you doing in Whitechapel on a weekday evening when you should be hard at your studies?'

'Sir, I was making my way home to my lodgings—'

'A likely tale.'

'When I came across this poor girl,' Chambers continued. 'She had been viciously attacked—ripped apart, even. And before she passed away she seemed to be muttering about the Duke of Clarence.'

At this, the old doctor grabbed Chambers and pulled

him to his feet. 'Leave this to me,' hissed Gull. 'Go home and bury yourself in your textbooks. And if you value your life, never speak a word of this matter to anyone. Do you understand?'

'I . . . I do,' Chambers agreed, shaking.

'Good.' Gull released him. 'Well? Go, boy. Go!'

Chambers backed away from Gull, then turned to go. He left the doctor bending over the woman, as if trying to decide what he should do.

The student rounded the next corner and noticed a carriage parked at the side of the street. For a moment, he swore there was someone watching him from the inside. He turned to look more closely, but the curtain was swiftly drawn across the window.

As he made his way back home, Chambers went through everything that had happened that night. The more he pondered it, the more he realised that however much he might learn about the world from his books, in the end, he didn't know Jack.

The ghost of Mary Ann Nicholls was more than a little confused as well. Somehow she had been left back in Regency times whilst her corpse had been blasted seventy years into the future. She had a feeling that this probably wasn't a good situation to be in.

No one seemed to realise she was there at all, apart from a slight shiver when she happened to walk through them.

'Oi, do you mind moving on a bit?' demanded a voice behind her. 'This is my pitch here.'

Mary Ann Nicholls turned and saw a headless female apparition standing behind her with an air of nonchalance. The voice came from the head she carried under her arm.

'Thank Gawd for that,' she said. 'Someone who can see me.'

'Yeah, I can see you all right. And you're standing on my pitch. So bugger off. Might be a punter along any minute.'

'Oh, I see what you mean,' said Mary Ann. 'Didn't realise that there were—you know—ghost 'ores like. I ain't been dead long, you see.'

'Ah. In that case, I'll let you off.' She held out a hand. 'Pleased to meet you. I'm the 'eadless 'ore.'

Mary Ann took the hand and shook it. Unlike everything else she'd encountered so far today, it seemed solid.

'Yeah, I'm quite notorious round these parts,' said the headless whore, with a superior smile. 'You should see what I gets up to with this.' She waved the head around in an unpleasant manner.

'Well,' said Mary Ann, her mind racing, 'it's nice to meet you, I'm sure. I'm Mary Ann Nicholls.'

'Thought I'd seen you around 'ere before.'

'So how come you're still — er — what's the word—unquiet?'

'I was just about to ask you the same question. But seeing as you asked me first I'll tell you. I got me head cut off by a falling gargoyle whilst walking widdershins round a church. Turns out your spirit don't get to lie down and rest with your body until the end of the world as predicted by your revelating John.'

'Bleeding hell. That sounds terrible.'

'Yeah well, it's a bugger to be sure. Still, at least I can keep me business going in the meantime. You'd be surprised how many lonely old phantoms there are round these parts.'

'I think I'm here because my body's been sent into the future,' said Mary Ann.

'Well, there's a thing,' said the headless whore. 'That's summat you don't come across very often.' She shook her head from side to side, and then tucked it back under her arm again. 'Can't you just sort of wait around to catch up with it then?'

'I suppose so. Not sure what I'm going to do for all that time, though. I expect you've got the 'oring covered.'

'True. But you could find a nice 'ouse to 'aunt. Or do good works. Like save people when they're about to be killed. Give them a mysterious warning just afore they're going to go on a journey that's going to end bad. So as they don't reach their final destination. That kind of thing. Depends on whether you want to be a good ghost or a bad one.'

'What sort are you, 'eadless?'

'Ha. That depends on who you ask. The Wanderin' Colonel what pops by every now and then says I'm a bad girl. But 'e also tells me I'm very good at it. So take your pick.'

'I think I want to be a good ghost,' said Mary Ann, brightening. 'Make up for me life of sin.'

'Good choice, me dear. World needs more good ghosts. And look. There's your chance to do some good now. Here comes young Annie Chapman. Keep an eye on her. She's a reckless young 'un.'

The Company's stables were situated in a mews at the back of Sloane Square. Wickham glanced to left and right, and when he was sure that he was unobserved, slipped in through the side door. He could hear a lot of clattering and muffled explosions coming from elsewhere in the buildings, but there seemed to be no one in the immediate vicinity.

He went over to a bench and picked up what appeared

to be an ornamental carriage clock. As he turned it over to adjust the time, a metal bolt shot out of the top of it, missing him by a fraction of an inch and embedding itself in the ceiling. The next item along was a ladies fan that emitted a noxious liquid when he squeezed the handle. He then picked up a chicken drumstick.

'Don't touch that!' came an urgent voice. Wickham froze and replaced the drumstick. 'It's my luncheon,' said Sir Humphry Davy, emerging from the shadows. He looked Wickham up and down. 'Rough cottager, eh?'

'Indeed,' Wickham agreed calmly. 'Hello, H. I've come to pick Jennifer up.'

'Step this way then. We've made one or two improvements since you last went on a mission.'

Wickham groaned inwardly. He followed H through to the building next door, where his horse was being restrained by two young men wearing full body armour.

'Now pay attention, Wickham.' He unstrapped the right side of the saddle, revealing what appeared to be a rifle dismantled into half a dozen of its constituent parts. 'Lee Van Enfield,' he said. 'Reassembles in under fifteen seconds, can bring down a speeding fugitive at a hundred paces.' He beckoned to Wickham to follow him around to the other side. He let down the other side of the saddle, enumerating the contents, one by one. 'Set of matching hunting knives, plus tool for removing stones from hooves. Full canteen of cutlery with a pair of goblets. Emergency flagon of claret and a pound of salt beef. Carrier pigeon. Carrier for carrier pigeon. And this—' he pulled out a small leather pouch, '—is most important.'

'Suicide tablets?'

'Certainly not!' said H. 'Sugar lumps.'

H took a couple out and offered them to Jennifer, who gobbled them up with apparent relish.

'Now watch this,' he said, motioning Wickham to move back slightly. He went over to Jennifer's side and slapped her firmly on the rump. The horse reared up, lifted its tail and then expelled something from its fundament with considerable force. The object flew across the room and landed a few feet short of the far wall, where it sat on the ground, steaming malevolently.

'You might want to duck now,' said H. Wickham looked around and realised that everyone else in the room had already done so. He was halfway towards the ground himself when the pellet exploded. It turned out that halfway to the ground wasn't nearly far enough and he took the full force of the blast in his upper body.

'Well,' said H, covering his face with a silk handkerchief. 'I think that completes the rough cottager look.'

He handed Wickham a flask containing a sticky brown substance. 'Fifty-fifty mixture of gunpowder and a powerful laxative. Add it to her feed every night and you shouldn't have any problems with footpads. Or indeed anyone who comes within ten feet of you.'

'Does she ride any differently?' said Wickham, once he had finished spitting out everything he had managed to catch in his mouth.

'She's like the wind, Wickham. Like the wind.'

Sir Humphry was right. Jennifer raced away like a thing possessed and they were in Rosings village well before nightfall. The first thing Wickham needed to do was obtain lodgings, and the obvious place to begin his enquiries was the inn on the green. He tied up Jennifer outside the Saucer and Tentacle, and went in. The bar was packed with locals, all making a noisy racket. But as soon as Wickham entered, the place fell silent and all eyes were on him.

He stepped up to the bar.

'Ah, my good man,' he said to the landlord, who was cleaning a tankard with a deliberate, thorough action. 'A pint of—' Wickham raised an eyebrow as if to ask what pints there might be available. There was no answer forthcoming, so he continued, '—a pint of your very best bitter ale, good sir.'

The landlord pulled a face, expectorated noisily into the tankard he had just finished polishing and then topped it up from one of the barrels behind the bar. He slammed it down on the counter and said, 'That'll be a groat and 'alf.'

Wickham fished in his pocket and withdrew some coins. He took a sip and tried hard to keep the foul liquid down.

All eyes were still on him, following his every movement. He realised that if he was to gain their trust he would have to go through with this to the bitter end, so he took a larger swig, then another, and then one final gulp until the glass was empty. Struggling to maintain his composure, he gingerly placed the tankard back on the bar and slumped down onto a stool.

This was evidently the cue for normality to resume once more. Conversations picked up where they had left off, and the hubbub was restored to its previous rowdy level. The landlord reached over the bar and handed Wickham a bucket.

'You might be a-needin' this,' he said.

Wickham tried to wave him away, but thought better of it as he felt his stomach begin to clench. Grabbing the bucket, he put it between his legs and heaved mightily into it. When he had finished, he handed the bucket back to the landlord. The landlord in turn inserted a funnel into the barrel from which he had served Wickham's pint before pouring the contents of the bucket back into it.

'Sorry 'bout that,' he said. 'You can't be too careful with strangers these days. There be some odd folk about these parts.'

'Really?' said Wickham.

'Really,' said the landlord, filling up Wickham's tankard from the other barrel. He handed it to Wickham, who eyed it with some suspicion.

'Go on, it's safe.'

'Really?'

'Really. So you be looking for lodgings?' asked the landlord as Wickham took his first nervous sip. Much to his relief and amazement, the ale was in fact remarkably pleasant.

'As it happens, I am,' he agreed. 'I intend to seek work at the Big House.'

There was a crack of thunder outside, and the whole inn suddenly became silent again.

'At the Big House, you say?' said the landlord, narrowing his eyes. 'Why'd you want to be going there?'

'I — er — hear that they have some work available in the hop fields,' said Wickham, aware that everyone was once again staring at him. 'I've always wanted to work with hops.'

'Interesting,' mused the landlord. 'Very interesting that a chap such as yourself with a mighty smart horse outside should be looking for hop work. Especially when hops is out of season. But,' the landlord relaxed a little ,'I guess it takes all sorts to make a world, don't it, lads?'

There were murmurs of assent from the rest of the clientele.

'I was evicted from my rough cottage only a few days ago,' began Wickham, before the landlord forestalled him.

'It's all right. No need to explain any more. No more questions, young man. You just take care up at the Big House. There be odd doings there, I'll be bound. And in the meantime, will you be wanting a room?'

'Well, yes, I will,' Wickham agreed. 'And another pint of your excellent . . .'

'Bishop's Todger,' supplied the landlord.

The dark shadow of Rosings loomed over the Collins' humble dwelling like some monster of the night, blocking out the moon. Elizabeth shivered as she stepped out of the carriage.

'Evening, Mrs Darcy,' said old Mrs Garson, emerging from the front door. 'Is Mrs Collins unwell?' she asked, peering into the carriage.

'She has a mild fever, that is all,' said Elizabeth.

'I understand,' said Mrs Garson. She picked up her skirts and climbed into the carriage, emerging a few moments later with Charlotte slung over her shoulder. 'Used to do this when she were a wee baby,' she said. 'I would end up with sick down me back even in them days.'

Elizabeth turned away. Poor thing. What was to be done with her?

'Mrs Darcy?' queried Garson, with Charlotte still swinging alarmingly on her back. 'I hope you don't think I speak out of turn, but has Mrs Collins ever spoken to you about any of her new friends?'

'New friends? I know nothing of any new friends, and she has certainly not spoken of any to me these past few days. I am sure that if she had new friends, she would be only too delighted to have told me, and I would have been delighted to have heard of them. I do hate the thought of poor Charlotte on her own here with only Mr Collins for company.'

'Aye, well, that's as maybe,' conceded Garson. 'And I'm not one to poke my nose where it don't belong, but them arty types ain't the kind of folk that a gentlewoman and wife of a holy man should be hobnobbing with, in my opinion.'

'Mrs Garson, please! I am sure that Mrs Collins exercises the utmost caution in all her dealings with the world, and if she has acquired some new friends of an artistic sensibility, well, I for one would welcome such a thing. Artists are gentle, sensitive people who can surely only enrich our ordinary everyday lives for the better?'

Garson shrugged and bustled off into the house with Charlotte's head just missing the doorway as they went through it. Elizabeth wondered what on earth the old woman could be talking about. Then, as she entered the house, she fancied she could hear music.

She followed the sound to the drawing room. Elizabeth knocked once and received no reply. Realising that the door was ajar, she nudged it open slightly and then knocked again. There was still no reply, so she opened the door and went in.

The room was full of a sweet-smelling smoke, evidently coming from the cheroot in the mouth of the young man plucking at the strange exotic instrument. As soon as he saw Elizabeth, he stopped playing and stubbed out his cheroot. He stood up, took her hand and bowed. As his hand touched hers, a strange spark of electricity shot through her entire being.

'I hope you don't mind,' he said, gesturing towards his instrument. 'I was just plucking at my bouzouki.'

'Well, if your . . .'

'Bouzouki.'

'If your bouzouki needs to be plucked, I would be the last one to try and stop you,' said Elizabeth, with a touch of nervousness.

'But soft, who is this vision of loveliness in front of me?' said the young man, as if taking in Elizabeth's appearance for the first time.

'Er—my name is Darcy,' she said, faltering a little as he seized her hand. 'Mrs Darcy. And who might you be, sir?'

'I will tell you,' he said handsomely. 'But first you must promise not to believe a word you hear about me. Some call me mad,' he carried her hand to his lips and kissed it, 'some call me bad,' he kissed it again, 'and yet others say that I am dangerous to know.'

He kissed her hand a third time before releasing it. 'But you may simply know me as Byron.'

Chapter Five

*The African Princess—A Woman's Hands—His
Lordship's Generosity—The Other Prisoner—
A Balmy Evening*

E LIZABETH BROKE HER fast alone the next day. Charlotte was still regrettably preoccupied, and the mysterious Byron was nowhere to be seen. Mrs Garson had
walked in just as he was about to demonstrate his bouzouki technique to her and he had immediately put it
away, deciding that an early night would be beneficial
to his muse. Mrs Garson had given Elizabeth a look that
suggested she would do well to steer clear of this extraordinary gentleman, and later reflection suggested that she
would probably be wise to heed this advice.

Fortunately a distraction arrived in the shape of a letter
from Jane.

> *My Dearest Lizzy,*
>
> *I hope that this reaches you. I trust all is well and
> Charlotte remains in high spirits. Have you visited Lady
> Catherine yet? I do so look forward to hearing all your
> news, as does Little Lydia, although of course she does not
> read yet or even understand the finer nuances of everyday
> speech.*
>
> *We have the Hursts staying with us at present, and it*

is good to see Louisa again, although Mr Hurst remains generally disagreeable. I have to say that their Damian is an unusual child. He seems to be forever making queer works of art out of anything he finds lying around. Only the other day he was asking cook for a sheep's carcass—can you imagine that?

Charlie is tolerably well, although his business venture with Mr Bradford seems to be running into difficulties already. To be perfectly honest, I am beginning to wonder if it was such a good idea to get involved with the man in the first place, as he keeps coming back to poor Charlie for more and more money in order to fund his mining venture. It would appear that the gold seam near Ashbourne has not yielded quite the amount that they anticipated and more exploratory holes will need to be made. Charlie has of course provided the funds, although I fear he is a little too trusting sometimes.

But dearest Lizzy, the most extraordinary thing has happened in the last week, because an African Princess has sent us a letter! Can you credit this? Apparently, she has been left an absolutely enormous fortune by her father, but it all seems to be tied up in groundnuts and the poor woman has medical bills to pay in the meantime. However, if Charlie can help her in the short term, she has offered to give him ten per cent of everything she owns! To be perfectly honest, I was unsure as to whether he should help the poor woman, but Charlie told me that it was our Christian duty to do so. Mr Hurst also pointed out that he could make enough out of his ten per cent to pay Mr Bradford. This would be useful, as his communications to Charlie are often brought to Netherfield by disagreeable men carrying big sticks.

Well, I must be going now. Damian and Lydia are playing at artists and models, and I should perhaps make

sure that they behaving themselves. I do hope you are well,
and I look forward to hearing again from you soon.

Elizabeth put the letter down and smiled. Lucky Charlie.
So good-natured and generous, and yet always falling on
his feet. She wondered if she should write to Jane immediately, but then decided that she should wait until they
had dined at Rosings later in the week. Something told
her it was going to be an interesting occasion.

As she stood up, she caught sight of a labourer walking
past the window, heading up the drive towards the great
house. There was something oddly familiar about him.

The man looked Wickham up and down and gave a dis-
dainful sniff.

'Sir, I seek work,' Wickham told him. 'I am a rough
cottager unjustly evicted from Lord Whitrow's estate. I am
skilled at coppicing, sedge-frotting and wither-mangling.'

'Show me yer 'ands,' said the estate manager.

'I beg your—I mean, you what?'

'I said, show me yer 'ands.'

Wickham shrugged and then presented his hands for
inspection, palms upwards. The man grasped them and
pulled Wickham towards him. As he did so, Wickham
caught a strong smell of rotting turnips. The estate manager
closed his eyes and rubbed Wickham's hands between his
own forefingers and thumbs. Finally, he scowled.

'These are a woman's 'ands!' he said, letting go with
some force.

'Sir, they are most certainly not!' exclaimed Wickham.
'These hands have worked as hard and as long as any man
in this great country of ours. They have worked in the
fields from dawn to dusk throughout many a harvest and

bitter winter. These are the hands of an honest English labourer.'

'Bollocks,' said the estate manager. ''Ands of a sodding ballet dancer, more like. Smooth as a baby's bottom, they are. Show me where the calluses are, then! Show me where the thorns of the haggleberry bush have pierced yer flesh! Show me the bruises from fencing whiplash!'

'Sir, I maintain that these hands — these 'ands — of mine are — despite appearances to the contrary — the hands of a man of the soil. And when I tell you why, you will be sorry you ever questioned my honesty, sir. For I —' Wickham paused for dramatic effect, '—worked for ten long years on Lord Whitrow's Aloe vera crop.'

There was a long silence, during which the estate manager looked hard into Wickham's eyes. Then he softened, and a look almost of pity came over him.

'Aloe vera, you say?'

Wickham nodded, lowering his head. The estate manager put his hand on his shoulder. 'Why didn't yer say, old feller? 'Tis notorious round these parts what the Aloe vera can do to an honest man's hands.'

'I know. They used to be coarse and gritty, my hands did. Young women would flinch when I touched them.'

'Aye, as young women should.'

'Then I started working for Lord Whitrow. I said I didn't want to work on the Aloe vera, 'cos I'd heard all the stories.'

' I know,' muttered the estate manager.

'But I was — I were — only a young lad then, and I couldn't say no. I stuck it out for ten years, and in that time my poor hands became so soft that even a cat would let me stroke it!'

'No! A cat?'

'It's true. And women used to say that they liked me to hold their hands.'

'Holding hands is no way for a rough cottager to carry on.'

'I know. I know.' Wickham waited for a moment and then looked up at the estate manager again. 'Sir, will you give me a chance to turn my life around? Will you let me use my wretched smooth hands for gorse-gathering? Will you allow me to pummel stones for her ladyship's rockery? Will you let me develop some proper calluses?'

The estate manager looked back at him and Wickham detected the faintest ghost of a smile. Then he patted Wickham on the back. ''Course we will,' he said.

Elizabeth was just about to ascend the stairs to her room when she noticed Mrs Garson coming towards her carrying a tray.

'Morning, ma'am,' said old Mrs Garson. 'I was just taking a little breakfast up to our other—er—guest.'

'Ah, the mysterious Mr Byron,' said Elizabeth.

'Lord Byron, I'll have you know,' said Mrs Garson, raising her eyebrows. She sounded as though she could scarcely believe it.

'Really?' said Elizabeth. 'I wasn't aware that he was a member of the nobility.' She looked at the contents of Lord Byron's breakfast tray, some of the details of which seemed unusual. 'I wonder, could you tell me what that is around the edge of the teacup there?'

'Ah, that is sugar, ma'am. His lordship says that a gentleman needs a good hard rim in the morning to wake him up.'

'Good Lord,' said Elizabeth. 'I have never heard of that before. I must try it myself some day.' She paused. 'Tell me, Mrs Garson,' she continued. 'Do you know how Mrs Collins became acquainted with Lord Byron?'

'Ah, that's an easy one. They both happened to be looking for some works of art in an auction not far from here, and his lordship offered to put Mrs Collins in touch with his dealer. Although,' and here her voice dropped to a whisper, 'I don't think he's on very good terms with this dealer any more, because I overheard him say the reason he's staying here right now is to avoid the man. Some dispute over a wicked skunk or some such.'

'Well, there's a thing!' said Elizabeth. 'So he trades in exotic animals as well?'

'Apparently so. But you know, ma'am, I'm a simple soul and I know little of the world beyond the garden gate. It all seems mighty queer to me, and the least said about it the better. All I know is he's not good for my mistress. And I worry about what he's doing to the carpet in his room, too.'

'I beg your pardon?' asked Elizabeth at this apparent non-sequitur.

'He's refusing to let the parlour maid in to clean his room,' explained Mrs Garson in an aggrieved tone. 'Says it's a bit of a mess 'cos of him dropping some bad acid last week. Well, I ask you!'

'So he is a man of science as well as a musician, then?'

'He writes poems, too. Filthy they are, some of them. I found one or two lying around last time I ventured in there. There's this one about a ship called Venus.'

'The goddess of love? But surely that is a delightful idea?'

'Ha! You might think that, but I can assure you that you wouldn't want to know what he says happened on that there ship. If that's what goes on in the English Navy, well, I'll tell you this for free: old Boney's won the war already.' She frowned and shook her head. 'But I will say this. Lord Byron can be a generous man. Only the other day he invited a couple of the young lads from the village in for a pork sandwich. He must have thought they were starving, poor mites.'

'So thoughtful!'

Mrs Garson's face brightened. 'And you know what? Only the other day he offered to give me a pearl necklace! At my age!'

'Great heavens! Is there no end to the man's generosity?'

''Course I couldn't take it,' said Mrs Garson. 'Wouldn't have been right.' She sighed. 'Anyways, I must be getting along, otherwise his lordship's tea's going to get cold. And Mrs Collins will be—er—needing her morning tonic.'

There was something a little over-familiar about the way Mrs Garson tapped the side of her nose, Elizabeth thought.

The prisoner looked at the latest arrangement of scratches on the wall, counted four and then drew a diagonal line through them. He stepped back and admired his handiwork. The entire wall in front of him was now covered, and a visitor who didn't know better might imagine that he'd been there for years. The truth was more mundane. He just liked drawing gates.

He sat down again on the cold granite and sighed. This was getting boring. He was almost beginning to look forward to the probing sessions, because at least you got to talk to someone, even if the conversation was not greatly diverting. He wondered what it was like outside. The only light the room received was from a small window high up near the ceiling, and the temperature was uniformly cold day and night. At least they'd given him a blanket to wrap round himself now, even if it did smell strongly of horse.

His reverie was interrupted by the sound of singing, far off beyond the opposite wall. He raced over and pressed his ear against the stone. He could just make out the words:

> *My Master has a ding-a-ling-a-ling*
> *and he plays with it all day long*

'Hey!' he shouted, slapping his hand against the wall. The voice stopped immediately. 'Who goes there?' he called, slapping the wall again. There was silence for several seconds and then the voice started up once more:

> *I wish I had a ding-a-ling-a-ling*
> *but he says it would be wrong*

It was a young girl's voice, tuneful and lilting. The prisoner found it uplifting and tantalising at the same time. He slapped the wall again.

'Hey! Speak to me, stranger!' he shouted. ''Tis a pretty tune you sing, young maiden, but I would much rather have discourse with you.'

There was another long silence.

'Please?' he said. He heard the sound of footsteps approaching the other side of the wall.

'Who goes there?' came the voice. 'Do you intend to probe me, sir?'

'No, madam. Sadly, I am the probee in these parts.'

'Ah, so you are a fellow prisoner, then.'

'I am indeed.'

There was a brief pause.

'May I enquire as to who you are?' asked the girl hesitantly. 'Do you know your name?'

The man sighed. 'No, I fear I do not.'

'Ah.'Tis the same with me. I fear my mind may have been befuddled. I remember nothing that happened before the day I arrived here.'

'And yet your voice—your voice—it reminds me of someone I used to know.'

'Really? How nice. I wonder who that was.'

'Yes, I wonder too.'

There was another silence, longer this time.

'Do you think they'll ever let us out of this dreadful place?' asked the girl.

'I don't know. Perhaps there are yet friends of ours striving to set us free. Surely we must have had friends once?'

'I am sure we must. We must have had friends. Everyone has friends. Even . . .'

And then it seemed that the effort of trying to keep her spirits up finally failed the girl, because all the man could hear now was sobbing.

'No, please don't start weeping, my dear—'

'It's all right. I merely have a mote of dust in my eye. Look! I rub my eye and blink once, then 'tis clear.' She paused. 'You are right, sir. We must be steadfast. We must dream of freedom.'

'Is it not true that the darkest hour is the one before the dawn?'

There was a moment's silence.

'But 'tis always dark in here, sir,' replied the girl, quietly.

It was a balmy evening. Elizabeth, Charlotte and Lord Byron sat outside in the Collins' little garden, replete after an excellent supper. The air was thick with the scent of cherry blossom, wisteria and the smoke from Lord Byron's extraordinary cheroots. Elizabeth took a fit of coughing and tried to waft away the smoke with her fan, but Charlotte didn't seem unduly concerned. In fact, she seemed to be positively inhaling it, and her chair was reclining at an alarming angle.

'Hey, Lizzy,' she said, breathing in deeply, 'Y'seem dis—dis—distracked, my dear. Relax. Jus' . . . be cool.'

'Cool?' repeated Elizabeth, gasping.

'Yeah . . . cool. Everything's cool. That right, Lord B?'

There was no response from Byron, who was staring up at the sky as if in a trance.

'Charlotte, I think—' Elizabeth began, but the clouds of smoke were starting to have an effect on her. She felt quite giddy. Yet after a while, a feeling of intense well-being flooded over her, and she started to imagine that everything was all right in the world after all.

Charlotte was trying to stand up and failing. 'Hey, Lord B,' she was saying, 'Don't Bonaparte that cheroot. Pass it over to me.'

'Wha' say?' said Elizabeth, struggling to locate her vocabulary, which seemed to have temporarily gone missing.

'Gimme smoke,' said Charlotte, waving at Byron. With one mighty effort, she heaved herself out of her chair and fell flat on the grass. She and Elizabeth stared at each other for a moment, and then started sniggering in perfect unison.

'Oi, Byron,' said Charlotte from her horizontal position. 'Want a smoke. Lizzy wants a smoke too.'

'I don't,' said Elizabeth, even though, much to her own astonishment, she found that she really rather fancied one.

'You so do,' insisted Charlotte.

'I so don't.'

'Lizzy,' said Charlotte, heaving herself up onto her elbows. 'You're my bestest friend ever.'

'An' you're mine, too,' said Elizabeth, kneeling down next to her. 'And Lord Byron's our next bestest friend, aren't you, Lordy B?'

But Lord Byron was still gazing up at the heavens. 'Moon,' he said, and then 'June'.

'Byron,' said Charlotte. 'You're a dead rubbish poet.'

Charlotte and Elizabeth both burst into giggles again, hugging each other in order to avoid collapsing on the ground. Byron ignored them.

'Someone once told me,' he remarked, 'that there is no dark side of the moon really. As a matter of fact—'

'Wassat?' demanded Charlotte, sitting up sharply. She was pointing up at the sky, where a vast saucer-shaped flying machine, blazing with lights, was passing overhead in a slow and stately trajectory.

'Whoa,' said Elizabeth, her mouth agape. 'That is . . . that is . . . so . . .'

'Totally . . .'

'Unbelievably . . .'

'Jus' amazing,' concluded Charlotte.

There was a brief silence. They watched as the great ship continued on its elegant way over towards the great house, where it drifted down towards the ground and disappeared.

'Charlotte,' said Elizabeth, when it had gone. 'Hassat ever happened to you before?'

Charlotte nodded frantically. 'Allthetime, Lizzy dearest. Allthetime.'

Elizabeth took a deep breath and then turned to Lord

Byron. 'Hey you,' she said. 'Think I'll try a smoke of that stuff after all.'

Meanwhile, in his room at the Saucer and Tentacle, undercover agent and would-be rough cottager George Wickham was oblivious to anything going on outside. He had had an utterly exhausting day in the fields at Rosings and was flat out on his bed fast asleep, having not even managed to take off his boots.

Chapter Six

Annie Chapman's Fate—Down the Rabbit Hole—Consequences—About Last Night—Phase Two

WELL, SAID THE ghost of Mary Ann Nicholls to herself, that went well, didn't it? Barely a couple of days into the job and she had managed to make a complete and utter mess of looking after Annie Chapman. In fact, barely half an hour had passed between her encounter with the Headless Whore and poor Annie being duped by that unpleasant Mr Collins into joining his Mission.

She'd tried everything. She'd kicked him, pinched her, shouted 'HELLO?' as loud as she could right in her face, but neither of them took the blindest bit of notice. It clearly wasn't anywhere near as simple as Headless had made out. Mind you, now she thought about it, taking advice from someone who didn't have their head attached probably wasn't the best idea she'd ever had.

Mary Ann had watched Annie subjected to the same peculiar probing that she'd been on the wrong end of. It wasn't a pretty sight from any angle. Once again she'd tried her best to distract the nurse whilst she was carrying out the procedure, and once again she'd completely failed to make any impression on the land of the living.

Then Annie was introduced to that cold, inhuman creature Mr Darcy, and Chosen, just like she had been. Oddly, this time Mary Ann noticed that it started with a capital letter. Maybe that was something that happened when you were dead. Perhaps when you walked through a few educated people some of the learning rubbed off on you. She stopped and thought about this for a moment.

'A', she said to herself.

'B'.

'C'.

Bloody hell. If only she'd known all her letters when she was still alive. She could have offered BDSM and charged extra for it.

She sighed. But all her new learning hadn't helped poor Annie, had it? And there was the proof, lying on the bed asleep in front of her. Annie was having a disturbed night, thrashing from left to right, drooling and sweating feverishly. Occasionally she would call out something like 'No!', 'Help!' or 'Tentacles!' and flail her arms about wildly. I must have looked like this, thought Mary Ann, the night before it happened. And the same thing's going to happen to her.

The worst thing was when Annie and Mr Darcy—she could hardly think of a word to describe what they did. It certainly wasn't anything on her price list, that was for sure. And something very odd had happened to Mr Darcy whilst it was going on. He'd seemed to change. Things had grown out of him: tentacle-y things, un-human things, things from a different . . . species.

As soon as she'd realised what was going on, she'd tried to stop it of course. And at one point, she almost felt that Mr Darcy noticed her, because for one brief moment, his eyes caught hers. There was the faintest glint of a smile, and then he returned to his grotesque business with Annie.

And now Annie was lying there, wracked by nightmares, with a strange unnatural thing growing inside her. Mary Ann leant over her and tried to stroke her hair to calm her down. As she did so, Annie's hand fell open and a piece of card tumbled out and landed on the floor. Mary Ann looked down at it and read the name *Lieut. Geo. Wickham, Dept of Unusual Affairs*, and an address where he could be contacted.

Perhaps this was a man who might be able to help.

The ground was definitely humming, thought Wickham. He lay spread-eagled on the rough grass of the paddock and pushed the side of his head down as far as he could. No, it wasn't so much a hum. More of a throb. Either way, it was more noise than paddocks usually made. And now that he pressed both of his palms flat against the grass he could feel the slightest hint of a vibration.

Kneeling up again, he carefully looked around to see that no one was watching. He reckoned he was pretty safe, as the paddock foreman tended to nip off for a swift half or two round about lunchtime. He wouldn't return for a couple of hours yet—if he managed to stagger back at all, as he seemed to measure his halves in gallons. Satisfied that he was unobserved, Wickham began to scratch away at the ground with his bare hands.

As he dug further and further into the earth, the vibrations increased and his hands began to tingle. Then, about six inches down, he came across something solid. It was smooth and warm to the touch.

Encouraged by this discovery, he scrabbled away at the hole until he had uncovered an area about a foot square. The surface underneath was unbroken, dull and metallic. But it was no metal that he'd ever come across, and he wondered if he'd manage to get a sample back to H for analysis. Unfortunately, that would mean trying to saw a piece of it off, and that could prove difficult. He'd have to come back under the cover of darkness.

Wickham became aware that he was being watched. He turned around and looked straight into the face of the estate manager.

'Been diggin' for buried treasure, 'ave we?' he asked.

'Er, n-no, no. I dropped my felching trowel down a rabbit hole.'

'A rabbit 'ole, eh?'

'Yes, and you know what rabbit holes are like, once you dig away at them, you just go further and further down. There's a whole matrix of tunnels down there.'

The estate manager squatted down next to Wickham and peered at his excavations.

'Funny ol' rabbit 'ole,' he said, looking at Wickham with one eyebrow raised.

'Yes,' said Wickham. 'Isn't it?'

There was a long silence. Then the estate manager stood up and methodically kicked all the earth that Wickham had dug up back into the hole.

'Wouldn't want any of 'er ladyship's fine 'orses catching their hooves in this, would we now?' he said.

Wickham stood up. 'I suppose not.'

The estate manager looked hard at Wickham and tilted his head on one side. 'Y'know, you're not soft, are you? But there's things go on here that don't concern the likes o' you and me. And if you take my advice, you don't want to go pokin' yer nose where yer nose ain't supposed to be poked. Right?'

'Right,' agreed Wickham. 'Right.' He really couldn't tell how much the estate manager knew.

'So, do we have an understanding?'

'Of course.'

'Good. Like I said, you're not soft, are you?' The estate manager relaxed a little. 'Anyways, the reason I came over was to say we need an extra 'and over by the cobber-mangling shed. So if you know what's good for you, you'll be getting your arse over there right away.'

He paused, as if trying to remember something important. 'Oh,' he added. 'An' I'll be dockin' you 'alf a day's wages for losin' a felchin' trowel, by the way. Those things cost a bleedin' fortune.'

As he said it, Wickham thought he caught the faintest ghost of a wink.

Elizabeth awoke with her mouth full of grass. This was to be expected, given that she had fallen asleep face down on the Collins' lawn, but it was quite some time before she established the connection between this action and its consequence. Likewise, it took Elizabeth several minutes to deduce the connection between the damp state of her dress and the presence of dew.

She spat out the grass and tried to sit up. This could not be considered successful, owing to the fact that her attempt was curtailed in short measure following an attack on her head by a renegade army of pickaxe brandishing midgets.

Her mouth had been used as a receptacle for cigar ash by some small creature of the night, and then as a location for its funeral pyre. She felt bad. Things were seriously amiss.

'Afternoon, ma'am,' came a voice from several miles above her.

'Urgh,' said Elizabeth by way of response.

''S'alright, ma'am. You don't need to get up for my benefit.' Through the fog that surrounded her brain, Elizabeth slowly recognised the voice as belonging to Mrs

Garson. Visual confirmation of this was impossible as her eyes were still firmly clamped shut. But as she listened harder, she thought she could detect undertones of either disapproval or disappointment.

'Urghmfthrgh,' she managed.

'I wouldn't have disturbed you,' said Mrs Garson. 'Only we've had word from the big house. Apparently Lady Catherine's guests arrived last night—foreign gentlemen, I'll have you know—and you and Mrs C are cordially invited.'

'Laycathdeburgh?' queried Elizabeth.

'That's the one.'

'Ohgogh.'

'Well, I wouldn't worry too much about it. Still plenty of time to get ready.'

Mrs Garson's cheery voice was several thousand shades too bright for Elizabeth's head. The clammy dress was beginning to annoy her, and once again she tried to move herself. Once again she admitted defeat. Then she suddenly remembered the previous evening, with Lord Byron and his horrible cheroots. And those extraordinary hallucinations about flying machines . . .

'Ohgogh,' she repeated.

'I know it's not my place to say so,' said Mrs Garson. 'But I did warn you about Lord B. He's a queer one and no mistake.'

'Iknowiknowiknowiknow,' Elizabeth agreed. Then she remembered something important. 'Charlottalrigh?'

'Sleeping like a baby. Heard her crawling up the stairs to her room in the early hours. I'll go in and wake her up the usual way I do when she's ga-ga. Poke her face, I do. Always works. I was all set to do the same to you, ma'am, begging your permission.'

'Urgh,' replied Elizabeth, satisfied with this news. She

didn't, frankly, care what state Lord Byron himself was in. The man was a menace and she fervently hoped the invitation to Rosings tonight did not include him. Heaven knows what he might get up to there.

'So what time do you think you might be getting up, ma'am?' asked Mrs Garson.

'Soosoosoosoon.' Elizabeth tried blinking her eyes open and immediately shut them again. The world was far too shiny a place for her to join at the present time.

'I only ask 'cos I've got a nice luncheon prepared for you here. Pickled eggs, diced carrots—'

At this, Elizabeth made one final attempt to sit up and this time she succeeded. However, the strain was too much for her delicate constitution, and she began to retch violently. She forced her eyes open and, to her absolute horror, observed the pool of regurgitated supper in front of her had apparently acquired legs.

'Don't worry, ma'am,' said Mrs Garson, looking down. 'Them shoes of mine needed a good clean anyway.'

By late afternoon, Elizabeth's head was feeling considerably better, although her coordination was still poor. She fervently hoped she would not be called upon that evening to perform on Lady Catherine's pianoforte—or at least anything more complicated than a couple of refrains of Mr Cobain's Maggot.

Charlotte joined her in the front parlour and seemed to be finding it difficult to express herself.

'Dearest Lizzy, about last night—' she began.

''Tis nothing. I have forgotten the occasion already. 'Tis as if it never happened.'

Charlotte looked at Lizzy in a hopeful manner and then shook her head. 'No,' she said. 'It is not a trifle. I have done you wrong, dearest friend. I have shared intoxicants with you, which are the gateway to the deep, dark void at the heart of my very being. You do not want to go there.'

'I most certainly don't, dearest Charlotte.' Elizabeth paused for a moment, pondering the depths of Charlotte's dark void. Then she came to a decision. 'I think you should dismiss Lord Byron from this house at once.'

Charlotte looked at her uncertainly. 'Must I?' she pleaded.

'Yes, you must. He is a corrupting influence. And what would your husband say if he knew?'

'Mr Collins is never home,' said Charlotte, coldly. 'How could he ever find out?'

'We-e-ell, that's not quite the point of my proposal,' said Elizabeth, fearing that Charlotte was not taking her suggestion in quite the way she had hoped. Then a question occurred to her that she'd always intended to ask.

'What exactly is it that Mr Collins does in his mission?'

'Dearest Lizzy, have I not explained to you before? Lady Catherine de Bourgh has charged Mr Collins to rescue the fallen women of Whitechapel.'

Elizabeth considered this. 'And do women fall a lot in Whitechapel?' she said. 'Are the pavements particularly badly maintained?'

Charlotte smiled. 'No, no, no. You know. Fallen women.' She made a gesture with her hand that Elizabeth failed to understand. So Charlotte whispered something in her ear instead.

'No!' said Elizabeth. And then, 'Really? How extraordinary. I had no idea that sort of thing went on in Whitechapel.'

'Yes, apparently it does. And Mr Collins tells me that some of them even—'

There was a cough as a newcomer entered the room,

preceded by a waft of exotic pomade. Elizabeth looked up in horror as Lord Byron loomed over her.

'So, ladies, are we all ready to depart?' he asked.

She turned to her companion in alarm.

'Charlotte, you can't seriously imagine that it is a good idea for—' she could scarcely bear to speak his name '—this man to join us at Rosings tonight.'

Charlotte gave a weak shrug and smiled thinly back at her. Elizabeth scowled. 'Sir,' she said, looking directly into his eyes. 'You are a cad and a libertine. You are a bad influence on Charlotte, and—'

'*Au contraire*, my dear,' he said. 'Any influence I have on your poor friend here is entirely for the better. And in any case, I understand the invitation extends to the gentleman as well as the ladies in this room. Fear not, however. I shall behave myself— unless the evening becomes a dreadful bore, in which case I may perchance undertake to spice things up a little.' At this, he withdrew a small vial from an inside pocket and tapped his nose.

Elizabeth turned away in disgust. Charlotte maintained an embarrassed silence.

'Hmmm. I wonder what they will serve us for supper?' continued Lord Byron. 'I rather fancy a roast.'

The cage containing the small tentacled animal sat on the desk between Mr Collins and Mr Darcy. The little beast was bouncing up and down and squeaking in an apparent attempt to gain the latter's attention.

'I think it wants a cuddle,' said Mr Collins, amazed at such a word issuing from his own lips. Up to this point in his life, he had shown little interest in children, being firmly of the view that they should neither be seen nor heard until they had reached middle-age. However, ever since he had rescued this one from recycling, he had developed a curious bond with it. 'Look,' he said, pointing to Mr Darcy, 'That's Papa!'

Mr Darcy made a face and pushed the cage away from him. 'Mr Collins,' he said. 'Please desist. I am not that creature's Papa, as you put it. That thing is merely the unfortunate by-product of a biological experiment, and because of your unwarranted fondness for it, we are low on our quota for grade C slop for tonight's supper.' At this, the creature stopped bouncing for a moment and fixed Mr Darcy with a watery glare.

'But Mr Darcy—'

Mr Collins was sure that this wasn't quite what he had agreed to when Lady Catherine de Bourgh—his beloved patroness—had asked him to set up the Mission. In fact the whole set-up was more than a little queer, and if it had been anyone other than Lady Catherine . . .

'Enough!' said Mr Darcy. 'I have received word from the High Command that we are to move on to Phase Two of the Experiment.'

Mr Collins blanched. 'Phase Two? Are you sure? We cannot possibly be ready for—'

'Ready or not, we must move on.'

A vision of Annie Chapman's ruptured corpse floated briefly through Mr Collins' mind and he shuddered. 'But Mr Darcy, as I'm sure you will be aware, we have had two—ah—rejections already.'

'I am fully aware of this. But the same thing may not necessarily happen to the Prime Subject. She is different. I may know more about this very soon, a fortunate coincidence has given two of our Technicians the opportunity to inspect her themselves this very evening. In fact, we have your wife to thank for this.'

Mr Collins gasped. He opened his mouth to speak but failed to fill it with anything approaching words. The creature in the cage tilted its head on one side and gave him a tender, sympathetic look.

'My wife?' he asked eventually.

'Yes. I believe you have a wife, Mr Collins?'

'I—well—but you have not involved her in this business, have you? I hasten to add of course that if this is what Lady Catherine de Bourgh wishes, then so be it. Lady Catherine's desires are coincident with mine, as always. But I did not think—'

'Mr Collins, we will take whatever steps we need to achieve our objective. However, in this case you may rest assured that your wife is an innocent bystander. She has merely been the vessel that has conveyed the Prime Subject to Rosings.'

'Ah.'

'I shall be leaving for Pemberley tomorrow,' continued Mr Darcy, 'to await the Prime Subject's return. And then Phase Two of the Experiment will commence.'

'I—I—am speechless,' said Mr Collins. 'I mean, I am in awe.'

Mr Darcy's lips straightened into a thin smile in acknowledgement.

'So does this mean that the other poor girls—'

'It means that they will have to be processed tonight, Mr Collins. Please therefore arrange for Elizabeth Stride, Catherine Eddowes and Mary Jane Kelly to be prepared and then brought to my chamber.'

Mr Collins grimaced and bowed his head. As he did so, the cage in front of him rattled from side to side and a tentacle shot out, giving Mr Darcy's nose a tweak. Mr Collins stifled a smirk, before noticing, to his chagrin, that an evil-smelling liquid was now leaking out from the base of the cage and burning a hole through his desk.

Chapter Seven

*Lady Catherine's Foreign Visitors — The
Information Superflyway — Resistance is
Useless — The Prisoner's Dilemma — Lord Byron
to the Rescue*

AN APPRECIATIVE SILENCE descended over the
heavy oak dining table at Rosings, as Lady Catherine de Bourgh's party quaffed their claret and tucked
into their roast beef. Lady Catherine herself sat at the
head of the table, presiding regally over the occasion,
whilst Charlotte and Lord Byron sat next to each other
on one side. Elizabeth was seated on the opposite side to
them, between the two curious foreign visitors. She had
been given their names, but despite several attempts all
she managed to grasp was that one of them was apparently called Cuthooloo. It was, however, possible that
she had misheard this.

Elizabeth cut off a slice of beef and was about to eat it
when she caught Charlotte's eye. Her friend was motioning with her head towards the gentleman on her right, so
Elizabeth risked a glance in his direction. He was struggling to put his food in his mouth, and in fact the more
that Elizabeth studied him, the more his mouth seemed to
be nothing more than a rather badly gouged hole in the

scarred flesh of his face. Her hand shot to her own in an involuntary motion.

'I hope you won't mind me asking, sir,' she said, trying to recover her composure, 'but would I be correct in deducing from your scars that you are a military man?' She had been warned that neither of the two gentlemen had a good grasp of The King's English, but she felt that it was the least that she could do to attempt to engage them in polite discourse. However, the man's red eyes registered alarm.

'Ek—ek—ek—ek!' he said by way of response.

'I see,' said Elizabeth, nonplussed. 'I do apologise, but I am unfamiliar with your country's language. Perhaps you could explain to me your meaning once again?'

'Eek! Ek—ek—ek—ek!' said the man again, more urgently than before. Elizabeth noted with some alarm that the same sound was now issuing from the gentlemen on her left as well, and she wondered if she had breached some important rule of etiquette. She looked up towards the head of the table and saw Lady Catherine glaring back at her.

'Mrs Darcy,' said Lady Catherine, 'Perhaps it would be better if you were to confine your experiments with conversation to those of us who understand your ways of speech?'

'I do apologise, your Ladyship. I had no idea—'

'These gentlemen have travelled far, and they are in no frame of mind to trade trivialities over the supper table with you, Mrs Darcy.'

Then why on earth have you brought me here, thought Elizabeth?

'They have merely expressed an interest in observing your manners,' continued Lady Catherine, as if reading Elizabeth's mind. 'They have little experience of young

English ladies, such as yourself, where they come from.' Elizabeth glanced from side to side and noticed that the two gentlemen were now staring at her with an intensity that was more than a little disconcerting.

For a moment, she was convinced that something tentacle-like had popped out of the collar of the one on her left. She looked ahead and noticed that Lord Byron had an odd little smile playing around his lips. Oh heavens, she thought. Has he put something in the drinks already?

'And may I say, Lady Catherine,' he said, 'That you have made an excellent choice in Mrs Darcy here.' Elizabeth grimaced and Lady Catherine de Bourgh fixed him with a gimlet eye, suggesting she was yet to make up her mind about this. There was an awkward silence, broken eventually by Lady Catherine herself.

'Lord Byron,' she said, 'These gentlemen would be very interested to hear of your exploits in the saddle. I believe you ride to hounds?'

Lord Byron smiled that curious little smile once more. 'Ah. Perhaps you misunderstood me. When I referred earlier to 'dogging', what I meant was—'

He had no time to finish his sentence. He was interrupted by Charlotte suddenly pointing at the gentleman on Elizabeth's left. She screamed and then fainted, head first, into her supper.

Wickham heard the scream as he crept round the side of the house, leading Jennifer behind him. As soon as he heard it, he tied the horse up to the nearest tree and raced over to the nearest window.

A peculiar sight met his eyes. Lady Catherine de Bourgh was seated at table with her back to him. To her left were a gentleman that he did not recognise and a lady who was almost certainly the author of the scream—now

incapable of making any sound owing to having a face full
of beef and gravy. To Lady Catherine's right were two
strange individuals, one of whom seemed to be struggling
to put his face back together. The penny dropped. Aliens!
Damned aliens in disguise!

Then Wickham noticed who was seated between
them. He gasped. Without a moment's hesitation, he ran
back to Jennifer and located the compartment containing
Colin, his pedigree White Emperor carrier pigeon. His
immediate instinct was to abandon his mission altogether
and race in to save Elizabeth, but he needed to check with
HQ first.

He scribbled a note to Colonel Sutherland, rolled it
up and attached it to Colin's leg. Then he unstrapped
a second compartment and withdrew a bottle, followed
by cylindrical object with a long wooden stick and a fuse
poking out of one end. The object was labelled 'Primary
Booster' and the sight of it caused the pigeon to start
hopping up and down in alarm.

'Sorry,' said Wickham, tying the booster to Colin's
back, 'but I need a response within a matter of minutes,
so we need to use the information superflyway. Just hang
in there until it burns itself out, all right?'

The pigeon shook its head violently and then put its
wings over its eyes as Wickham placed the booster in the
bottle and lit the fuse. After a few seconds, the rocket lit
up the sky as it soared aloft, carrying its avian passenger
towards London.

'God speed you, White Emperor,' said Wickham.

He had only been pacing up and down for a few
minutes before he heard a squawking in the sky above
him as Colin returned, tumbling out of the sky in a mael-
strom of flapping wings, before impaling himself in the
ground, beak first. In the moonlight, Wickham could just

make out a wispy plume of smoke from the bird's tail and the faintest whiff of cordite in the air.

Wickham went over to where Colin had landed and prised him out of the ground. The pigeon seemed relatively unharmed, but his little heart was going nineteen to the dozen. 'Sorry,' said Wickham again.

Colin fixed him with a malevolent glare and nipped his finger as he was untying Colonel Sutherland's reply from the bird's leg. 'Ow!' said Wickham, and for an instant, he was convinced Colin was grinning. Without further ado, he put the bird back in his cage in Jennifer's saddle.

Colonel Sutherland's response was terse. It simply said, 'Rescue ED at all costs.' Wickham had already worked out his plan of action, and he knew exactly what equipment he needed.

He let down the other side of Jennifer's saddle and removed his Lee Van Enfield musket, complete with the custom super-soaker attachment. Having assembled this, he returned to the window.

Peering in, he could see that the woman who fainted was now having smelling salts administered to her by the gentleman sitting next to her, whilst Elizabeth Darcy was leaning over and touching her on the arm. As she did this, Elizabeth was evidently oblivious to the the aliens extending their tentacles towards her. Wickham had to act fast.

He smashed the window with the butt of the musket and pumped a high-pressure water stream over each of the candles, plunging the room into darkness.

Inside the dining room, chaos reigned. Voices were raised in alarm, and footsteps clattered in every direction. Elizabeth was trying to make her way towards where she thought the door was, but her path was blocked.

'Excuse me,' she said, 'But I need to—urgh!' She felt something clammy against her face.

'Ek—ek——ek,' said a voice in the darkness in front of her.

'Oh, it's you,' she said, trying to remove the clammy hand—no, it wasn't a hand, more of a—no, surely not?—well, whatever it was—from her face. But someone else was approaching from behind her.

'Ek—ek—ek.' came another voice.

'I do so wish you would stop doing that,' said Elizabeth, turning around, 'Because—yeech!' Great heavens! What was happening now? There seemed to be two lots of slimy things crawling around her face now. Then, all of a sudden, she heard footsteps and a familiar voice bellow:

'Unhand that lady, sir, or you shall feel the power of my fist!'

'Wickham?' cried Elizabeth. Then the man behind her collapsed, having evidently been punched hard in the mouth. She took this as her cue to turn on the other one and made a grab for his face, which unexpectedly came away in her hands.

Dropping the horrible thing on the floor, she stood transfixed as her eyes, which were now adjusting to the gloom, saw what her mind could not begin to comprehend. The person in front of her no longer had a face at all, but tentacles!

It wasn't in front of her for much longer, however, because another hefty blow from Wickham sent it swiftly in a direction towards the horizontal.

'Mrs Darcy, are you all right?' asked Wickham.

'Y—es,' stuttered Elizabeth, although her answer was inaccurate in almost every single respect. What had that man Lord Byron put in the drinks? What on earth was happening? Surely this couldn't be real?

'—sure?' Wickham was saying.

'I am perfectly well, Mr Wickham,' she stated, recovering her composure, 'But—' her hand went to her mouth—'Lord Byron! Charlotte! Where's Charlotte?'

There was no reply.

'Charlotte! Where are you?'

The room was completely silent now. Then the tiniest whimper came from the doorway. Wickham whirled around towards the source of the sound, raising a finger towards Elizabeth. Peering into the gloom, she could observe nothing apart from a couple of indistinct shapes. She saw Wickham reach into his pocket and withdraw something, which he proceeded to strike on the sole of his boot. When he brought his hand up again, it held a flame.

Holding the light, Wickham slowly approached the door, with Elizabeth following behind at a short distance.

As they got nearer, she saw Lord Byron lying on the floor, apparently unconscious. Well, serve him right, thought Elizabeth, immediately regretting it.

Then she looked up and saw Lady Catherine de Bourgh standing in the doorway, her arm firmly gripping the neck of Charlotte Collins.

'Well, Mr Wickham,' said Lady Catherine, 'What a fine mess you've made of things. And not for the first time, either.'

'Let her go,' said Wickham. 'She's no threat to you.'

'Give me the Darcy woman instead.'

'No!'

'It's all right, I don't mind,' began Elizabeth, once again being less then strictly accurate about her frame of mind.

'No!' repeated Wickham.

'In that case, I have no alternative but to incarcerate you all,' said Lady Catherine. 'I have sounded the alarm. Within a matter of minutes, this place will be overrun and

81

you will be powerless. Resistance is useless! Prepare to be probed!'

In the dungeon, the prisoner stared at the open door, wondering when they were going to come back with his food. This was so annoying. He had a feeling it was going to be the nice light grey gruel tonight too, which was his favourite, marginally ahead of the dark green stodge. In fact he was becoming so accustomed to it that he was thinking of asking for the recipe when — if? — he was ever released from this place.

And he really, really wished someone would stop ringing those bloody bells.

It was the bells that had caused the problem. The guard called Bob had just come down with his evening tray. He'd unlocked the door to the cell and was just about to enter when the bells started, causing both of them to jump several metaphorical feet in the air.

In Bob's case, the jump was literal as well as metaphorical, albeit only several inches, but sufficient to cause him to scatter the prisoner's food all over the floor of the corridor outside.

'Bugger,' said Bob, running off without stopping so much as to tidy up the mess. Clearly the bells meant something important. But that had been several minutes ago, and there was no sign of Bob returning.

The prisoner stared at the open door again. The bell outside the cell was getting really annoying, and he wondered if there was any way of muffling it somehow. Perhaps he could use some of his blanket as a damper.

He removed it and picked away at a corner, intending to tear off a small square. Unfortunately, in the process of doing this, he managed to remove a strip down the whole of one side. This left a frayed edge on the rest of the blanket, which without any further human intervention, managed to completely unravel itself into a tangled ball of coarse wool.

'Oops,' he said to himself, looking at the sad remains of his clothing.

The bell was still ringing.

Finally, he shuffled to the door. He peered out into the corridor. There was no one there. He went over to where the bell was, reached up and stuffed the strip of blanket into it. At last the dreadful sound stopped and there was silence.

Silence, that is, apart from the bells ringing further away in the building. The prisoner examined the remains of his food congealing on the stone floor. He bent down, put his finger in and then licked it. It was the light grey gruel!

He looked up and down the corridor again. There really was no one there. No one to stop him just leaving. Walking out. Escaping.

But if he escaped, he'd miss out on the light grey gruel.

He really had been looking forward to it.

It was quite a dilemma.

Then he thought of the probe, sighed and shut the cell door behind him. He prevaricated a further moment, wondering which way to go, before heading off in the direction of the bells.

He briefly wondered if he should do something about the prisoner in the cell next to him, but remembered he wasn't exactly dressed to meet a lady. He could always come back for her later. Once he'd got some clothes.

'You'll never get away with this!' said Wickham.

'Oh, I rather think I shall.' replied Lady Catherine de Bourgh. Elizabeth was rooted to the spot, desperately trying to think of something to do. Then she happened to glance down at the prostrate form of Lord Byron and, in the half-light, she was sure she saw him wink at her. She quickly looked back at Lady Catherine, hoping she had not seen this.

'Lady Catherine,' she said, suddenly feeling quite emboldened, 'I am more than a little surprised you find this an appropriate way for someone of your standing in society to behave.'

'What impudence!' said her ladyship. 'How dare you—urgh!' She reeled backwards as Lord Byron hurled the phial of liquid at her. Her reaction was not unusual, but nothing compared to what happened next.

Her body was suddenly transformed into a mass of writhing tentacles. 'Ek—ek—ek!' screamed Lady Catherine.

'My God!' shouted Wickham. 'A shape shifter! Stay back, evil beast from Hell!'

'Charlotte, my dear,' said Elizabeth, trying to stay calm, 'I think you may find this could be an excellent opportunity to free yourself.' As if in a dream, Charlotte gently moved aside the tentacles and fell forward. Elizabeth caught her and pulled her away to safety.

The four of them started to back away from the many-tendrilled monster that was gradually reasserting itself into the form of Lady Catherine.

'When I give the word,' said Wickham, 'Get back to the window.' He waited for Lady Catherine to advance a little further and then kicked the door back in her face. There was a muffled imprecation from the other side. 'Now!' he shouted. Elizabeth and Byron turned and ran for the window, dragging Charlotte after them. Byron gave Elizabeth a leg up and she leapt through, landing on the ground outside. Then Byron passed Charlotte down to her, and finally the two men followed.

'Stop!' came a cry. It was one of the Rosings footmen, appearing from the side of the house, closely followed by Lady Catherine herself.

'This way, Mrs Darcy,' said Wickham. 'I have Jennifer parked over by that tree.' He turned to Byron. 'Take care of Mrs Collins, sir. They will not follow you, but you would be wise to go to ground until this damnable business is over.'

'Fear not', replied Byron. 'I shall take most excellent care of her.' He winked again, slung Charlotte over his back and ran off into the night, her head bashing against his back with every pace that he took.

'He seems like a decent fellow,' said Wickham to Elizabeth as he lifted her up onto the horse.

'I—' began Elizabeth, but her reply was interrupted by an explosion just above their heads.

'They're shooting at us!' cried Wickham, leaping onto Jennifer and urging her away. There was another loud bang next to them. 'Slap her on the—er—rump,' he said.

'Why?' said Elizabeth.

'Just do it!'

Elizabeth did so, and H's fifty-fifty mixture proved just as effective in live use as in tests. 'Great heavens!' she said, looking back at the stunned figures of Lady Catherine and her footman, who now looked as if they had crawled out of a midden heap. 'That was most unseemly.'

They rode on in silence for a while. Elizabeth deep in thought.

'Mr Wickham,' she said finally, in a small, uncertain voice. 'When we were in the dining room—Lady Catherine—for a moment, I had the unaccountable impression she had grown tentacles.' She paused for a moment. 'Mr Wickham, what is going on?'

Chapter Eight

Inside the Department — Clothes — Keeping an Eye on Mr Darcy — Ghosts — Old Ale, Brassicas and Cowpats

A T A LITTLE after nine of the clock on this fine summer's morning, the ghost of Mary Ann Nicholls walked through the front door of the *Department of Unusual Affairs* and paused for a moment to clear her throat. She still hadn't got used to walking through things and she especially disliked the strange woody taste in her mouth after she'd passed through a door. Still, it was better than brick dust, which made her sneeze terribly. The guard on duty inside didn't give her a second glance.

The entrance hall was cavernous, with staircases leading off in all directions, and the marble floor echoed with the footsteps of various uniformed men striding across it with great purpose. How on earth was she going to find this Wickham person? What if he wasn't even in?

As she was trying to decide what to do, a man barged through her on his way towards a staircase, shivered and gave a nervous glance around. Serve you right for being so rude, she thought to herself. On a whim, she decided to follow him.

The man led the way up to the second floor and then down a long corridor decorated with paintings of men striking heroic poses. At the sixth door on the left, there was a plaque bearing the legend *Capt. Maberly, Special Projects*. The man knocked and a voice commanded, 'Come!' He went in and Mary Ann Nicholls followed. What she saw on the desk chilled the ghost to her non-existent bones.

It was a cage. And inside the cage was a small creature. A creature with tentacles.

'What do you think?' the man in the room was saying, gesturing towards it. 'Caught it in Whitechapel last night. Don't say a word to anyone, though. Very hush hush. Orders from the colonel.'

'Does it talk, Maberly?' asked the other man.

''Course not. It's only a baby. To be perfectly frank with you, Briers, I'm not even sure what I should be feeding it on.'

'Rusks, perhaps? Or maybe a spot of gin. My nanny always used to swear by gin. Never did me any harm. Apart from the incident with the goldfish.'

'Your nanny used to swear by gin for most things, if I remember correctly,' said Maberly. He was interrupted by a buzzing and looked up. 'Damn that fly!'

The two men broke off for a moment to track the course of the insect on its wild trajectory around the room and then gawped in amazement as the thing in the cage sent out a tentacle, grabbed the fly and consumed it in one seamless movement.

'Well, I'll be damned.' said Briers. 'There's your answer, Maberly.' But Maberly had gone quite pale and seemed at a loss for words.

Mary Ann Nicholls was transfixed, too, but for a different reason. Something was stirring deep within her. Something primordial. Something that she couldn't ever have any hope of controlling.

The little tentacled creature in the cage was staring right at her, its head tilting slightly to one side, round eyes wide and innocent, with the tiniest of smiles playing around its mouth.

It was asking for her approval.

And now she understood what she was feeling, and why it felt so utterly confusing. She was glowing with maternal pride. It was bad enough being a ghost. But now she was a ghost with responsibilities.

Seth Moriarty slowed his horse to a halt and dismounted.

'Stay there, Harley,' he said.

Crouching down on the ground he found what he was looking for. It was camouflaged well, but old Seth knew exactly what it was. A trap. Fresh, too, by the look of it, but empty so far.

Well, that's something, he said to himself, watching as a couple of rabbits bounded across his line of sight, their fluffy white scuts flickering in the morning sunshine. His Lordship would have something to say to him if there wasn't any game for next weekend's shoot, and he made a mental note to return later with one of the mantraps. Give the bastard poachers a taste of their own medicine.

He spat on the ground in disgust.

Looking up, he saw something unexpected on the horizon. It was a man, heading straight for him, waving at him. Even more unexpected was that the man appeared not to be wearing any clothes. Seth screwed up his eyes and peered into the distance. Yup, he said to himself. Stark bollock naked.

Seth was a man of simple rules. He knew where he stood with most of the things that encroached onto his Lordship's lands. Foxes, for example, were most definitely bad. Poachers were bad, too. But he wasn't one hundred percent sure of the correct line to take with naked men.

He was only a hundred yards or so away now, and Seth could see he was a fine figure of a man with well-toned musculature; a big man, in every respect, and almost certainly a man of high standing in society. The man waved again, and Seth raised his arm and gave a weak reply.

'You there!' called the naked man as he drew near. Seth looked around. There was no one else. This person really was addressing him. 'I said you!'

'Sir?' inquired Seth.

'I need your clothes, your riding boots and your stallion.'

It was a cultured voice, although it was undermined to some extent by the man's matted hair and straggly beard.

'Beg pardon, sir?'

'I said, I need your clothes, your riding boots and your stallion.' There was a hint of exasperation in the voice, as if the owner was well within striking distance of the end of his tether.

Inside Seth's head, deference struggled against the opposing twin forces of outrage and confusion—and deference won. He looked around again. There was no one watching.

'Hold on a minute, then,' he said. He sat down and took off his boots, grumbling to himself as he did so. Finest leather, they were.

Then he unbuttoned his jacket and removed his trousers, handing them over to the stranger, who put them on without another word.

'Forgot to say please,' he muttered to himself.

When he had pulled on Seth's riding boots, the patrician newcomer put his left foot into the horse's stirrup and swung his leg over. With barely a backward glance, he rode off.

Seth stared after him, dazed at what had just happened. Then he snapped out of his trance and called after the man, 'Will you be back?'

But there was no reply: just the wind picking up and the leaves on the trees softly swaying backwards and forwards. It was getting chilly and he hugged himself for warmth. Now he thought about it, this was going to take some explaining to Mrs Moriarty. And the sky was beginning to turn grey.

'Bugger me,' he said out loud. 'Looks like there's a storm coming, an' all.'

Elizabeth Darcy woke up late, in an unfamiliar bed, with the sun streaming in through an equally unfamiliar window. For a moment she had no idea where she was or how she had got there, but her discombobulation soon passed as she recalled the extraordinary events of the previous evening at Rosings. Her recollections also went some way to explaining why she was still in her evening gown.

Heavens! She could not possibly go home dressed like this; it would be as if she were taking what Kitty and Lydia used to refer to as 'the perambulation of shame'. Then she caught herself and gasped. Lydia! She had become so caught up in her own adventures that she had scarcely given her missing sister a second thought these last few days. But these ruminations were interrupted by a knock on the door.

'Er—come in?' she said. Wickham entered, bearing a package.

'I have some day clothes for you, Mrs Darcy,' he said, handing the package to Elizabeth. It smelt musty.

'Why—I thank you, Mr Wickham. At least I think I do.'

'I understand that they should be a good fit. I had our local agent make the necessary adjustments.'

'How—?'

'It's a skill I have. I can assess a lady's measurements in a matter of seconds.'

'Really?' Elizabeth pulled the covers up around herself. 'You become more surprising with every minute that passes, Mr Wickham.'

There was an awkward silence. 'I have checked the timetable for the coach and one is leaving in two hours. The route is clear, apart from a short stretch near Nuneaton where the road is impassable.'

'What shall I do instead?'

'Apparently, there is a replacement sedan chair service.'

'Ah—'

She stopped in mid sentence. Wickham was looking at her. 'Mrs Darcy, are you sure that you wish to return to Pemberley?'

'Why of course, Mr Wickham. Why ever not? It will soon be time for our Midsummer Ball, and—'

'I think you should keep an eye on Mr Darcy.'

'I beg your pardon? Keep an eye on my husband? Mr Wickham, I think I must ask you to leave before you say anything you may have cause to regret!'

'I apologise, Mrs Darcy. I was speaking out of turn. It's just that I—that is, one of our operatives—thinks that he may have seen him somewhere—somewhere where he shouldn't have been.'

'Enough, Mr Wickham!' Elizabeth was outraged; her every instinct leapt to her husband's defence. 'Are you seriously suggesting that my husband is mixed up in this alien nonsense?'

Wickham began to back towards the door.

'Great heavens, no—although, as you have seen for yourself, it is far from nonsense.'

'As I have already made clear to you, Mr Wickham, what I saw last night was a mere fancy, which was itself a direct result of Lord Byron corrupting my drink. There are no aliens, any more than there are magical flying machines in the sky over Rosings. It is true that Lady Catherine was behaving strangely, but was she not bound to react most vigorously when confronted with a gentleman appearing unannounced at her dining table via the window, waving a water pistol about his head?'

'Please, Mrs Darcy, be assured that I was acting purely in your best interests.'

'Mr Wickham, I think you should leave. I need to prepare for my journey to Pemberley.'

'As you wish, ma'am. But please be careful.'

'Mr Wickham, I am always careful.'

She watched as Wickham bowed and hurriedly left the room. As soon as she returned home, she would write to Lady Catherine to explain everything. Yes, that was the right course of action. There was no problem that two ladies could not resolve between them when the spirit was willing. It was only when foolish men such as Wickham and Byron got involved that things started to go wrong.

Colonel Sutherland sat at his desk, skimming through Wickham's report. Every now and then, he would mutter something unintelligible to himself and shake his head.

When he finished reading, he frowned at Wickham.

'Bad,' he said. 'Very bad.'

'Sir, I—'

'Very bad indeed.'

'Sir, I must—'

'First, I have to transfer you from the Whitechapel investigation because of your insinuations about a former rival.'

'Sir, it was definitely—'

'Wickham, there have no further sightings of the man since! And please do not interrupt.'

'I apologise, sir.'

'Secondly, a mere forty-eight hours after arriving at Rosings, you manage to blow your cover and wreck any chance of finding anything out about what may be going on there.'

'I did request your permission first, sir.'

Colonel Sutherland had stood up and was pacing up and down the room. 'You told me that Mrs Darcy was in imminent danger,' he said, pointing at Wickham for extra emphasis, 'when the only thing she was in danger of was a slight biliousness as a result of over-eating! And then, finally, you come here with a cock and bull report about Lady Catherine de Bourgh being some kind of—what's the phrase you use?—shape shifter!'

'But that's exactly what happened!'

'Will Mrs Darcy corroborate your story?'

Wickham was silent. Colonel Sutherland looked him straight in the eye, and then continued, in a more reasoned tone of voice. 'Wickham, I know as well as you do there is something fishy going on at Rosings. But we have to follow due procedure in order to establish beyond any reasonable doubt what manner of fishiness is going on.'

'But there was something humming under the ground!'

'Wickham, I think we need something a little more solid by way of evidence than 'something humming under the ground'. Did you bring back any samples?'

Wickham was silent again. Colonel Sutherland put his

hand on his shoulder. 'I'm sorry, but I'm going to have to take you off this case as well.'

'I really don't know what to say, sir. Am I to be disciplined, then?'

Colonel Sutherland smiled for the first time since Wickham had come into his office. 'Great heavens, no!' he said, shaking his head. 'I have a much more interesting job for you.' He paused for a moment and then gave Wickham a curious look. 'What do you know about ghosts?' he asked.

'Ghosts?'

'Yes, ghosts.'

'As in the spectral manifestations of the souls of the dead, sir? Wanderers in the ethereal plane 'twixt the living and the departed? Spooky things that go 'Whoo'?'

'Exactly! I knew you'd get the picture. Capital, Wickham!'

Wickham looked puzzled. 'But what's this got to do with the Department, sir?'

'We think there's a ghost in this building. Quite a persistent one, too. Young girl, not particularly well off, by the look of it. Plenty of sightings — mainly in the corridor near Special Projects on the second floor. Between you and me, old Captain Maberley's scared out of his wits.' The colonel narrowed his eyes. 'Do ghosts bother you?'

'I'm not afraid of any ghosts,' said Wickham.

'Good,' said the colonel.

'All right, I'll do it,' said Wickham. 'But who am I going to call on?'

It was late in the evening when the coach reached its destination, and Elizabeth was exhausted, although the part of the journey covered by the replacement sedan chair service was, at least, mercifully short.

She had been forced to share with a travelling non-conformist entertainer who had insisted on demonstrating how to keep a ferret down his trousers for as long as it took to recite the opening chapters of the book of Genesis.

'You can always tell when they're going to bite you,' he had explained, 'because the little buggers give you a lick first.'

'Really?' Elizabeth said, trying very hard not to visualise the precise details. 'How fascinating.'

Fortunately, that part of the journey came to an end before he had time to perform his encore, which seemed to involve several doves, a blazing rabbit and most of the Revelation of St John the Divine.

She was now alone in the village square, wondering how she was going to make her way back to Pemberley. She almost resigned herself to walking the few miles remaining when a horse and cart trotted past.

'Ha-har, Mis' Darcy!' said a familiar voice. Elizabeth's heart sank. It was old Mr Firth. 'You be wantin' a ride, Mis' Darcy?'

'Well, actually, it's all right, I'm—'

''Cos it be a dark and grim night out there, Mis' Darcy. There be farrow-manglers and nadge-cutters abroad.'

Oh dear, sighed Elizabeth. Still as crack-brained as ever. Then again, perhaps the old fool had a point after all. The wind was beginning to pick up and she wasn't sure if she hadn't felt the first few spots of rain. It wouldn't be good to be caught out on a night like this.

'Are you sure, Mr Firth?' she called up to him.

''Course.'Op on.' He caught hold of her arm and hauled her up. As she drew close, she was enveloped in a heady scent of old ale, brassicas and cowpats. 'Ha-har, Mis' Darcy!' he repeated, greeting her with a broken-toothed smile. 'I been seein' things around these parts, that I 'ave, oh yes.'

'Really?' she said, immediately regretting the automatic instinct to respond.

'That I 'ave, Mis' Darcy, that I 'ave. I seen 'im again. Ol' snakey boy.'E thinks I don' see 'im but I do. Thrutch, scabbard and cordwainers, if you knows what I mean. Behind the old barn.'Im and all the others. All of 'em, dancin' around.' He broke off to chuckle inwardly at something. 'All of 'em,' he repeated, 'wearing nowt but a thong.'

Elizabeth raised her eyebrows, but resisted the temptation to comment further, and there was silence for a while as they trotted along the lane towards Pemberley. Then old Mr Firth gave a conspiratorial wink and leaned closer to her. 'She's evil, that one, y'know. Evil. She'm gonna take over the whole world, that's what she thinks.'

'Who?' asked Elizabeth.

'Ha-har, Mis' Darcy. Ha-har,' was all he would say by way of reply. 'Ha-har!'

Elizabeth found the conversation unsettling, even if it was largely gibberish. She did not get the opportunity to question Mr Firth any further because they arrived at the great house.

As the horse and cart drew up outside the main door, Dench and Hollander appeared and helped her down. She thanked old Mr Firth and offered him a glass of gin in the servants' quarters. Eizabeth paused for a moment to take in the moonlit glory of Pemberley once more. It was as if she had been away for months, and it was good to be home.

'Is everything in order?' she asked Dench.

Dench hesitated before replying. 'Everything is satisfactory, my lady. Entirely satisfactory.'

'Good.'

'Satisfactory,' reinforced Hollander. 'Everything is satisfactory.'

'Well, then,' said Elizabeth, walking towards the house. But there was another figure in the doorway; a dark, brooding presence, familiar and yet unfamiliar at the same time.

'Good evening, my dear,' said Mr Darcy, stepping out from the shadows.

Chapter Nine

The Fishing Trip—The Presence in Maberley's Office—Preparations for the Ball—Steam—A Game of Cards

E LIZABETH HAD GONE straight to bed, being too tired for any kind of social intercourse with her husband. The next day, however, she rose early, feeling thoroughly refreshed and with a strong sense that the rest of her life was about to begin. After breaking her fast alone, she went out into the garden to read some letters that had arrived in her absence.

The first of these was troubling.

> *Lizzy,*
> *This is your MOTHER here. I HOPE that you remember me—the one who BROUGHT you into this world? I only ask because it has been MANY LONG WEEKS since your FATHER and I last heard from you. We understand that you are a VERY important LADY now and that you have a BUSY life but we would like, if POSSIBLE, to see you once again before the GOOD LORD takes us to a BETTER place. As I am sure you can imagine, all this WORRY about Lydia has only served to make my PALPITATIONS worse, and I am convinced that Jane is HIDING something from me*

as well. Oh, it is all too MUCH, Lizzy! It is all TOO MUCH! I shall of course say nothing at all about Mary as the whole AFFAIR with her is far too DISTRESSING for me in my present DELICATE state.

Your father sends his love. His GOUT continues to trouble him.

Mother.

Elizabeth was stricken with a complex mixture of anger and shame, to say nothing of perplexity at the unexpected comment about her middle sister. To divert herself, she turned to the other letter, from Jane. However, this proved to be no less concerning.

My Dearest Lizzy,

I write in some haste as Mr Bradford's men with sticks are once again harassing poor Charlie and I must go to his aid. Sadly, we have let several of the staff go owing, to what Charlie refers to as, 'transient cashflow problems' so there is no one here, apart from myself, to protect him from these ruffians.

As you will have surmised from the foregoing, our affairs have taken a temporary turn for the worse. The African Princess who Charlie invested so much trust (and indeed money) in has vanished from the face of the Earth and we have no way of knowing whether we will ever see our capital again.

However, I can tell you, my dear Lizzy, we have had at least one piece of good fortune! A Russian financial expert, who happened to be passing Netherfield the other day on a fishing trip, offered to investigate what he called our 'security arrangements'. He established that we were in imminent danger of having all of the family silver stolen, along with the deeds to the estate!

Luckily it turns out that this gentleman owns what he refers to as a 'secure facility' in Novosibirsk, which he is prepared to let Charlie use for a very small emolument. He is to return tomorrow to arrange to take all of our valuable goods away, so that we may once more sleep easy in our beds. Once more I bless the serendipity that surrounds my Charlie and protects us all from disaster!

Dearest Lizzy, have you heard from Mary recently? I only ask because Mama is concerned for her wellbeing. She will not unfortunately say why she is so concerned, and if pressed she will protest that she is suffering from the vapours. And poor Father is no use whatsoever in this respect. I am sure there is nothing to be worried about, but I would like to know for certain.

Elizabeth put the letter down and frowned. It was good to know the Bingleys' financial affairs were at last going to be in good hands—and she made a mental note to suggest Fitzy should also seek the services of this Russian gentleman—but what were all these rumours about Mary? As if she didn't have enough on her hands with trying to find Lydia!

Nine o'clock in the morning, and it was time for the ghost of Mary Ann Nicholls to visit her child again. She'd spent the previous night doing a bit of light haunting and had quite enjoyed herself, now she was getting the hang of it. Evensong at St James' had been particularly fun—she'd managed to get all the candles to go out every time the young vicar said the phrase 'Holy Ghost'. The poor lad ended up running out the church screaming.

But now it was time for her maternal duties. The more she thought about it, she believed that children were the future. You should teach them well, she thought, and let them lead the way. She would have to show that tiny thing of hers all the beauty it possessed inside—because, frankly, the little bastard was no oil painting on the outside, what with all the tentacles and stuff.

As she approached the cage, it waved one of them at her in greeting and her heart melted.

'I will always luv you,' she whispered.

Behind her, the door opened, instinctively she turned and backed into the corner, crouching down next to a cabinet. It was pointless, she knew, although she had a feeling that Captain Maberley was somehow aware of her. He'd certainly developed a habit of twitching whenever she crept up close to him.

Maberley was accompanied by another man in uniform. Bit of a looker, she thought to herself.

'So you think you've felt a presence in this office?' the newcomer was saying.

'Look, I know this sounds stupid, Wickham—'

Wickham? This was Wickham!

She had to make her presence felt, but how? The only trick she'd picked up so far was the candle one, and it was broad daylight right now. Bugger.

'—right there,' Maberley was saying.

'There?' said Wickham, pointing to the creature in the cage. Then he stopped, as if he'd only just registered there was something unusual in the room. 'Maberley, there's something queer on your desk.'

'Yes, I know.'

'It's got tentacles.'

'So do lots of things.'

'Why hasn't anyone told me about this?'

'Possibly because you're on ghosts now?'

'But I do tentacled aliens!' said Wickham. 'I've always done aliens.'

'Not any more, according to the colonel. Sorry, but Special Projects are handling this one.'

'Where did you get it from?'

'Can't say. More than my position's worth.'

Wickham advanced grabbing the other man by the lapels. 'Where?'

'Steady on, old man' spluttered Maberley. 'It's only a baby anyway.'

Wickham released him and slumped into a chair. 'Sorry,' he said. 'It hasn't really sunk in until now. Ghosts, I ask you. Not exactly the frontiers of investigation, is it?' He shook his head. 'Bloody ghosts!'

Excuse me, said Mary Ann, standing up and waving. Halloooo! Over here!

But she was wasting her time. The man wasn't the slightest bit aware of her. She might as well have been invisible. Actually, she was.

'All right, then,' said Wickham, standing up again. 'Let's do this, so I can finish it and get put back onto a proper job. So you have this 'sort of creepy feeling' around—'

'—here, yes.' Maberley made a vague gesture.

Wickham sighed. 'Are you absolutely sure it's not because you have a baby alien sitting on your desk?'

'Let's leave the alien out of it.'

Yeah, you do that, thought Mary Ann.

'In that case,' said Wickham, 'We had better get the specialist team in to give the place a sweep. H claims he's got some detector thingy almost ready to try out. Just hope it doesn't explode,like most of his stuff does.'

I'll be watching you, said Mary Ann, unheard. No one was going to explode anything around her baby.

Elizabeth was busy all week preparing for the Pemberley

Midsummer Ball. It had taken all her skills of persuasion to convince Fitzy it might be a nice idea to hold any kind of event that involved dancing, but it was now a firm fixture on the social calendar. Fitzy himself had even gone to the extent of taking dancing lessons and was now well-known in local circles as an expert proponent of the flying volte-fetlock.

And what about Fitzy? thought Elizabeth. Since her return to Pemberley, her husband had been behaving in an unusual manner, at once cold and then—well, a trifle over-familiar. He had raised the question of an heir on more than one occasion and Elizabeth's suggestion that such a diversion might best be left until after the ball had met with a chilly response. Ah, there was so much about men that she still did not understand, even now.

The one really excellent piece of news was she had heard from Charlotte. Lord Byron had been as good as his word and removed her safely from Rosings, she was now living in a communal dwelling in Glastonbury along with several of his artistic friends. Here she was learning some valuable new skills, such as tie-dye bonnet-making, tofu-herding and playing the green tambourine.

And yet Elizabeth still felt out of sorts. She had thought much about poor Lydia this week. In her mind, she went back to that dreadful day when Wickham arrived at Pemberley to inform her of the abduction. There was an ugly scene as he talked of lights in the sky over their cottage and of visitations by men with tentacles from another world—great heavens, why was the man so obsessed with tentacles? Fitzy took a horsewhip and threatened him with it, and yet he still insisted on spinning this ridiculous yarn. In the end, he only ceased when her husband chased him out of the house.

The only explanation for it was that Wickham had

succumbed to some kind of madness, some wild fancy that had, in all probability, been induced by over-indulgence—heaven knows, she had observed similar behaviour in Charlotte.

Then Elizabeth reflected that she had seen some curious things herself lately. That night at Macfadyen's quarry, had not Wickham fought with such a tentacled man? Oh, but it had been dark, and such nights played tricks on the eyes, did they not?

But none of this brought her anywhere nearer knowing what had happened to Lydia, and at times like this she wondered if she would ever see her little sister again.

Her thoughts were interrupted by a knock on the door.

'Come in,' she said, turning round. It was Dench.

'I've come to enquire about the buckets and sawdust, ma'am,' he said. The old butler raised a quizzical eyebrow.

'I beg your pardon?'

'The—ah—buckets and—ah—sawdust, ma'am. For the drinks area. When the gentlemen have had—'

'Oh, I see,' said Elizabeth, hurriedly, realising the significance of his remark.

'So shall we say a dozen buckets and a couple o'hundredweight of sawdust, then, ma'am?'

Elizabeth's eyes widened for a moment, then she nodded. 'If you say so, Dench. If you say so.'

'Very well, ma'am. Very well.' Dench bowed and reversed out of the room. Elizabeth shook her head and tried very hard to remove the image of Lord Rutherford dancing naked in the orchard at last year's ball, soliciting passers-by to have a nibble at his russets.

Men. They could always be guaranteed to let you down.

Wickham looked at the contraption H brought into

the office. It was a rectangular polished mahogany box, around four feet high, with ornate brass fittings. On the top was a large red button and on the side was a crank handle.

'Ready?' asked Sir Humphry Davy.

'I suppose so,' said Wickham. 'Are you sure this thing's safe?'

'Safe as houses.'

Yes, but your last house burnt down, thought Wickham, although he kept this to himself.

'Here we go then,' said H, pressing the button on the top. At this, the top of the box divided into four sections and a panel containing several dials, a pair of regulators and a whole array of knobs and switches sprang out. He reached down and gave the crank handle a couple of turns and Wickham heard the unmistakeable sound of a steam engine starting up. The regulators began to spin furiously in opposite directions and the dials started to flicker backwards and forwards.

'So far, so good,' said H. He leaned over and turned one of the knobs a few degrees clockwise. A whistle blew, and a faint wisp of rose-coloured gas wafted from a vent at the back of the box. If Wickham had to think of a name for the precise colour, he would have called it 'steam pink', but he didn't have time to do this because the box started shaking from side to side in an alarming manner.

'H, are you sure—?'

Several of the dials now began to whizz round at a frantic speed. The right-hand regulator went 'ping' and flew off, embedding itself in the ceiling. The rose-coloured steam now turned into belching clouds of black smoke and there was a strong smell of burning in the room.

'H, I really think—' attempted Wickham, before he was overcome by coughing.

One of the brass handles on the front of the box shook itself loose and narrowly missed Wickham's ear. An alarm bell began ringing somewhere and a slick of oil started seeping out of the bottom. The atmosphere was now positively toxic.

Then without any warning, everything went quiet and the air cleared. The machine was quietly humming to itself and the remaining regulator whirred happily around. H smiled at Wickham. 'Forgot to activate the dampers,' he said, pointing to one of the switches.

'Ah—good,' wheezed Wickham, gasping for breath. He watched as H opened up a compartment on the front of the box and withdrew a long length of hose with a funnel on the end.

'H? What on earth is that?'

'Ghost detector. Uses the power of the steam engine to generate ether waves that amplify the presence of supernatural objects. Damn clever if I say so myself.'

'Fine. Fine. Well, go ahead, then,' said Wickham.

'I already am.' Sir Humphry waved the end of the hose in the direction of Maberley's desk. 'Wickham, would you mind awfully flicking the third switch on the left, please?'

Wickham looked at H in horror. 'Are you sure?'

'Of course.' H paused, and then hit the side of his face with his hand. 'Sorry, old man. The fourth one. Yes, definitely the fourth one. Third one would have blown us all to kingdom come.' He seemed to find this incredibly amusing.

Wickham leaned towards the machine, keeping as much distance as he could between it and himself, and flicked the switch. He leapt back as quickly as he could, but then felt a little foolish as nothing untoward happened after all. Then he turned and looked at where H was pointing his device.

The image of a woman was forming in the air next to the desk; a young woman, dressed in shabby clothes but with an air of wounded pride and self-respect.

'About bloody time, Mr Wickham,' she said.

The man with no name entered the inn, surveyed the scene and then sat down at a table where three of the locals were playing cards.

'Deal me in,' he said, accidentally nudging the table so that the pint of beer belonging to the man opposite splashed a few drops into his lap. With a scowl, the man leaned over the table as if to grab the newcomer by the throat, but his hand was stayed by the man to the left of him.

'Now, now, Jed. Let's not be unwelcoming,' he said, motioning to him to sit down again. Then, turning to the man with no name, he added, 'So what be you called, then?'

'I don't have a name. I used to have one once.'

'A man with no name, eh?' said the one called Jed. 'That won't end well. Last time we had a man with no name around here, he did nowt but stir up trouble between the Rogers and the Baxters. Right bloody mess, weren't it, Ebeneezer? Bodies everywhere.' The last comment was directed at the man who had first spoken.

'I assure you I mean to cause no trouble. I merely seek to chance my luck with a game or two so I can perhaps afford a night's accommodation before going on my way. I have been sleeping rough these last few nights and am in urgent need of a bed.'

'And where might you be on your way to, then?' said Ebeneezer.

'I'm not sure. I have forgotten so much.'

'Dear, oh dear,' said Ebeneezer, with the slightest suggestion of a glint in his eye. 'So what you got to bet with, then?'

The man with no name took off his boots and placed them on the table.

'That's bad luck,' said the one who hadn't spoken yet.

'Shut it, Montmorency,' said Ebeneezer, examining the leather. 'Nice boots, they are. Bonham-Carter weekend casuals, if I'm not mistaken. All right, then. Portugese six-card wazzock?'

'Hapsburg rules?'

'If you wish.'

This seemed to satisfy the trio, and they each threw a few coins on the table. Ebeneezer dealt them six cards each and the man with no name looked at his hand.

'One for his nob,' he said.

'Pass,' said Montmorency.

'Pass,' said Jed, shaking his head.

'Double whammy,' said Ebeneezer.

'Blocked flush.'

'Pass.'

'Pass.'

Ebeneezer paused, and then a smile began to play on his lips. He laid down the Jacks of Hearts, Clubs and Spades in turn. 'Three skins,' he said.

There was an audible intake of breath from Jed and Montmorency. All eyes swivelled towards the man with no name. Then he laid down his entire hand, one card at a time and leant back in his chair, arms folded.

'Royal wazzock,' he said, with an air of triumph.

'Bollocks,' said Ebeneezer. He looked the man with no

name firmly in the eye and then slowly pushed his coins towards him. The other two followed with great reluctance. The man with no name took his boots off the table, picked up the money and began to stand up.

'Wait one moment, Mister,' said Ebeneezer. 'Don't you think you ought to give us the chance to win it back off you?'

The man with no name detected the underlying threat, shrugged and sat down again. This time he won when his whiffy trump beat Jed's ace-up-the-jacksie, much to the latter's annoyance.

They played on for a few more hands, by which time he had won a whole fistful of cash and the others had all but run out.

Choosing his moment, the man with no name grabbed his winnings, went to the bar and paid for a room for the night. Now feeling quite exhausted after his long journey, he staggered up the stairs to bed. He was asleep within seconds of his head hitting the pillow.

But in the early hours of the morning, he woke suddenly, sweat pouring off his brow. A single word filled his head.

'Pemberley!' he said out loud.

Chapter Ten

Mary Ann Tells All — Dreaming of Tentacles — Status Report — Up On the Roof — Home

S IR HUMPHRY DAVY'S ghost detection engine
chugged away happily with occasional puffs of smoke
and the odd chirpy whistle. The woman in front of them
shimmered in and out of sound and vision as he and
Wickham attempted to stabilise the signal, a process
which appeared to involved flicking switches at random,
remembering to duck in case anything happened to dis-
lodge itself.

'—tentacles . . . Mr Collins . . . Mission . . . position
. . . Mr Darcy—'

'Hold on, H, did she say 'Darcy'?' asked Wickham.

'Sounded like it, old man,' said H.

'—lousy food . . . bedsores . . . chest bursting open—'

'Look H, can you try and get the sound sorted out? She
really isn't making much sense.'

'One moment,' said H, passing the detector handset to
Wickham and disappearing behind the engine. There was
a sound like someone kicking the back of the machine
hard, followed by a yelp. As he emerged again, Wickham
noticed that H now walked with a pronounced limp.

'—anyway, then he says to me—'

'That's it!'cried Wickham.

'Good,' said H with a noticeable lack of enthusiasm. He sat down and began to massage his foot.

'—so I says to him, where's you going to put that thing anyway? And he says—'

'Excuse me, miss?'

'Hoo—bloody—ray! So you can hear me, now, can you, Mr Wickham? Bleedin' hell, you're hard work. Thought you was ignoring me.'

'Great heavens, no, Miss . . . ?'

'Mary Ann Nicholls at your service, sir.' The ghost bowed slightly. 'I found Annie's card. Told me to come here, it did.'

'Annie?' Wickham racked his brains. Then he felt in his pocket and took out Annie Chapman's card. 'This Annie?' he said, with a sinking feeling.

'Yeah, that's the one. I'm afraid she ain't in good shape now herself. In fact, I wouldn't be surprised if her spectre wasn't following on behind. You could have a whole load of us to deal with soon.'

Wickham sighed. 'So tell me what happened at the Mission, Mary Ann.'

Mary Ann told him. Her story was punctuated by grunts of disbelief from both Wickham and H, who was now sitting up and paying attention. When she finished her story, they both looked at each other.

'If this is true,' said Wickham.

'We'll have to rewrite half the laws of science!' said H, rubbing his hands together. Wickham shook his head.

'I was thinking in terms of more immediate concerns. What this means is that Mrs Darcy is in grave danger.'

H smacked his temple. 'Ah, silly me. Of course you are right. You must go to Pemberley at once.'

'But I'm off that case, H. It would be a gross dereliction of duty.'

H winked. 'Well, it wouldn't be the first time, would it, old man?' He stood up and pressed the red button on the top of the ghost detection engine once more. There was a hiss of steam, then the regulator gently stopped spinning and all was quiet. He gathered up the hose to the ghost detection handset and packed it away. No one noticed the ghost of Mary Ann Nicholls frantically waving at them as she disappeared from view.

'Come on, then, Mr W,' he said. 'Might have one or two new trinkets for you to play with.'

The two men left the room, speaking to each other in furtive whispers. As they did so, they were both completely oblivious to Mary Ann's gesticulations towards the cage on the desk, as well as her cry of 'Oi! You two! What about my baby?'

Elizabeth was annoyed. She shouldn't be feeling like this on the day of the Midsummer Ball. It should be a jolly occasion, with lashings of good humour and merriment, but at the present moment, she felt neither good humoured nor the slightest bit merry. What was worse, she wasn't even sure why it was she felt like this.

In the old days, when she'd felt out of sorts, she would simply pour her heart out to Jane. But Jane was tied up with Charlie's financial complications and wasn't coming to the Ball this year. Mary was—well, she had lost touch with Mary lately—not that she was ever much help in this type of circumstance. Besides, Jane had hinted that all was not well with her either.

As for Kitty, the least said about her the better. This year's invitation to the Ball had gone unanswered until the arrival of a bow-tied messenger running up the drive the previous afternoon. Elizabeth had groaned at the sight of him, wondering how much Kitty was spending on tux'd messages.* She knew all the young girls were obsessed with them, but they were hideously expensive, even when you paid for them in a monthly bundle. The message was almost unintelligible anyway:

'CANT DO BALL TOMOZ. GOIN 2 MRYTN DNCE W BF CAPT MULLIGAN HES WELL FIT LOL. SOZ'

Elizabeth read it three times before giving up. Frankly, the only one of them who ever managed to understand Kitty at all was Lydia and who knew where she was now? Poor Lydia. Would she ever see her again?

Perhaps that was what was distracting her, deep down. For the first time in her life, she was truly alone in the world. She had no sisters to turn to, she had managed to offend her mother and even dear Charlotte was many miles away in Glastonbury, in the company of that dubious Byron fellow.

Fitzy, of course, would have been no help to her what-

---

* Tux'd messages became briefly very popular in civilian life during the early nineteenth century, but as with so many modern inventions, they were in fact military in origin, going back to the Peninsular War. During the brief siege of the town of Tuxedo, a messenger was sent out to request help from Wellington, who was stationed thirty miles away.

The task of carrying the message fell to a local fishmonger named Rojo d'Arenques, who set off wearing his traditional outfit of black suit and white shirt. On the journey, his neck was grazed by a shot from a French sniper, whereupon he tore off a strip from his jacket and tied it around his neck to staunch the flow of blood. He barely survived until the end of his journey, but he succeeded in delivering his message to Wellington, who immediately changed his plans and came to the relief of Tuxedo.

In honour of Rojo d'Arenques, all messengers from that day forth were ordered to dress in the same 'Tuxedo' style, with the black suit, white shirt and black neckerchief—subsequently formalised into the bow tie that would have been familiar to Elizabeth Darcy and her sister Kitty. Of course, towards the end of the nineteenth century, when the tux'd messenger service became obsolete with the arrival of the telegraph, their uniform became popular as a type of gentleman's formal attire instead.

soever, even if he had been behaving normally—and his behaviour at the moment was curious indeed. For one thing, he was presently refusing to take any meals in her company, preferring to stay in his room instead. And he would insist on continually raising the question of his heir in a most unbecoming manner.

Elizabeth looked out of the window and observed the willow trees by the lake swaying in the breeze.

She suddenly realised what was disturbing her.

Tentacles!

Last night she had dreamed again of tentacles. Hundred of slimy tentacles swarming over her, caressing her skin. Oh, where were these frightful nightmares coming from? It all seemed so real—as if some ghastly alien creature had been lying next to her. This was madness!

She turned away from the window and then became aware of something that she had failed to notice before.

There were trails of green slime on the bedclothes—made by tentacles swishing back and forth.

She almost screamed but managed to gag herself in time.

There had to be a sensible explanation for this. Gothic fantasies of monsters in the night were for impressionable girls like Kitty and Lydia, not for her. Surely she was made of sterner stuff?

But try as she might to dismiss it, in her deepest being she knew something was wrong. She felt different.

Something had happened to her during the night—something unnatural.

Something alien.

The awful truth began to dawn on her. There was only one person who could possibly help her now.

'Oh, Wickham,' she said out loud. 'Where are you?'

Lady Catherine de Bourgh rearranged her tentacles and pressed the button on the communications device. Another alien figure appeared on the screen in front of her.

'Ek — ek — ek — ek.?' it said, waving. (**Greetings, k'Ek! I trust you are well. How goes the project?**)

'Ek — ek — ek — ekkitty — ek.' replied Lady Catherine. (**Very well, k'Ekk! I have news.**)

'Ek — ek — ek — ek — ek.' (**Well? Go on then. I haven't got all day, you know.**)

'Ek — ek — ek — ekekekekekek!' (**The target has been fertilised!**)

'Ek — ek — ek — ek — ek.' (**Are you sure? Seem to remember that your man made a bit of a cods of the last few trials.**)

'Ek — ek — ek — ek — ekky — ekky — ek.' (**Yes, but don't forget we have had more time to refactor his DNA for full compatibility with her. There shouldn't be any problems with rejection this time.**)

'Ek — ek — ek — ek — ek.' (**Fair enough. But do try to make sure you don't turn this one inside out. She is the key to our plan.**)

'Ek — ek — ek — ek — ek.' (**I know, I know.**)

'Ekky — ekky — ekky?' (**Any word on our escaped prisoner?**)

'Ek.' (**No.**)

'Ekekekekekek.' (**Bugger. That's a bit unfortunate. What if he remembers who he is? Couldn't half be embarrassing, that.**)

'Ek — ek — ek — ek — ek.' (**Very unlikely. He was a bit dim to start with, if you ask me, that one.**)

'Ek — ek — ek — ek — ek.' (**Never underestimate a human, k'Ek.**)

'Ek—ek—ek—ek—ek.' (Pah. You should try living here. Thick as pig poo, most of them, and twice as sloppy.)

'Ek—ek—ek—ek—ek!' (Well, with any luck, I will be living there very soon and I will know more of these pigs of which you speak. Once you and your advance party have finished breeding the new race of hybrids who will quash resistance for us, the pitiful remains of our once-great civilisation can leave this wretched base camp on Mars and establish a colony on Earth, where we can re-build Once again we will rule the galaxies with a fist of iron!)

'Ek—ek—ek—ek—ek—ekkacha-ekkacha-ekk.' (That would be nice. I've missed you.)

'Ek—ek—ek—ek—ek?' (What about Wickham?)

'Ek—ek—ek?' (What about him?)

'Ek—ek—ek—ek—ek?' (Is he a threat?)

'Ek—ek—ek—ek—ek.' (To his own safety, yes. To us, no. He's a fool, to be honest.)

'Ek—ek.' (I thought as much.)

'Ek . . . ek—ek—ek—ek?' (So . . . what's it like there?)

'Ek—ek—ek—ek—ek.' (Red. It really is very red. There's pretty much no other colour apart from red. Just bloody red wherever you look. Which is fine if you like red, but I'm getting a bit bored with it now.)

'Ek ?' (Really?)

'Ek—ek—ek—ek—ek.' (And it's pretty much the same shade of red, too. It's not as if there were some nice subtle shades here or there. I could cope with that. But the same dull, bland red, over and over again, in every bleeding direction.)

'Ek.' (I see.)

'Ek—ek—ek—ek—ek.' **(Not even the slightest hint of crimson. Or rose. Or magenta. Just the same rusty shite whichever direction you look in. You know, sometimes I slice off one of my own tentacles, just to mix the colours up a bit? It's awful. Just awful.)**

'Ek—' **(It must—)**

'Ek—ek—ek—ek—ek—' **(So I think what I'm saying, k'Ek, is whatever you do, please don't cock this up. If I have to stay in this dump much longer, I'm going to go mad. Have you any idea—)**

Lady Catherine sighed and switched off the communicator. There was a limit to the amount of maudlin self-pity she could take. Still, let's hope it does work this time, she thought to herself.

Wickham trotted up the drive on Jennifer, weaving unnoticed in and out of the carriages delivering their occupants to the Pemberley Midsummer Ball. He hadn't banked on there being so many other people heading the same way as him and was grateful that Jennifer had been daubed all over—much to her evident dismay—with H's experimental new stealth paint. Arriving at the mansion, he tied her to a lightning conductor and unbuckled her saddlebag.

He needed to get onto the roof somehow, so he rummaged in the bag for something suitable.

The first thing he came across was the miniature steam-powered gyrocopter, which he discarded on the grounds that it appeared to be, on the basis of H's disappointing demonstration, a somewhat unstable mode of transport. He could still remember the look of terror on the face of the pilot, during the ascent, as the device spun him around at increasingly high speeds before flinging him off in the rough direction of the Thames.

Instead, Wickham opted for a more conventional musket-powered grappling iron, and set about assembling his trusty Lee Van Enfield.

Fortunately, no one was around the back of the mansion when he fired it, because the explosion made by the musket was deafening.

When Wickham picked himself up off the ground again, he observed the hook embedded in the guttering. He gave it a good tug and was pleased to note it seemed to be secure.

He stowed the musket out of sight, strapped his sword to his belt, and began to climb.

When he had almost reached the guttering, he heard voices below him. He saw, to his horror, there were a man and a woman approaching.

He quickly scrabbled his way to the top and hauled the rope up behind him. Looking down at what was now taking place beneath him, Wickham realised he probably hadn't needed to be so careful.

The couple from the Ball were oblivious to anything else going on around them, as they were very soon engaged in an energetic *bête aux deux dos*. Nice footwork, thought Wickham to himself.

He began to make his way around the parapet, hoping the revellers would be too occupied to see him. Every now and then he dislodged a small piece of masonry, forcing him to crouch down and hold his breath until the danger passed.

After several minutes of negotiating his way across the roof, he found himself by the skylight above the great ballroom.

Looking down, he could see the dancing was in full

swing, with the orchestra playing enthusiastically and several groups performing *Sir Roger M'Gently's Eightsome Quadrille*. But where was Mrs Darcy?

Wickham scanned the twirling crowd, but he could not find her anywhere. Then he caught a glimpse of someone else: Darcy himself, striding through the ballroom with his usual haughty demeanour. Wickham felt a shiver run down his spine.

Then Darcy stopped suddenly, turned and tilted his head up towards where Wickham squatted above him. He ducked down, wondering if he'd been quick enough to avoid being seen.

After a few seconds, he raised his head again — just enough to be able to see over the lip of the skylight. Darcy had gone.

Wickham scurried over to the front of the roof and looked over. Ah, there he was! Darcy was outside the front of the mansion, issuing orders, left right and centre, to two nervous-looking footmen.

Damn the man!

With a sickening feeling in the pit of stomach, Wickham realised he had been seen.

He cursed his own incompetence. He should have realised someone as evil as Darcy would sense his presence — they always could. And he still hadn't located Mrs Darcy. What to do?

He waited until Darcy disappeared inside and watched as the footmen below him seemed to be arguing about what they should be doing. The conversation grew quite animated, with much gesticulation towards the roof, and it was clear that neither of the men seemed particularly keen to venture up there.

But at that precise moment, something happened that threw them, and him, into complete confusion.

The man with no name reined in his horse and dismounted, preferring to walk the last few hundred yards of his journey. He needed to feel the earth beneath his feet. Even though it was dusk, he knew where he was now: the old field. He unstrapped the saddle and took it off. He leaned close to Harley's ear and whispered:

'Go, boy, go! You've been a good companion to me. I'd rather be with you than—' He stopped. The horse was giving him an odd look, as if he was trying to work out what on earth the peculiar human was on about. Then it gave a horsey shrug and trotted off into the night. The man with no name smiled to himself and turned back towards his ultimate destination.

He soon came to the lake. For a moment, he had an urge to throw off all of his clothes and dive in—to feel the chill of the water against his flesh, and then to roll naked on the grass afterwards, like the time when he wrestled in front of that blazing log fire with . . . or was his fractured memory deceiving him? The more he thought about it, that didn't sound quite right.

In any case, the water looked bloody freezing.

He continued on into the twilight, until he could see the great house in front of him. There were lights blazing everywhere and sounds of music and merriment. I know this place, he thought to himself. I know these people! This is where I belong. He began to run now. He was laughing. He was smiling. He was happy.

He was almost there now. He just had to cross this last field and he would be there. His journey had not been in vain after all. All the privations he had suffered over the last few days were nothing to him now. All was joy. All was bliss.

As he reached the mansion, he could see that there was an altercation in progress. There was a man who looked oddly familiar remonstrating with two footmen. From time to time, he would point towards the roof, as if there was something there that shouldn't have been. Then the angry man turned and went back into the house.

The man with no name could feel the satisfying crunch of his feet on the gravel. As he neared the house, the two footmen, who had been arguing with each other, turned towards him. He waved at them.

'Hello!'

'It's him!' said one of them to the other. In perfect unison, they both frowned, turned in the direction of the house, shook their heads and looked back at him.

'Of course it's me!'

'But you're——' said the younger of the two footman.

'——in——' continued the older one.

'——there.' finished the younger one, scratching his head.

'What on earth do you mean?' said the man with no name, looking down at himself. 'I rather think you'll find that I'm here.'

'No, sir,' said the younger footman. 'Begging your pardon, sir, but we just saw you go inside.'

'Now look here!' said the man with no name, advancing on the pair.

The older one put his hand on the younger one's shoulder. 'Doesn't matter,' he said. 'Funny things happen in the dark, don't they?'

'Yes, but——'

'It doesn't matter, laddie. Important thing is, he's here now. So what can we do for you, sir?'

He stood there for a moment, immobile. There was still something important he hadn't worked out yet. It was on the tip of his tongue, but still elusively out of reach.

'This is going to sound a bit odd,' he said, finally. 'But

I'm just wondering if you could perhaps remind me who I am?'

The two footmen exchanged glances again.

'Why sir,' said the older one, with a smile. 'You're Mr Darcy. That's who you are. Mr Darcy.'

It was as if a bolt of lightning hit him. Of course. That's exactly who he was. He was Mr Darcy. And he was home at last.

Chapter Eleven

*The Changeable Mr Darcy — Confrontation in the
Ballroom — Trapped in the Closet — Not the Man
She Married — Mrs Darcy's Needs*

ELIZABETH BUSTLED HER way through the throng of
ball goers, searching for Mr Darcy.

'Excuse me, have you seen — ?' she asked a passing
servant, but her words were drowned by the music starting up again. The orchestra were playing the opening bars
to Young Montague's Cotillion Arabesque, a gay dance
which involved a sequence of intricate hand gestures.

This was one of Elizabeth's favourites and she had so
looked forward to dancing it with Fitzy, hoping it might
help her forget everything else that was going on. But
he was in a strange mood — tonight of all nights! — and
had been brusque to the point of rudeness with several of
their guests.

'Fitzy? Where are — ah, there you are!' He was march-
ing past her on his way to the main staircase, entirely
oblivious to her until she tugged at his sleeve.

'I need to —'

'Nonsense, my dear, you're coming with me.'

Elizabeth grabbed her husband and dragged him
towards the ballroom. They found a group who were a

couple short. She positioned him opposite her and they joined in the dance.

'So what is it so pressing you cannot bear to dance with your wife?' she asked with a playful smile. 'I do hope it's not some fancy mistress of yours?' She raised her eyebrow mockingly.

'Good heavens, no—look, I must leave!'

Elizabeth looked on in amazement as Fitzy ran out of the room. However, only a minute or so later he returned. His boots were now spattered with mud.

'I'm back!' he exclaimed, clearly struggling to work out where they were in the dance.

'So you are. I feared you were going to be away much longer. Right foot, left arm, dear. Right foot, left arm.'

'My dearest Lizzy, I have been travelling for days!'

'I hardly think so. I agree that Pemberley is a more than usually large residence, but surely—'

'They kept me in a dungeon!'

'A dungeon? Are you referring to the cellars? I asked Dench to arrange for them to be cleaned out, but I would hardly refer to them as a dungeon. Left foot, now. To me. To me.' She broke off and looked at him. He seemed about to faint, and was having trouble standing up, let alone dancing. 'My dear, are you well?'

'I am—I am—I don't know—I'm so—Lizzy, they used a probe on me! They stuck it up my—'

'Fitzy, dear, people are looking at us. Do you wish to retire for a moment?'

'I ran naked across the countryside to be here'

'Fitzy, that's enough now.' She flashed him a warning look. 'Well?'

'I think I need some fresh air. Yes, that's what I need. I'll just go outside for a moment. I do apologise, my dear. I will return presently.'

Elizabeth was abandoned by her husband for the second time in a matter of minutes. But much to her surprise, he reappeared at her side almost immediately. His jacket was now torn, but at least he had brushed the mud off his boots. He was perspiring heavily and seemed a little distracted, constantly looking up at the skylight.

'I know he's up there somewhere,' he said.

'Who, dear? Fitzy darling, you are behaving in the most abominable manner this evening!'

'Elizabeth, there is a man on the roof!'

'That's it, Fitzy, you've gone mad. You talk about being kept in a dungeon and running around naked, and then you say there's a man on the roof. You are clearly unwell. I really think you should—'

She didn't manage to complete her advice.

There was the sound of breaking glass above them. The dancers dived for cover as shards rained down upon them.

Elizabeth looked up to see a man sliding down a rope attached to the ceiling, He brandished a sword in an heroic manner.

'Wickham?' she said.

The man had gone too far this time. It was time to put an end to this nonsense once and for all.

'Wickham,' commanded Elizabeth. 'Sheath your weapon immediately! There are ladies present.'

'Mrs Darcy, I must explain myself!' The music stopped and everyone looked in their direction. 'This man next to you is an imposter. An alien imposter.'

There was a shocked intake of breath from all those present. Wickham approached Mr and Mrs Darcy, his sword outstretched before him. Mr Darcy took hold of Elizabeth's arm and stepped in front of her.

'Wickham,' he said in a firm voice. 'I must ask you to leave. You are embarrassing yourself.'

'Am I indeed, Mr So-Called Darcy? I think we'll soon find out exactly who is embarrassing himself, and it won't be George Wickham.'

'Enough! This is quite intolerable!' Darcy's voice had begun to quaver, and he was clearly becoming agitated.

'Intolerable for whom, Mr Not-Quite Darcy? Only yourself, sir.' Elizabeth was astonished to realise Wickham appeared to be enjoying himself. It was as if he was deliberately goading Darcy.

'Mr Wickham, you are behaving as if you are drunk-k-k-k!' The voice was rising now, and he had developed a slight twitch.

Wickham tilted his head on one side and raised a single eyebrow. 'Did I hear you correctly, Mr Whoops-I-Don't-Think-This-Is-The-Real-One Darcy? Did you say 'drunk-k-k-k-k'?'

'Stop it!' said Elizabeth, trying to push in front of her husband. But Darcy held her back with a firm grip.

'Stay there, my dear,' he said. 'I shall deal with this blag-k-k-k-k-k-ard!'

'This what?' said Wickham, laughing. Several of the others in the ballroom joined in, with varying degrees of nervousness.

'This blag-k-k-k-k-k-k-k-' Something decidedly queer was happening to Darcy. As he grew more and more angry, his head was beginning to shake violently backwards and forwards. His hold on Elizabeth's arm was growing stronger. For a brief second she thought she felt something slimy creeping around her waist.

'Exactly how are you going to deal with me?' said Wickham, a smile playing around his lips. 'Will you give me a kick-k-k-k-k-ing?'

'I shall have you—ek!'

'Ek? You shall have me ek? Dear me.'

'Ek! Ek!'

'Fitzy?' said Elizabeth, looking up at him in alarm. 'Are you all right, my dear? And could you perchance loosen your grip?'

'Ek—ek—ek—ek !'

Darcy began to move backwards towards the doorway, dragging Elizabeth with him.

'Mrs Darcy,' said Wickham. 'Free yourself! Now!'

'Ek—ek—ek—ek—ek!'

'Fitzy, let me go!' said Elizabeth. 'Let me go!' She tried to wrestle herself free, but it was no use. He held her firmly in his grasp. Then some long-suppressed instinct for self-preservation asserted itself and she kicked him hard in the shins.

For an instant, Darcy mutated into a revolting mass of writhing tentacles, before his shape quickly restored itself to human form once again.

There was a scream from the dance floor as one of the ladies fainted.

The sound distracted him for a moment, permitting Elizabeth to break free and run towards Wickham.

Darcy turned and fled up the stairs towards the upper floors. Wickham followed, leaving Elizabeth behind in the ballroom. She turned towards her guests, who were all now staring at her, as one, open-mouthed.

'My husband is unwell,' she said by way of explanation. Then she turned, picked up her skirts and ran after the pair of them.

The fresh air wasn't doing any good. The events of the last couple of weeks had finally caught up with him. He needed to sleep.

Whatever it was up in the sky above Pemberley couldn't possibly be real. The strange flying machine was decorated with coloured lights that twinkled as it twirled around and, every now and then, it emitted a mournful,

'Ooo—laa—laa!'

'Probably French,' thought Darcy. 'Not that it exists anyway.'

Whether it was real or not, there wasn't a lot he could do about it. He sighed and headed back towards the house.

There seemed to be a bit of a commotion in progress, which was the last thing he wanted to get involved in at the moment, so he eschewed the main entrance and went in by the side door instead.

Darcy plodded up the back staircase until he found his bedroom. He went in and was about to lie down when it struck him the room wasn't in anything like the state he'd left it. There were unfamiliar clothes scattered everywhere, a curious trail of slime on the rug and a smell hinting at the presence of a long-dead animal.

'Who's been sleeping in my bed?' he wondered. But his thought process didn't get much further, because he decided to lie down anyway and, within a few seconds, he was asleep.

He was rudely awoken minutes later by voices shouting up and down the corridor outside his room. Darcy recognised one of the voices as his wife's. The other one was male. It was familiar as well, but not in a good way. Who on earth was it?

'He's not here!' he heard it say.

'I'll try the billiard room!' came his wife's voice in reply.

'Take care! I'll check out the bedrooms. He can't have gone far.'

He heard running feet disappearing into the distance. What the deuce was going on?

There was a knock on the door. He was about to tell them to come in, but it occurred to him they might not be friendly.

Who was the owner of that voice? Was it someone who owed him money? Did he owe him money?

The best policy was to take no chances. He leapt out of bed and hid in the closet.

'Anybody there?' said the man. 'I know you're in here somewhere. Come out and we can deal with this like gentlemen.'

Darcy could hear the person moving around the room, rustling through clothes and opening and shutting cupboards. Finally, he could hear the man's breathing outside the closet.

'Aha! So that's where you are!' There was a triumphal tone to the voice. 'If you don't come out of the closet in the next ten seconds, I shall run you through.'

Darcy burst open the closet, knocking the intruder over as he did so. He tried to make a break towards the bedroom door, but the man grabbed his ankle as he went past He crashed downwards.

He was too tired to put up any more resistance, his opponent straddling him and pinning him to the floor.

'Wickham?' he gasped, finally recognising the face looking down at him.

'The same. Now no more of your slimy tentacle tricks—you're coming back with me to the Department. Sir Humphrey's in the mood for a little dissection, I think.' Wickham produced some rope and began to bind Darcy around the chest.

But he was interrupted by a loud thump and a crash above them, followed by a woman's scream. There was a brief silence, broken only by the awful keening sound that Darcy thought he had imagined earlier:

'Ooh—laa—laa!'

On the roof, Elizabeth was more than a little vexed to discover her beloved Fitzy was no longer behaving like the man she had married. She was prepared to acknowledge that the Fitzy she used to know could be cold, aloof and altogether difficult to deal with at times, but if she had known he concealed tentacles under his skin, she might well have called the whole thing off.

'Let me go!' she tried to say, although because this man held his hand over her mouth, it actually came out as 'Mmfth mm mfth!'

Below her, she could hear the orchestra playing a vigorous accompaniment to a Threesome Rumpy Pumpy; there was no chance anyone would hear her cries.

'Be quiet, Elizabeth,' said Darcy. ''Tis for your own protection. Because of the blundering fool Wickham's intervention, I will have to take you away to a place of safety.' He broke off and started to make strange noises into a device mounted on his wrist. 'Ek—ek—ek—ek!' The device answered back in kind. Then there was a loud booming noise from above and a great flying machine began to descend.

Great heavens, thought Elizabeth! It was just like that machine they had seen that night at the parsonage—that night when . . . that night when . . .

So she hadn't imagined it after all. Strange things were indeed happening and now she was caught right in the middle of them.

She wriggled again in a bid to escape once more from Darcy's grip, but this time he held her firm. Both of his arms, as well as half a dozen tentacles, bound her to him.

131

Elizabeth looked up in horror as a rope with a hook on the end was slowly being lowered towards them and real-ised what was happening. She was going to be kidnapped and taken away in that flying machine. If that happened, she might never see her loved ones ever again.

'Stop right there!' Two figures emerged from a trap-door onto the roof a few feet in front of them. The first was Wickham, brandishing his sword as ever. The second figure was quite unexpected.

It was Darcy.

She looked from him to the one who was holding her and back to him again.

Whoever — whatever — it was that was holding her was clearly rattled by this new development. 'Get back, imposter!' it said, without much conviction. It gave an anxious look upwards towards the rope, which now almost reached them.

Come on, do something, thought Elizabeth! But the new Darcy looked ill and out of sorts, and Wickham seemed uncertain as to when he should make his move.

'Too late!' cried her captor, grabbing hold of the hook. It attached the hook to its jacket and gave a tug on the rope. The great flying machine boomed out an 'Ooh — laa — laa!' and the pair of them began to ascend.

But before they had gone very far, another flying machine suddenly appeared out of the night sky — a curious kind of balloon with a steam engine mounted on it, puffing out clouds of black smoke. She tried to wave at it and she thought a man in British Army uniform waved back.

Then she heard a shot ring out and one of the arms that were grasping her went limp . . .

. . . and then she was falling . . .

. . . falling . . .

. . . falling . . .

Wickham watched in horror as the scene unfolded before him in terrible slow motion; the alien flying machine above him winching alien Darcy's limp body aboard, the strange inflatable steam-powered newcomer descending to where they were standing, and Mrs Darcy tumbling out of the sky towards the roof. This could only end in disaster. He would never forgive himself for failing to act more quickly.

And then another sudden movement, knocking Wickham aside with the force of a dozen men.

It was Darcy himself.

Somehow, he seemed to have located an inner reserve of strength and was hurtling towards where his wife was plummeting.

He arrived just in time to catch her in his arms, steady her and then fall over backwards in a graceful heap.

Up above them, the flying machine gave one last 'Ooh—laa—laa!' and disappeared into the night, whilst the strange balloon gently touched down on the other side of the roof, surrounded by billows of thick smoke. Two familiar figures emerged out of the twilight, coughing and wheezing.

'Wickham, old man!' said Colonel Sutherland. 'How're you doing?'

'Very well, sir,' said Wickham, beginning to feel a little better about the situation. 'I take it that you haven't come here to court-martial me, then?'

'Good Lord, no. H here and his—ah—spectral friend have explained everything. Good job, man. Good job.'

There was silence for a moment.

'Everyone all right?' inquired H, sounding slightly concerned. There was a groan from Darcy, echoed by his wife. Wickham thought he could detect a sort of 'Phew' sound from H.

'Jolly good show,' said Sutherland. 'Jolly good.'

'Bit of a risky shot though, sir, if you don't mind me saying so,' said Wickham.

'Nonsense, man, nonsense. I was certain that one of you chaps would be able to catch Mrs D. And so you did. Capital!'

There was another awkward silence.

'Nice new toy you've got there, H,' said Wickham.

'Ah, that thing. Dirigible, they call it. Didn't make it myself, though. Inherited it from a Prussian fellow called Fuchs.'

'What? *The* Fuchs?'

'Yes, the Flying Fuchs. Dead now of course.'

'Really? I thought he'd go on for ever.'

'So did I. No, he went the same way as that other chap, half Italian — what was his name?'

'Gunther Bugari?'

'That's the fellow. Poor blighter bought it trying to fly across the channel with wings strapped to his arms. I ended up with his dirigible. Felt I had to carry on his work.'

'For Fuchs' sake?'

'Indeed.'

Sutherland coughed. 'Well, that's as maybe. But I'm afraid there's no time for gossip. We need to get going again, chaps. All five of us. This place is no longer safe. Our alien friends will very likely return soon with reinforcements and next time they may be armed.'

'Excuse me, sir.' The three men turned towards the voice as Mrs Darcy disentangled herself from her husband. 'But may I remind you we have a houseful of guests here tonight?'

'I understand, madam, but—'

'And also 'tis the first I have seen my real husband for some considerable time. I am a woman and I have needs. He is a man and he has needs also.'

Sutherland gave a cough and looked deeply embarrassed. 'Er, yes, well—I'm sure—one night—we can leave—in the morning, yes that's right, we'll leave in the morning.'

'Good,' said Mrs Darcy. 'That's settled, then. Come, my dear.' Her husband groaned as he made to stand up. With considerable effort he eventually made it to his feet and, supported by his wife, staggered towards the trapdoor that led down from the roof.

Chapter Twelve

The Council of Pemberley—Cover Art—The Mission Arrives at the Mission—Ecky Ecky Ecky—Mr Collins is Discarded

THE PARTY REASSEMBLED itself over breakfast the next morning—at least all of the party except Mr Darcy.

'My husband is still a-bed,' said Elizabeth by way of explanation. Colonel Sutherland raised his eyebrow for the briefest of instants. 'The poor man is quite limp after his ordeal,' she continued. 'In fact, he is completely drained.' There was a strangled, choking sound from the colonel as he struggled with a mouthful of Bath bun. The other two men tried very hard not to catch each other's eye.

'So what's the plan, sir?' asked Wickham, after his superior's discomfiture resolved itself. 'Do we have any more information about these creatures?'

'We think they come from Mars,' said H.

'Mars?' asked Wickham. 'Great heavens, what are the chances of anything coming from there? Must be—'

'A hundred to one' said the Colonel. 'So obviously we cannot hope to attack them on their home ground—at least not until H here has finished work on his space machine.' (here H looked slightly annoyed and shook his head) 'So instead, we must penetrate their base on Earth.'

'Rosings!' said Wickham.

'Indeed. However, we believe that a frontal assault on the house will be too risky now. They know that we know about them. In fact, they probably know that we know that they know that we know.

'Until now they have refrained from using force against us, but we must assume they possess weaponry far more advanced than anything we have. So we must employ subterfuge instead.'

'Subterfuge?'

'Yes. And this is where your husband comes in, Mrs Darcy.'

Mrs Darcy looked shocked. 'Surely you aren't suggesting he should visit Rosings and pretend to be an alien?'

'No , of course not. Far too risky. For all we know, your husband's alien copy may be dead or mortally wounded, and we can be sure that Lady Catherine will be all too aware of this. However, if we move quickly, we may just be able to convince a certain third party that our Darcy is their Darcy, so to speak.'

'Mr Collins!' said Wickham.

'Precisely. And if we can feed him the right story to take back to Rosings, then we can use him to get us in there without any blood split.'

'A brilliant plan, sir! What can possibly go wrong?'

The colonel smiled. 'What indeed?' he said. 'So the three of us will go with Mr Darcy to Whitechapel, having sequestered Mrs Darcy in a place of safety along the way.'

'Excuse me,' said Mrs Darcy. 'But if my husband is being involved in a dangerous undercover plot, then I should be by his side. I shall come too.'

The colonel shook his head, 'No Mrs Darcy.'

'Sir,' said Wickham. 'Perhaps she—'

'Wickham,' the colonel rolled his eyes. 'I'm sure that

you will agree with me this is no job for a woman. It is said the heat of battle can fry the brains of the fairer sex. She may lose control of her bonnet!'

A new voice now entered the argument. 'Colonel, I beg to differ.' Everyone turned towards the doorway, where Darcy was leaning against the wall. 'If my wife insists on coming, then she shall. You may rail against it until you are quite puce with the trying, but 'tis of little use. She will have her way in the end.'

It sounded like the voice of bitter experience.

There was a brief silence as the colonel digested this. 'Well then,' he said eventually. 'There we have it. We shall all go to Whitechapel. H, fire up the dirigible! Let's hit the sky!'

The little dirigible pitched, rolled and yawed as it chugged its erratic way towards London. Wickham and Sutherland maintained a watch on either side of the prow, whilst H stood in the middle, turning the wheel this way and that.

Darcy, however, was clearly less comfortable with this mode of transport; he lay supine on the deck of the gondola, tossing from side to side and groaning.

Elizabeth fared even worse, spending most of the time leaning over the side, losing more of her breakfast each time she heaved.

Great heavens, it's a long way down, she thought.

'Why couldn't we have taken the carriage?' she wailed.

No one answered her.

'Can you see him yet?' called H.

'Not yet,' said Sutherland.

'Who?' asked Elizabeth.

'Hold on, I think I see something,' said Sutherland. 'Pass me that spyglass, will you, Wickham?'

Sutherland held the glass up to his eye and squinted into the distance. 'Yes! There he is,' he said, pointing.

'Who?' said Elizabeth again. She lifted herself up from the side of the dirigible and peered into the distance ahead of them. She couldn't see a thing. Meanwhile, Sutherland returned the spyglass to Wickham.

'Good Lord, so he is!' said Wickham.

'WHO?' demanded Elizabeth. This time, Sutherland took pity on her, and beckoned for her to join them in the prow. She gingerly made her way forwards until she could grip the bow of the gondola, and stood there for a moment, trying to steady herself again.

'Here,' said Sutherland, passing her the spyglass, 'Take a look.'

Elizabeth put the glass up to her eye and looked towards where Sutherland indicated. What madness was this?

There was another balloon in the sky ahead of them, except this one was tethered to the ground by an impossibly long rope. In it was a man dressed in a smock. To one side of him was an easel. The man appeared to be holding an artist's palette in one hand and a brush in the other.

'See?' said Sutherland.

'Y—e—es,' said Elizabeth, nonplussed. 'But who is he and what is he doing up here?'

'He's an artist,' replied Sutherland, as if it explained everything.

'Yes, I can see that. But what is he painting? The clouds?'

'No, he's painting us!' said Wickham.

'Us?'

'Yes,' said Sutherland. 'Us. Let me explain. One day, when all this ghastly business is over, it may fall to some great writer to tell the tale of how we defeated the alien menace that threatened the very existence of our magnificent country.'

'Great writer? Not that dreadful Austen woman, I hope?'

'I know her not. Who is she?'

'The one who writes those ghastly Gothic romances about the undead.'

'Well, for one thing, I hardly think this would be a suitable job for a woman,' said Sutherland with a laugh. Elizabeth shot him a look, but he ignored her. 'And for another, I think we would be looking for someone with a little more class.'

'That still doesn't explain the artist,' she said, although she had a horrible feeling it probably did.

'Well, obviously such a book will require illustrations.'

She stared at him.

' And we felt that a picture of H's revolutionary mode of transport—'

She continued to stare.

'—would be particularly—particularly—'

'Appealing?' interjected Wickham.

Elizabeth looked at the three men in charge of the flying machine and noticed each of them now adopted an heroic pose as they were approaching the balloon.

Good grief, this was preposterous. 'Are you therefore telling me, sir, our sole reason for utilising this absurd mode of transport is to provide an airborne artist with a picture opportunity?'

'Well, not in so many words, but—I suppose—' Sutherland's voice reduced to a mumble as he finished with a tiny, 'Yes'.

Elizabeth folded her arms and flounced back to where her husband was still moaning on the deck. As they passed the other balloon, she distinctly heard Wickham call out 'Good show, sir!'

It was nearing twilight when H damped the boiler down, let the engine cool and opened the valve to let the last of the steam escape. Silently, the dirigible drifted down towards the roof of the Mission in Whitechapel.

There was a crash and a thump as H and his two colleagues in uniform fought to stop the vehicle sliding off the roof. They threw grappling irons at any chimney that happened to be within range. Finally it shuddered to a halt, with an ear-shredding scraping, a few feet shy of the edge.

'Well, that went well, eh?' said Sutherland, clinging on to the side.

The look that Mrs Darcy gave him would have felled an ox. She hauled herself to her feet and assisted her ailing husband to his.

H busied himself setting up some kind of contraption involving lots of rope and gearwheels. Then he threw one end of the rope over the side of the gondola, letting it drop down to the ground. Sutherland went to swing his leg over the side, but Wickham spoke up.

'Sir, let me go first. We don't know what we may run into down there.'

'I thought you all said that nothing could go wrong,' said Mrs Darcy.

'Well, best to be careful, all the same,' said Sutherland. But he didn't sound terribly convinced and seemed to be entirely comfortable with the idea of Wickham leading the descent.

Wickham sat on the rail of the gondola and grabbed hold of the rope, testing that it was secure. Once he was happy that it would bear his weight, he began to climb down. When he reached street level, he drew his sword and looked around.

Satisfying himself there was nothing untoward lurking in the gloom, he gave two sharp tugs on the rope to indicate the all-clear.

A few seconds after that, he heard the unmistakeable sound of a miniature steam engine starting up, followed a minute or so later by the arrival of a wicker basket attached to the rope by a complex system of pulleys. In the basket was a somewhat bemused Mr Darcy. He looked paler than ever.

Next to descend was Mrs Darcy, followed by Colonel Sutherland.

The plan was for H to stay in the machine, ready for immediate take-off in the event of anything going disastrously wrong. Which of course wasn't going to happen at all. There was never any chance of that.

Once all four of the party were assembled, Sutherland whispered to them to follow him.

'Sir,' said Wickham. 'I believe the entrance is this way.' They all turned round and followed him instead.

'I knew that,' said Sutherland.

Creeping round to the front of the Mission, they located the front door. It was locked.

'Do we knock?' asked Wickham.

'Of course not,' said Sutherland. 'Damn blighters might hear us. No, we break it down instead.'

'Wouldn't that—oh never mind,' said Mrs Darcy. She still sounded peeved.

'Any other suggestions?' said Sutherland. There was no reply, apart from a vague groan from Darcy.

'Is he all right?' inquired Wickham. 'The success of this endeavour does rather depend on him.'

'Nonsense,' said Sutherland. 'All the man has to do is keep upright for long enough to give his story to Collins.'

'But—' said Mrs Darcy.

'Enough,' said Sutherland, choosing a place on the door to take aim with his shoulder.

He took a couple of steps back, charged and went flying straight through the doorway, past a bemused man with a slight stoop and greasy unkempt hair.

'Mr Darcy!' said the man. 'And Mrs Darcy?' he added, with evident surprise. 'Your face looks familiar too, although I remember not your name,' he said, turning to Wickham. He held out a limp hand and bowed from the waist. 'Mr Collins,' he said 'At your service. Welcome to my humble Mission.'

Mr Collins led the way down the corridor, followed by Darcy, Wickham and Sutherland, with Elizabeth bringing up the rear. Sutherland seemed less than sure of foot and was clutching a kerchief to his brow at the point where he had recently made contact with the wall beyond the front door.

Even though it was still a warm summer evening outside, Elizabeth shivered. Something inside her knew that bad things happened here. The flickering light of Mr Collins' candle up ahead caused strange shadows to dance on the walls. She could easily imagine a more suscepti-ble creature than herself perceiving ghosts and phantoms in a place such as this. Every now and then, she even managed to convince herself there was another set of foot-steps behind her.

At the end of the corridor, Mr Collins ushered them into a room, shut the door and bade them seat themselves in front of a large desk. He took a seat opposite them, clasped his hands together and turned to look at Darcy with an expectant air.

'So, Mr Darcy,' he said, 'What can I do for you?'

Something was wrong. Elizabeth couldn't quite put her finger on it, but Mr Collins wasn't behaving the way she would have expected. The usual oleaginous fawning tone was absent.

'I need to take Mrs Darcy to Rosings,' said her husband, exactly as he had been primed by Colonel Sutherland.

'Indeed?' asked Collins. 'So pray why did you bring her here, accompanied by two agents of the Crown?'

Great heavens, he knows, thought Elizabeth! We are in mortal peril!

'These two agents, as you call them, are aliens in disguise,' said Darcy, sticking to his script. This was the least convincing part of the deception, thought Elizabeth.

'Eck,' said Wickham, without much conviction.

'Ecky ecky,' said Sutherland.

'Ecky ecky indeed,' said Collins. 'Ecky ecky.'

We need to get out of here, thought Elizabeth. 'Excuse us, Mr Collins.' She began to rise from her chair.

'Sit down, Mrs Darcy,' commanded Collins. 'Stay right there.'

'Now look here!' said Darcy, making as if to stand up. But before he could do so, a pair of metal bands erupted from the arms of his chair and pinned him to it. At the same time, similar devices were activated and made prisoners of the other three.

'I demand—' began Sutherland, but he was cut short by Collins.

'Be quiet, you blundering old nincompoop. Did you imagine I was so ill-informed I would be taken in by your deception? That I would somehow be unaware that my alien friends' replacement for your Mr Darcy here was wounded whilst escaping from Pemberley last night?'

'Replacement?' said Elizabeth.

'Well, he's certainly an improvement on the original, don't you think?' said Collins. 'Just think, my dear Mrs Darcy, you could have had me instead.'

'How dare you speak to my wife like that, you revolting little man!'

'Cease!' Collins was on his feet now, pacing up and down in front of them.

'Now the question is, what shall I do with you all? I fear the only one of you who is not completely expendable is indeed the lovely Elizabeth here.' He bent down to stroke her chin, but she shook her head away in disgust. 'I wouldn't be so quick to disown me, my dear. Our new masters have promised you to me when this is all over.'

'No!' cried Elizabeth.

'Oh yes,' said Collins.

Darcy and Wickham were both squirming in their seats by now, taking turns to fire insults at Collins, who merely laughed at them. 'You poor pathetic humans, look at you! Mankind is finished!'

'Traitor!' shouted Sutherland.

'I am but a realist,' said Collins, with a sad shake of his head. 'The first of many such realists, as you will soon see, once my masters show their true colours!'

The door opened behind them, and Collins' familiar obsequious demeanour returned in an instant. 'Ah! Lady Catherine!' he said. 'So delightful to see you once more. See, I have your prisoners!'

Lady Catherine de Bourgh swept into the room and surveyed its occupants. 'Well, well, well,' she said. 'What do we have here?'

'My Lady, 'tis—' began Mr Collins.

'Oh, do be quiet, Collins, you snivelling wretch,' said Lady Catherine. He flinched and gave an uncertain smile. 'As you wish.'

'Of course I wish. Now be quiet until I ask you to say something, and even then make sure your answer is of the highest quality before you venture to respond. Is that understood?'

Collins made to reply, caught himself and ended up giving a passable impression of a particularly absent-minded goldfish.

'Good,' said Lady Catherine. 'So, I see we have almost a complete hand to play with here, even if most of them will ultimately be discarded.'

'You'll never get away with this!' said Wickham.

'Wickham, do you ever say anything else? Or does your conversation consist of selections from a limited set of tiresome stock phrases?'

'You have to admit he was right last time,' said Elizabeth. Lady Catherine turned on her with an evil eye.

'Ah, the feisty Mrs Darcy! I wonder, will you be so bold when I probe your husband to within an inch of his life?'

'No! Not the probe!' said Sutherland. Lady Catherine blinked and stared at him.

'And who on earth are you?' she said. 'Do I know you? Perhaps I should probe you first.'

Sutherland gulped. 'Madam, it would be an honour,' he said, his voice rising to a squeak.

'Enough!' said Darcy, twitching against the metal bands that held him in his chair. 'If I am to be probed, let it be done now.'

Lady Catherine laughed. 'Ha! You poor fools. There

will be no probing tonight. There is no need for any more probing at all. The probes have done their work.'

There was an audible sigh of relief from all four prisoners.

'No,' said Lady Catherine. 'I shall simply dispose of all of you except Mrs Darcy. Her destiny is yet incomplete.' She reached into her bag and withdrew what appeared to be a small firearm — albeit one that was far smoother in shape and more compact than anything Elizabeth had seen before.

Lady Catherine pointed it at each of the four of them in turn, and then — to everyone's astonishment — at Mr Collins, who stood up and began to edge away from her.

'Lady Catherine!' he said. 'Pray wh — wh — what are you doing, ma'am? Have I not served you faithfully all these years? Have I not obeyed every command, followed every whim and indulged every nuance of your desires? Please, I beg you!'

He seemed uncertain as to whether to abase himself before her or to try to make a run for it.

'Mr Collins, you tiresome, repulsive little man, I thank you for delivering this band of deluded idiots to me and thus ensuring the success of our great plan. But now victory is in sight, your life serves no purpose to me. Moreover, I am tired of your wretched fawning and, if I have to spend one more minute in your company, there is every chance that I shall strangle myself with one of my own tentacles.'

'Lady Catherine!'

'Enough!' She raised the firearm and pointed it at Mr Collins' body. Panic-stricken, he turned and looked at Elizabeth, pleading at her instead.

'Mrs Darcy!' he said. 'Go to my wife. Ask her — ask her about — about the potting shed.'

'I beg your pardon?' said Elizabeth, taken aback. But before he could elucidate, there was a sharp crack, a blinding flash and the room filled with smoke. When it cleared, there was no sign of Mr Collins at all.

Chapter Thirteen

*Mr Collins' New Career — Poltergeist! — Bath
Time for Mr Darcy — Stowaways — Strange
Happenings in Bath*

'Aaaaaaaaaaaaaaaaaaaaaaaaaaaaaaaaaaaaaaaaaaaaaaaaaaaaa
agh!'

Mr Collins was flying, but he knew not how nor where, nor even—now he came to think of it—when. The aliens' ray gun—even in the hands of such a skilled practitioner as his esteemed patroness, Lady Catherine de Bourgh—was an unreliable device at the best of times. The fact that he had apparently survived its use was not necessarily a useful indicator that he was still on the same planet or in the same period of history.

'Aaaaaaaaaaaaaaaaaaaaaaaaaaaaaaaaaaaaaaaaaaaaaaaaaaaaa
agh!'

The shock at his treatment by Lady Catherine had dissipated somewhat during his journey into the unknown. In any case, no doubt she had a point. He must have let her down somehow—although he was at a loss, for the moment, exactly how—and she was fully entitled to exact punishment. It was, however, a shame to lose such a gracious and beneficent patroness.

'Aaaaaaaaaaaaaaaaaaaaaaaaaaaaaaaaaaaaaaaaaaaaaaaaaaaaa
agh!'

The wind rushed past his ears, and he flailed his arms, trying to slow himself down. When was it going to end? Did this kind of thing happen every time? He hadn't yet dared to open his eyes, so he had no idea what was going on around him, and there was every chance that the eventual landing could be an unpleasant experience. It was in fact entirely possible that he would not survive this.

'Aaaaaaaaaaaaaaaaaaaaaaaaaaaaaaaaaaaaaaaaaaaaaaaaaaaaaa agh!'

Come on now, he thought to himself, pull yourself together—what's the worst that can happen? However, this did not prove to be a helpful line of enquiry. There were very many bad things that could happen to him right now and he decided, on balance, he would prefer not to think about any of them.

'Aaaaaaaaaaaaaaaaaaaaaaaaaaaaaaaaaaaaaaaaaaaaaaaaaaaaaa agh!'

He risked opening one eye, and almost immediately saw a tree heading straight for him.

He put out his hands in front of him and somehow managed to cushion the impact. For a second, he dangled from a branch, ape-like, and then dropped heavily onto the ground.

Silence reigned, broken only by the tweeting birds of the dawn chorus. A damp country smell filled the air.

'Morning,' said a voice.

Collins looked up towards the direction it came from. 'Er . . . yes.'

'You all right, mister?' A face peered down at him. It was florid, male and chewing a long piece of grass.

'I believe I am.'

'Is that so? Is that so indeed? Strikes me as an odd place for a gentleman such as yourself to kip down for the night? Missus kick you out?'

'Great heavens! The impertinence! I shall report you to the authorities for insulting a minister!'

He struggled to stand up, but his foot was caught in one of the lower branches and his efforts merely resulted in him ending up with his face in the mud.

'So you a man of the cloth, eh? Well, ain't that a coincidence? 'Cos they're a-looking for a new Rector 'round these parts. You come for the interviews?'

Collins thought for a moment. He was going to have to make a living somehow. He softened his tone a little. 'Maybe I was a little hasty just now. As you see, I am in a difficult position here.' He paused. 'This may sound a curious question, but which year is it?'

The face frowned. 'You don't know? What a peculiar gentleman you are to be sure. Well, sir, 'tis the year of our Lord 1906.'

Collins finally managed to extricate his foot from the tree and succeeded in standing up. He looked long and hard at the yokel in front of him. 'And where is this place?' he said.

'Why, sir, this be Stiffkey! 'Tis the finest place on God's own earth is Stiffkey.'

Stiffkey, thought Collins. I like the sound of that. He really had fallen on his feet this time—just when he thought he might have ended up walking into the proverbial lion's den.

Elizabeth gaped in astonishment at the empty space where Mr Collins had been.

'You killed him!' she said. 'How could you?'

Lady Catherine de Bourgh shook her head. 'I am sure he would see it as merely being sent to a better place. He was of no further use to me.'

'But surely you are not going to kill us, though?' said Wickham.

'Ah, Such optimism, Mr Wickham.'

'What is it that you want from us?' said Sutherland.

'Want? I want nothing from you, colonel.'

'Perhaps you expect us to talk?' said Darcy.

'No, Mr Darcy. I expect you to die,' said Lady Catherine. She took aim at each of the three men in turn. 'So, who is to be executed first?' she said. 'The bumbling colonel? The dashing, yet idiotic lieutenant? Or the pompous and rather dull Mr Darcy?'

The silence in the room was palpable.

For a moment it seemed as if Lady Catherine settled on Wickham. Then she changed her mind and aimed at Darcy.

But then her choice was rendered moot by the unexpected appearance of an airborne teapot that struck her arm with some force, knocking the pistol out of her hand.

For an instant, a tentacle appeared from her sleeve and flailed about for a moment, then her human form reasserted itself.

'Damn you!' she cried. 'Where are you now?'

'Where is who now?' said Elizabeth, thoroughly confused by this new development.

Lady Catherine reached down to pick up the gun, but was knocked off her chair by an ornamental vase smashing against the side of her head.

Elizabeth felt a draught of air whistle past her and something sounding like the rustle of skirts.

'Great heavens,' said Sutherland. 'A poltergeist!'

'How extraordinary! What are the chances of that happening, I wonder?' said Wickham.

Darcy, however, sounded a cautious note. 'This is all

terribly interesting, but I'm sure you will be aware that we are still manacled to these seats.'

There was a sudden 'ping' sound.

'Well, we're not any more,' said Elizabeth, getting to her feet. Lady Catherine was stunned on the floor.

'Come on, then, let's get moving!' she said. The men were all standing up now, and looking at each other, trying to decide who was going to take charge of the situation.

'Yes, let's go!' said Sutherland.

'Yes, let's!' said Wickham.

Darcy was looking pale again, and didn't say anything.

Elizabeth was already halfway down the corridor by now. 'Come on!' she cried. All four were making their way towards the exit now, but Lady Catherine had apparently regained her senses and was now in hot pursuit.

And then, once more, Elizabeth felt that strange draught of air and a rustle of skirts next to her. She was also convinced that she heard the word 'Duck!' whispered to her by an unseen voice.

So she did, and the next thing she knew, an unflattering china bust of the Prince Regent suddenly materialised in mid air and was spinning madly in the direction of Lady Catherine. It caught her right on the temple, stopping her in her tracks once again.

'Did you see that?' said Sutherland. 'Dashed good aim, what?'

By this time, they had all reached the door. Wickham heaved it open, and they burst out into the night.

Then they made their way round to where the steam lift was waiting to carry them up into the dirigible again.

Wickham helped Elizabeth into the basket and gave a tug on the rope. There was a tense couple of seconds before they heard the unmistakeable sound of the engine chugging back into life.

When Elizabeth reached the top, H helped her out of the basket.

'Everything go according to plan?' he asked.

Once Wickham, bringing up the rear, was aboard, H fired up the burners and the dirigible soared upwards into the night sky. Fiddling constantly with the controls, he held her steady — or as close to steady as he could manage, which wasn't in fact remotely close — as they told him everything that had happened to them inside the Mission. Or at least three of them managed to recount their respective tales. Darcy was looking distinctly unwell again and was only capable of groans from where he lay in the bowels of the gondola.

'So what do we do now?' said Sutherland. 'We seem to be once more without a plan.'

'Surely our aim remains the same as it ever has been — to get into the house at Rosings?' said Wickham.

'Yes, but our means to achieve that aim was vaporised not half an hour ago. Extraordinary business. To think that he was in front of us one moment and then, not.'

'That's as maybe, my good sirs,' said Elizabeth. 'But for the moment my main concern is closer to home. I am exceedingly vexed about my husband. All this excitement and adventure is too much for him in his present frail state.'

'I agree,' said Sutherland. 'The man needs a rest cure.'

There was silence for a minute or so.

'How about Bath?' said Wickham.

'What an extraordinary suggestion!' said Elizabeth. 'I hardly think that sitting in a tub of water for half an hour is likely to do him any good.'

'No, I meant the City of Bath.'

'Oh, I see.' She thought for a moment. 'He does not view that place with much pleasure, I fear. But 'tis also true that the waters may revive his spirits.'

'So 'tis agreed, then,' said Sutherland. 'We shall go to Bath. And once Mr Darcy is placed in the care of the healing springs, we may resume our quest to steal our way into Rosings unnoticed and put an end to this hideous alien intrusion of our English way of life.'

'But how are we to do that?' asked Wickham.

'What was it that Mr Collins said before he—as you say—vanished?' inquired H.

'I think he said that we should ask his wife for the key to the potting shed,' said Wickham. 'Perhaps 'tis a clue.'

'Great heavens!' exclaimed Sutherland. ''Tis indeed a clue! What if the potting shed was Mrs Collins' nickname for Rosings?'

'She must have a secret key!' said Wickham. 'Collins must have needed to enter the great house without knocking on the front door, so to speak, so he would need a key to some other entrance.'

'Brilliant!' said Sutherland. There was a slight pause.

'That is indeed an exceptionally astute piece of deduction, gentlemen,' said H. 'But I yet perceive a problem.'

'Why so?' asked Sutherland.

'We have no idea how to locate Mrs Collins.'

Elizabeth coughed. 'I think I may be able to help you there. I have lately had communication from Charlotte Collins. She is staying in Glastonbury, in a commune for artistic people.'

'Is she of the artistic persuasion herself?'

'Thankfully not,' said Elizabeth.

Wickham suddenly clicked his fingers as if something

extraordinarily important had just occurred to him. 'Is not Glastonbury only a few miles from Bath?'

''Tis true,' said H. 'It seems that our twin paths do indeed run parallel. I shall set a course for Bath immediately. Once Mr Darcy has disembarked, we shall proceed thenceforth to Glastonbury.'

'I love it when a plan comes to—' began Sutherland.

'I hate Bath,' said Darcy with a groan.

'Nonsense, Fitzy dear,' said Elizabeth. ''Tis for your own good. Now lie down again and get some sleep.' As she bent down to tuck a blanket around her husband's supine form, she shuddered. For a moment, she was convinced she heard the rustle of another woman's skirts.

The dirigible floated on through the night air towards Bath. The only sounds apart from the soft chugging of the engine were the snores of Colonel Sutherland as he lay dozing in the rear of the gondola and occasional groans from Mr Darcy. Mrs Darcy was asleep too, but she maintained a ladylike silence.

Keeping watch at the prow, Wickham had plenty of time to think. What he was mainly wondering about was how on earth did they manage to escape from the Mission. They had surely all been doomed to certain death until that poltergeist had appeared.

Or was it a poltergeist? Maybe it was simply a ghost with a bad attitude? How could you tell? Of course!

Abandoning his post for a moment, he went to the middle of the ship and found H, busy checking the course to Bath.

'How much do you know about ghosts, H?' he asked.

H narrowed his eyes. 'You've heard it too, haven't you?'

'Heard what?'

'The rustling.' H twitched slightly.

Wickham frowned. 'No, I haven't heard anything. I was just wondering how we managed to evade Lady Catherine.'

'Yes, I was wondering about that. Queer business and no mistake.' H suddenly stiffened. 'Did you hear that?' he whispered.

'Hear what?'

'Listen! There it goes again!'

This time, Wickham heard it — a definite rustle of skirts. And was he imagining it, or was there a whiff of cheap gin in the air?

'H?' he said.

H put a finger to his lips and opened up a panel in the bulkhead. He motioned to Wickham to hold the wheel and started rummaging. Eventually he emerged, triumphantly clutching a device Wickham recognised; the funnel at the end of H's ghost detection engine.

'Good Lord!' he whispered. 'What else do you have stashed away on board, H?'

H smiled. 'You'd be surprised, young man. Never underestimate Sir Humphry Davy.'

'I most certainly won't.'

The conspiratorial silence was rudely broken by H starting up the engine. Sutherland sat up briefly, scratched his head and then lay down again, muttering. The Darcys slept peacefully on, undisturbed.

'So what's the plan?' asked Wickham.

'First of all, keep your hands on the wheel and your eye on the sky ahead. For my part, I will carry out a sweep of this vessel to see if we are harbouring any spectral stowaways.'

H pulled out a length of hose from the machine and began to wave the funnel from side to side, moving slowly forwards, until a pair of female feet suddenly appeared. Unexpectedly, a second pair of female feet then appeared next to the first pair, followed by a third and a fourth.

H tilted the funnel upwards, revealing four women, each of whom was regarding Wickham and himself with some interest.

'Evening, Mr Wickham,' said Annie Chapman. 'Nice to see you again.'

Wickham found himself unable to speak.

'Wickham?' said H. 'Do you know this person?'

'I—I—yes, that is to say—'

'Oh, don't worry, Mister,' said Annie Chapman. 'He don't know me in the biblical sense.' She paused. 'Even if he did ask if I did Prussian.'

'He did what?' said the girl on her left.

'Filthy bugger,' said the one next to her.

'But he is handsome, like you said,' remarked the fourth one. 'So I might—'

'Now listen to me, Mary Jane Kelly,' said Annie Chapman. 'You wanna be careful, my young lady. You don't let no one ask you for Prussian. More than your life's worth.'

'Even if I'm dead?' said the other.

'Annie's right, Mary Jane,' said the one to Annie Chapman's left. 'You wanna look after yourself.'

H held up his hand. 'Ladies!' he said. 'Please calm down. I'm sure that my colleague's enquiry was entirely innocent—'

'Yeah, right!'

'But be that as it may, I would be very interested to know what you're doing here. I'm not altogether certain if this vessel can cope with four extra passengers.'

'Us?' said Annie Chapman, with a hint of indignation. 'We only went and saved Mr Wickham here's life. Not so say those other geezers what were with him. Although we still don't know what's up with that Mr Darcy.'

'I can explain that,' said Wickham. 'But who are you all?'

'Just four 'onest 'ores what got caught up in bad business, Mr Wickham,' said the one on Annie Chapman's left. 'Elizabeth Stride, at your service,' she added, with a curtsey, 'And that there is Catherine Eddowes. And the cheeky one on the end is Mary Jane Kelly. And us four ain't going anywhere right now, Mister.'

As the five travellers disembarked from the dirigible, which was now safely secured in a field just outside Bath, Wickham turned to Elizabeth.

'Why does Mr Darcy hate this place so?' he said.

She thought for a moment, and then shook her head. 'You'll find out,' she said with a sigh.

'Oh. That bad?'

'I'm afraid so.'

The party headed off towards the city. It was early morning, and the streets were full of people bustling around on various errands. Sutherland and H, supporting poor Darcy between them, led the way, followed by Wickham and Elizabeth.

Elizabeth was getting ever more concerned about Darcy. In truth, she was not confident the famous spa waters would cure his ailments, but there seemed to be no choice, other than leaving him here while they continued their journey. H said he would stay and look after him, but she suspected the man's motives. She did not wish her husband to become a mere guinea-pig for whatever quack cures he might come up with. Better surely to treat him conventionally with some light blood-letting or perhaps a mild trepanation?

The presence of the four ghosts was also a worry. She didn't have a problem with believing in them — particularly after a brief demonstration involving a pair of dividers and Colonel Sutherland's buttocks — but she was not yet comfortable with the idea of being so overtly in the company of dead people. Particularly ones that kept themselves invisible. H had taken her to task over this, accusing her of being 'deadist', although this just gave her one more reason to regard the man with suspicion.

'Don't wanna be in Bath,' Darcy slurred, turning around. He looked awful.

'It's all right, dear,' she said. 'You'll be well cared for.'

'Don't like Bath. Full of odd people.'

'Now you know that's not true.'

They were getting curious glances from passers-by now.

'I'm so sorry,' she said to a lady in an expensive bonnet. 'My husband is ill.' The woman sniffed and crossed to the other side of the road.

'How much further do we have to go?' she asked Sutherland, leaning forward.

'I believe we're close now,' he replied. 'Look, there's the Jane Austen Emporium!'

'The what? Are you telling me that dreadful woman has her own souvenir shop now? It's bad enough that her residence here attracts all manner of unsavoury people to the city.'

'She's terribly popular, you know,' said Wickham. 'I—I—' He suddenly looked somewhat embarrassed.

'Mr Wickham, I do hope you're not going to admit to reading books about zombies!' Elizabeth was shocked. But there was never any accounting for the reading tastes of men.

Even her Fitzy had been known to read some of the

most appalling tripe, such as—what was the name of that book about the Italian painter? Or the ones by that woman from Jordan? Revolting stuff.

'Well—I—never mind, never mind,' said Wickham, attempting to bring the topic of conversation to a swift close.

'As if anyone could imagine such creatures as zombies being real!' Elizabeth was getting into her stride now. 'The undead walking the earth!'

'Zombies,' muttered Darcy.

'Indeed,' said Elizabeth, surprised to find her husband joining in the conversation.

'Good Lord, he's right!' said Wickham. 'Zombies! As if we don't have enough to contend with already!'

All five of them had stopped and were looking in the direction where Darcy was pointing.

In the road ahead of them, as far as the eye could see, were a vast array of rolling-eyed creatures that could only be described as zombies.

The creatures were lurching towards them with a sinister shambling gait. Wickham pushed his way past Darcy, and his two supporters, and unsheathed his sword.

Chapter Fourteen

What a thriller!—Mr Wickham's Obsession—Autograph Hunting—Status Update—Miss Austen's Secret

THERE WAS NO escape from the crowd of zombies converging upon them. Wickham stood poised, his sword raised, ready to slice the heads off anyone who got close to them. Elizabeth knew she had to act fast.

'Put your sword away, Wickham,' she commanded.

'I beg your pardon, Mrs Darcy?' said Wickham, wavering.

'Trust me. You won't be needing it with this lot.' She turned to the two lead zombies. 'And you are?'

The pair of them looked at each other, both apparently waiting for the other to do the talking. They were the most immaculately-dressed zombies she'd ever seen.

'Well, I'm Billy, Madam' said the one on the left, eventually.

'And I'm Jean,' said the other.

'A French name?' said Elizabeth. 'A bit risky, I would have thought.'

'It's only his stage name, Madam,' said Billy.

'I'm in character. I do the Method.' said Jean. 'When I'm a zombie, I am Jean. Very macho is a French zombie. The ladies love a French zombie, don't they, Madam?'

'Excuse me?' said H.

'What on earth—' began Sutherland.

'—is going on?' finished Wickham, finally sheathing his sword.

'Zombie parade,' said Elizabeth, with more than a hint of contempt. 'Every year, round about now, there's a big festival in Bath to celebrate that woman—the one who writes those dreadful books. And all these idiots come and dress up as zombies and parade around the place. There's even a zombie ball at the end, and some of them stay in costume all week. Awful.'

'The woman that Madam refers to—' said Billy.

'Miss Austen,' added Jean, 'Madam.'

'Miss Austen, yes, is our greatest living author.'

'Of zombie stories, maybe.' said Elizabeth.

'Our greatest living author, full stop. Madam.'

'*Rien ne vas plus,*' said Jean, in an unconvincing accent.

'Pah!' replied Elizabeth.

'In any case, I see at least one of you is a fan,' said Jean.

'Well—' said Wickham, uncertainly.

'Lovely to see you again, Sir, Mr Wickham, Sir.'

'What?' said Wickham, with a double-take. 'Do I know you?'

'Of course you do, sir,' said Billy.

'Sir was an excellent rough cottager, wasn't sir?' added Jean.

Wickham looked non-plussed for a moment, and then slowly turned a slight shade of red. 'Ah,' he said.

Sutherland looked at Wickham and narrowed his eyes. 'Do you know these two fellows?' he said. 'I didn't realise—not that there's anything wrong with that, obviously—'

'Surely you remember, sir? You sent me to this pair of clowns to be disguised.'

Sutherland frowned. 'Why would you want to be disguised?' he asked.

'I needed to become a rough cottager.'

Sutherland's eyes widened. 'That sounds remarkably unlikely, Wickham. Why would I ask you to do that?'

'Well, to be fair it was actually their suggestion.'

'Well, there you are. If you go around with people who dress as zombies, then all sorts of peculiar things can happen. Best not to, in my opinion.'

'No, sir. Billy and Jean here weren't dressed as zombies then.'

'And I certainly wouldn't have sent you to anyone with a French name!'

'They weren't called Billy and Jean then!'

'Or anyone who went around changing their name. Wouldn't know what was going on. Still,' said Sutherland, with a tolerant smile. 'Takes all sorts of chap to make a world.'

Wickham tried to say something else, but no words came out apart from a vague bluster.

'Sir had a wonderful beard, too,' said Billy. 'I bet the ladies loved that beard.'

'Suited you sir.' said Jean.

'Oh, just beat it,' said Wickham.

'Certainly sir,' said Billy. 'A pleasure, sir.'

The pair staggered off to join the rest of the parade.

There was an awkward silence.

'Told you I didn't like Bath,' said Darcy.

The party resumed its progress towards the Baths, but Wickham hesitated.

'Are you all right, Wickham?' asked Colonel Sutherland.

'Yes, yes, perfectly well, sir. It's just—just—look, I'll catch you up. Yes, that's it. I'll catch you up.'

Elizabeth narrowed her eyes. 'Where are you going, Mr Wickham? If it's somewhere interesting, I'm sure we could all spare the time.'

'No, no, no. It's nothing interesting,' said Wickham. 'You definitely won't be interested at all. In fact, you've already said you don't like—I mean—Blast! I didn't mean to say that!'

'It's about the Austen woman, isn't it, Wickham?'

'Well—'

'Damn it, man, what is this all about?' demanded Sutherland.

'Let me explain,' said Elizabeth. 'As we now know, Mr Wickham here is a—what is the modern parlance?—fanatic of the works of the well-known writer of cheap, tawdry zombie stories, Miss Jane Austen.'

'They're not that cheap, actually ' said Wickham. Elizabeth ignored him.

'It is patently obvious, since there is currently a festival in celebration of this dreadful woman, there is every likelihood that she herself is in town.'

'How did you—?'

'—and he is now wondering how to impose himself upon her. Am I right?'

Wickham was lost for words.

'I'll take that as a 'yes', then. Oh, Mr Wickham, I am so disappointed in you. You really are no better than that absurd pair we had the misfortune to encounter not five minutes ago.'

'I say, steady on,' said Sutherland, rushing to Wickham's defence. 'At least he's not an actor!'

''Tis true,' said Wickham.

'Oh, but he might as well be,' said Elizabeth. 'I bet

if you take a look in the inside pocket of his tunic—'
Wickham's hand, which had unconsciously strayed to that
very place, immediately shot out again '—you will find
a much-thumbed copy of 'Zombie First Impressions' or
some such rubbish.'

'It's 'Sensei and the Insensibles', actually,' said
Wickham, reluctantly withdrawing the novel in question
from his pocket. 'The one with the ninjas,' he added.

'For heaven's sake!' cried Elizabeth.

'It's really good, you know. There's this brilliant fight
scene where two ninjas take on an entire army of zombies,
armed with nothing but a single set of nunchucks between
them. They have to keep throwing the nunchucks at each
advancing zombie in turn, so they decapitate them, and
fly back again so that they can catch them.'

'And in what way is this remotely believable?'

'Well, strictly speaking—' said H.

'Oh, do keep out of this,' said Elizabeth. 'Begging your
pardon, Sir Humphry.' She turned back to Wickham,
who was hugging his book like a favourite. The man was
like some besotted girl!

'You want to her autograph, don't you?'

'Well, it would add to the value of the book.'

'Except you'd never sell it in a million years, would
you?'

'No.'

Elizabeth sighed. 'When she's in town, she stays in
rooms above the Jane Austen Emporium we just passed.
They give them to her rent-free.'

'Really?' said Wickham. 'I would have thought she
could afford far better accomodation!'

'She could afford to buy most of the street. But if
that woman senses any opportunity to take advantage of

someone else's good nature, believe me, she'll pounce on it.'

Wickham looked shocked. 'You surprise me, Mrs Darcy.'

'You have no idea, Mr Wickham.' She turned to the other three. 'You carry on with my husband to the Baths. I'll go with Mr Wickham. He might need protection.'

The Jane Austen Emporium was doing a roaring trade. Elizabeth looked at the wares on offer and gave a deep sigh. There was a big display devoted to the Great Author's works, of course, with particular prominence given to her latest offering, 'The North Abbey Hanging', which seemed to involve a brotherhood of zombie monks.

But there were also blood-spattered tea-cosies for sale, and little crocheted keepsakes in the shape of various internal organs.

The whole place was quite unseemly in Elizabeth's opinion, although Wickham was entranced. He had already picked out a neckerchief bearing the slogan 'Hack away here if you want to survive' and was proceeding towards the counter, where a young lady wearing a gruesome mask was in charge.

'Excuse me,' she said, placing herself in front of Wickham, 'But I wonder if you could possibly tell me if Miss Austen is in residence?'

'I'm hafraid that it would be himpossible for me to give you that kind of information,' said the young lady behind the counter, her voice muffled by the mask.

Elizabeth narrowed her eyes. 'In other words, she is in residence. For if she were not, then you would have simply denied it.' She turned to Wickham. 'Come on, let's get this over and done with.'

Wickham paused, holding his purchase in one hand and trying to find his wallet with the other.

'Wickham, put that ridiculous neckerchief down and follow me.'

But the sales assistant had now interposed herself between them and the doorway. 'Hay'm sorry, but hay can't let you go up there,' she said.

'Ah. So she's upstairs then, is she?' said Elizabeth.

At that moment, there was an altercation above them, followed by heavy footsteps descending the staircase. The footsteps paused for a moment, and a male voice called out, 'You have three days, Miss Austen! Three days!' Then the footsteps resumed and eventually a tall, dark figure appeared in the hallway. Elizabeth and Wickham watched as the man strode past them and out through the front door, muttering angrily to himself.

'Hexcuse me,' said the sales assistant, tearing off her mask and rushing after him. 'Don't move,' she warned as she left. 'Sir!' she called after the man, 'Sir, please sir! Please don't do this to Miss Austen, sir! Please!'

'What was that all about?' asked Wickham.

'It's an opportunity,' said Elizabeth. 'Come on, let's go.'

Making sure that no one was following them, they climbed the staircase. From somewhere on the second floor, they heard the sound of a woman weeping. Elizabeth motioned to Wickham to stop. Then they heard a male voice.

'You heard what he said.'

'Oh, leave me alone,' came another voice, this time female.

'According to the schedule, you have three days left.'

'No!'

There was silence for a moment, and then the woman

continued. 'He said I couldn't spell. If I can't spell, why does he want me to keep writing this stuff for him?

'Calm yourself, Miss Austen.'

'Five minutes. Please.'

'Two.'

Elizabeth glanced at Wickham. 'I hate to tell you this,' she whispered, 'but—'

Wickham looked concerned. He started, 'You're going to say—'

'Hush,' said Elizabeth, shooting him a look. He stopped immediately. They both turned and peered upwards. A woman was watching them from the landing above with desperate, pleading eyes.

Wickham started to back away.

'Don't go,' said the woman. 'Please don't go. Don't leave me on my own. I don't like it on my own.' She edged down the stairs towards them, until she was two steps above them. 'Can I help you?' she asked.

'I—I—I've come for your autograph,' said Wickham, fishing in his pocket for the book.

The woman gave the saddest of smiles.

'I suppose you'd better come on up, then.'

'Wait!' hissed Elizabeth. But it was too late.

Lady Catherine de Bourgh hesitated before answering the call. This was going to be an awkward conversation. Oh well, she thought, here goes. She pressed a button on the communications device in front of her. The screen flickered and her opposite number appeared. He didn't look happy.

'Ek—ek—ek—ek—ek?' she said. (**Greetings k'Ek! Good to hear from you again! How is the Red Planet?'**)

'Ek—ek—ek—ek—ek.' came the response. **(Yeah, whatever. Still sodding red. No change there.)**

There was an awkward silence.

'Ek—ek—ekky?' she asked, eventually. **(How is k'Ekkk?)**

'Ek?' **(He has sustained considerable damage to his third and fourth inner tentacle and his perianal thrust bladder has been perforated in several places. What kind of a weapon was that maniac using?)**

'Ek—ek—ek—ek—ek—ekekekekekekek?' **(I know not. Some kind of gunpowder-powered device. But at least k'Ekkk still lives?)**

'Ek.' **(He lives, yes, but he'll never play the flugelhorn again. Still, I imagine you've caught the swine who did it.)**

'Ek—ek—ek—ek—ek—ek—ekekekekekekekek—ekkity—ek . . .' **(Ah . . .)**

'Ek.' **(I'll take that as a 'no', then.)**

'Ek—ek—ek—ek—ek.' **(Well, yes and no. Mainly no. Collins and I had them cornered in the Mission.)**

'Ek?' **(What were they doing there? Oh, never mind. I'm losing the will to live here. What happened?)**

'Ek—ek—ek—ek—ek—ekka—ekka—ek.' **(Well, I started off by disposing of Collins.)**

'Ek?' **(An interestingly surreal opening gambit. Were you perhaps intending to confuse them to death?)**

'Ek—ek—ek—ek—ek.' **(He had outlived his usefulness. There was a chance that he might turn against us.)**

'Ek.' **(Still seems a bit harsh.)**

'Ek—ekkity—ekk.' (**You didn't have to deal with him on a regular basis.**)

'Ek?' (**Fair enough. So what of the others?**)

'Ek—ek—ek—ek—ek.' (**Well, they had reinforcements.**)

'Ek?' (**I'm having a bad feeling about this. What reinforcements?**)

There was a pause.

'Ek. Ek. Ekekekekekekekekekekekekekekekekekekekek!' (**Poltergeists!**)

'Ek? EK?' (**You what?**)

'Ekekekekekekkekkekkekkkkkkkkkitty ek.' (**I said: poltergeists.**)

'Ek.' (**Bollocks!**)

'Ek—ekekek—ek.' (**No, really. Things started flying around the place. Ornaments. Teapots. All sorts of things.**)

'Ek?' (**And you're expecting me to believe this was the work of poltergeists?**)

'Ek—ek—ekekekekekek.' (**The afterlife seems to operate according to different rules down here. Some of them seem to hang around for a while. It's very annoying.**)

'Ek.' (**Er . . . right. So perhaps I can sum up what you're trying to tell me in four words: you let them escape.**)

'Ekekekekekekekekekekekekekekekekekekekekekekeke kekekekek.' (**Basically, yes.**)

'Ek?' (**So where are they now?**)

'Ekekekek—ek—ek—ek—ek.' (**Our agents have reported sightings in Wiltshire.**)

'Ek?' (**Swindon?**)

'Ek—ek—ek—ek—ek.' (**Possibly. As long as they don't go near Glastonbury.**)

'Ek?' **(Why not?)**

'Ek—ek—ek—ek—ek.' **(Don't get me started. Plays havoc with our equipment, that place. And it's full of weirdos.)**

'Ek.' **(Fair enough. So what's the plan?)**

'Ek—ek—ek—ek—ek.' **(All our agents in the West of England are on full alert. As soon as there is any sign of the Darcy woman, they will pick her up and bring her in. Anyone travelling with her will be terminated without prejudice.)**

'Ek.' **(Well, let's hope that your people have more success than you did ourself, k'Ekk. I'm sick of this place.)**

'Ek—ek—ek.' **(Here we go.)**

'Ek?' **(What?)**

'Ekekekekekekekekekekekekekekekekekekekekeke kek.' **(Nothing.)**

'Ek. Ekek.' **(It's all right for you. You don't have to stay on this bloody awful boring planet. You've got fields and birds and stuff. Dogs. Cows. Living things that move around and make interesting noises. We've got a load of red rocks.)**

'Ek—ek—ek—ek—ek.' **(I know. Must be terrible.)**

'Ekek.' **(And the food's rubbish.)**

'Ek—' **(Anyway—)**

It was time to bring this to an end. Lady Catherine pressed the button again and the screen went blank. She wrung her tentacles in frustration. This time there must be no mistakes.

As soon as Elizabeth and Wickham were inside Miss Austen's study, the door closed behind them and there was the sound of an unseen hand turning a key in the lock.

'Excuse me?' said Elizabeth, waiting for Wickham to back her up. But he was simply staring at Miss Austen with his mouth open. 'Wickham, we seem to be locked in,' she said to him. 'Once again we are trapped, only this time there do not appear to be any poltergeists at hand to save us.'

'Did you say poltergeists?' said Miss Austen, narrowing her eyes. 'What do you know about poltergeists? Are you familiar with the supernatural? Tell me about the supernatural! I want to know everything you know. Everything! This could be the answer! At last! I can be free! Poltergeists! Ghosts and ghouls! Spectres! Wraiths! Apparitions!' Her eyes were now ablaze with a wild fervour.

She leaned close to Elizabeth. 'I hate zombies. Really hate them. But all they ever let me write about is zombies. Old zombies, young zombies. Lady zombies, gentleman zombies. High society zombies, poor as muck zombies. French zombies even! Can you imagine that? And they never give me any money either. They just keep me locked in this horrible place.'

'Who's 'they'?' inquired Elizabeth.

'Sometimes I think to myself, wouldn't it be nice to go out to the Milliner's and buy myself a nice bonnet? You know, a really nice pretty bonnet? Like the nice pretty bonnet you're wearing.'

She reached out towards Elizabeth, who backed away. A small amount of spittle was dribbling from Miss Austen's mouth. This isn't right, thought Elizabeth.

'Please, Miss Austen. I beg you —' began Wickham, snapping out of his reverie and looking distinctly alarmed. Miss Austen began to sob.

'I really do hate zombies,' she said again, her shoulders heaving.

'I — I like the zombie books,' said Wickham. 'Especially 'Sensei —''

Wickham took out his copy of the book, ready for her to sign. At the sight of it, Miss Austen shrieked and collapsed into floods of tears again. Wickham looked nonplussed for a moment and then quickly put the book away.

'So let me get this straight,' said Elizabeth. 'You're kept locked in here to force you to write about things you don't like and you don't get to see any of the money you make? But they're the most popular books in the whole world!'

'I hate those books' said Miss Austen, sniffing. 'I want to write about something else.'

'Such as ghosts, perhaps?' said Elizabeth, remembering the earlier part of their conversation.

'No, ghosts would be a silly subject for a book. Everyone knows ghosts don't exist. I want to write nice books. Books where people fall in love.'

'You mean romances?' said Elizabeth, barely suppressing a smile.

'Yes! Maybe with vampires too! That would be brilliant, wouldn't it?'

Wickham looked aghast. 'Madam, I fear it would be the twilight of your career!'

'Perhaps you are right. So realistic romance it is.' She looked from Elizabeth to Wickham and from Wickham back to Elizabeth, eyes wide. 'Well, then. Has anything interesting ever happened to either of you? Anything romantic?'

Chapter Fifteen

Miss Austen Regrets — Gin and Tonic — The Road to Glastonbury — Street Theatre — Mary, Mary, Quite Contrary

ELIZABETH WAS BEGINNING to get extremely anxious about the time. It had taken over an hour for Wickham and her to tell their story.

'Miss Austen, I really do think—' she said.

'Hush!' Elizabeth ceased talking and held her breath. The only sound in the room was of Miss Austen's quill scratching away. Then that stopped, too. 'So, then,' said Miss Austen, 'Is that it?'

Elizabeth and Wickham both nodded.

'Good,' said Miss Austen. 'Good.' She sat for a moment in silence.

'Right then,' she said. 'First of all, I don't like all this alien nonsense. It's just silly.' She took her pen and began crossing out large swathes of the text.

'But!' began Wickham.

Miss Austen held up her hand. 'And I'm not sure I like your character either, Mr Dickham.'

'Wickham.'

'I think I might have to change the whole thing to make you look the villain. That would be fun!'

Wickham was completely at a loss for words and all he could do was gape back at her.

'I'm not sure I like the tiresome haughty one either. He's going to have to go.'

'But surely he's essential to the story?' said Elizabeth, wounded by this slant on her husband's character.

'No. He's dull and boring. If I'm going to write romances, I want them filled with nice people. Not boring old fuddy-duddies like this Arsy person.'

'Darcy.'

'But wait!' She paused. 'What if I used your story and added zombies to that?' She considered this for a moment, then shook her head. 'No, that's a really dreadful idea, isn't it? Oh, this is hopeless!'

There was an embarrassed silence. Elizabeth and Wickham glanced at each other.

'Well, if you don't require our services any more,' said Wickham eventually, 'it's probably time for us to be leaving, so if you would be so kind to ask someone to let us out?' He stood up and moved to the door. Elizabeth made to follow him.

'They won't let you, you know,' said Miss Austen.

'What do you mean?' she asked.

Miss Austen shrugged. 'They just won't. They're quite ruthless.'

'Well, that's as maybe,' said Wickham, turning so that his right shoulder was now facing the door. He leant forward and charged. The door came clean off its hinges and flew open.

'Ha!' said Wickham, turning to face Miss Austen. 'See?'

Elizabeth shook her head. 'Oh dear,' she said. 'This isn't so good.'

A man with a pistol pointing at them walked slowly into the room.

'If you think for a moment,' said the man, 'I am going to let you two take your material elsewhere you've got another thing coming.'

'Why does everyone insist on waving guns at us?' said Elizabeth. 'And who are you anyway?'

'You may think of me as her editor,' said the man. 'And I'm just about to edit you two out of the story.' He snickered unpleasantly at his own joke. No one else laughed.

'It's really not fair, you know,' said Wickham. 'I'm Miss Austen's biggest—'

'Shut up, you tedious man,' said the editor. 'I despise Miss Austen's fans. And because of that, I've just decided I'm going to shoot you first.'

Miss Austen's editor took aim. Just then, however, a teapot struck him on the side of the head and he crumpled to the floor.

'About bloody time too,' said Wickham.

By the time Elizabeth and Wickham made their way towards the Hotel Romero, it was getting dark. The inns along the way were packed with revellers and the gutters were already filling up with zombies.

'I won't be sad to leave this place,' said Elizabeth. 'I only hope my dear husband will be safe here.'

'He is in good hands,' said Wickham. 'H knows what he is doing, and the waters will be a tonic.'

'Wickham, have you actually tasted the stuff? There's a reason why they use so much gin here, you know.'

'A gin always helps a tonic, so I've heard.'

They swerved to one side to avoid a zombie who lurched towards them clutching his mouth, before emptying its contents over the road behind them.

'Evidently,' said Elizabeth, quickening her pace. 'Ah, here we are,' she said as they turned a corner and saw the hotel ahead of them.

It was with some relief when they entered the lobby and found the front desk. After a brief enquiry as to the location of Darcy and H's suite, during which it became clear that there was a significant misunderstanding as to the nature of the relationship between Darcy and H, they ascended the main staircase and knocked on the door.

The door was opened by Colonel Sutherland, who put his finger to his lips and ushered them in. 'Your husband is asleep,' he said.

'Is he well?' said Elizabeth, anxiously.

'He is perfectly well,' said H, emerging from the bedroom with an enema hose in his hands. Elizabeth stared at it with some curiosity.

'I thought it was more conventional to take the waters orally?' she said.

'Not when the patient has been probed,' said H.

'Ah. Of course.' Elizabeth flushed slightly, wishing she hadn't drawn attention to the appliance.

'Gather you had some trouble with Miss Austen,' said H.

'Yes, that's r—' began Wickham, before breaking off. 'Hang on—how do you know?'

H smiled a smile suggesting he was far too pleased with himself. 'Annie told me,' he said.

'Annie who?' said Wickham.

'Annie Chapman, of course,' said Sutherland. 'Do try to keep up, old boy. H here taught himself to talk to ghosts this afternoon. Doesn't even have to use his machine thingy any more. Dashed if I know how he does it.'

'Oh, it's a simple matter of bifurcating the mucous vectors of a polynomial determinant and—' said H.

'Yes, yes, yes,' said Sutherland. 'Jolly clever. Jolly clever. Anyway, good thing he did, because I rather get the feeling that you two were heading for an early exit.'

'I don't know what to say, Sir Humphry,' said Elizabeth. 'You appear to have saved our lives.'

'Did I?' said H, with a faraway look on his face. 'Well, then. I suppose I did. Although it was mostly Annie's work, of course.'

'Of course,' said Elizabeth, looking around the room.

'She's over there,' said H, nodding towards the fireplace.

'Ah,' said Elizabeth, turning round. 'Er—thank you, Miss Chapman,' she said, feeling more than a little self-conscious to be addressing her remarks to thin air. There was a short pause.

'She says it was no trouble,' said H eventually. 'And—what's that?—ah yes, she says best to stay clear of them writer types in future—nutters the lot of them, apparently.'

'I fear she may be right,' said Wickham, with some feeling.

'Anyway, 'tis time to retire,' said Sutherland. 'Come along, gentlemen! Plenty of space on the floor here. And after we break our fast tomorrow, we go to Glastonbury.'

'To Glastonbury!' said Wickham and Elizabeth in response.

As her rental horse trotted along the road to Glastonbury, Elizabeth felt torn between delight in leaving Bath and sadness at leaving her poor husband behind. He hardly said a word to her all night, apart from a vague muttering, very little of which made much sense apart from a long and detailed description of the Eton version of the offside rule. Elizabeth noted it was inaccurate in a number of significant respects.

'Horse all right, Mrs Darcy?' asked Sutherland, turning round.

'Perfectly fine,' she said.

'Jolly good. Glad I managed to get you a free upgrade to a leather saddle. Are you keeping an eye on those oats? Need to fill them up before we hand them back.'

Elizabeth nodded. Rental horses were a whole new world for her, and she had watched in fascination as Wickham and Sutherland examined each beast in turn, marking off various minor scars on a picture given to them by the agent. There was a discussion about whether or not to take out insurance against one of them going lame during the journey or somehow having an injury owing to a collision with another horse.

If the truth were to be told, however, the old nag she ended up with had seen better days. It could barely stagger into a rising trot, let alone a canter, but Elizabeth didn't mind. She was just glad that they weren't in that awful dirigible. In this respect, it was most definitely a good thing H was needed back in Bath to attend to Darcy.

Elizabeth turned around to see how Wickham was fairing. He was more than a little quiet this morning, and she surmised this might have something to do with suffering a restless night. He was reticent about the details, but it seemed he was bothered by one of the ghosts who was taking quite a fancy to him. Elizabeth refrained from enquiring further.

Every now and then, they would chance upon a group of travellers on foot. More often than not, these folk would be carrying musical instruments, and after a while, she asked one of them why this was.

'Why, we be musicians, ma'am,' said one, a sallow-faced young man carrying a mandolin, with his flaxen hair in curious ringlets.

'I can see that, sir, but where do you intend to play?'

'Why, ma'am, we be going to play in a muddy field just outside of Glasto. They be watering it special, 'cos of there being so little rain of late.'

'And why would you wish to play there? For surely you will have no audience in such an unpromising location?'

'Ah, begging your pardon, ma'am,' said his colleague, a lad with a wispy beard and a tin whistle. 'But the folks what come here love the mud. They come from all around, from genteel homes an' all.'

''Specially the genteel ones,' said the one with the ringlets. 'You should see some of the women in their smart frocks.'

'They roll around in the mud whilst we play tunes for them. And then after three days, they go home and get cleaned up.'

'Is that so?' said Elizabeth. ''Tis a strange world we live in, to be sure.'

The three of them trotted slowly on towards their destination, which appeared before them around mid morning. As they reached the outskirts of the town, they dismounted and conducted a brief conference.

'So what's the plan, sir?' said Wickham.

'Simple,' said Sutherland. 'We locate Mrs Collins, relay her husband's final words to her and convince her to translate their meaning to us.'

'There's only one small problem,' said Elizabeth. 'I have no idea where she is living. She gave no address.'

'Isn't she staying in some place full of peculiar arty types?' said Sutherland. 'Shouldn't be hard to track down.'

'Colonel Sutherland, this is Glastonbury. Around here, we are the peculiar ones.'

It was late morning in Glastonbury, and the streets were bustling with folk going about their daily business. Many of them wore the traditional local attire of a rough smock emblazoned with the seven-leaved plant that made up the town's insignia. The air was thick with traditional cries such as 'Finest Acapulco Gold!', 'Tastiest hash cakes in town!' and 'Get yer bongs 'ere!' The air was also thick with curious, exotic scents which made the three visitors feel quite giddy.

Elizabeth had oft pondered the meaning of these cries, ever since her parents had brought her and her sisters here many years ago on a day trip from Bath. Why, for example, was this the only town in the entire kingdom that seemed to trade in South American precious metals? She also remembered being disappointed that they wouldn't buy one of those nice cakes for her, as her stomach had been rumbling at the time. And what exactly was a bong—some type of horological device, perhaps? It was one of those things that she felt it best not to enquire on, but she was still curious.

'You there,' said Sutherland, pointing to a gentleman who was standing in a space apart from the crowd. 'Can you tell me where we can find Lord—what's the fellah's name?'

'Byron,' said Wickham.

'—Lord Byron?' finished Sutherland.

By way of reply, the gentleman cocked his head on one side in an exaggerated manner, grabbed hold of his earlobe with his index finger and thumb, and pulled his face into an unnatural rictus with both eyebrows raised.

He held this pose for a few seconds, then raised one triumphant finger into the air, gave a broad smile and shook himself upright. He then leant forward, shielding his face with one hand on his forehead and then swung his whole body from side to side as if scanning the horizon.

Elizabeth sighed. 'I think this may take some time,' she said, indicating the three of them should move along. 'In future, it may prove to be more helpful to choose someone other than a mime to ask for directions.'

'A mime?' asked Sutherland, perplexed.

''Tis a type of theatrical performer who communicates through gestures, sir,' explained Wickham.

'Ah! Like charades!' said Sutherland, brightening. 'I do enjoy a game of charades. Jolly good fun. Perhaps we can join in?' He made as if to go back, but Wickham restrained him.

'Perhaps some other time, sir.' 'Twould perhaps be better to ask someone who can actually talk to us, I think.'

'What about those chaps over there, then?' said Sutherland, heading over to a group of men wearing elaborate costumes. One of them was holding a bladder on a stick.

'Er, maybe not,' began Elizabeth, but it was too late. Sutherland was already in discussions with one who seemed to be the leader of the troupe.

'You sir!' he was saying. 'Can you tell me where I can find Lord Byron?'

The man struck a pose, with his hand on his chin. His companions did likewise.

'He's not another mime, is he?' whispered Wickham to Elizabeth.

'No. Far worse than that. Street theatre.'

'Dear me. I had no idea.'

The lead actor had now come out of his pose, and was looking very pleased with himself.

'Why, sir,' he said to Sutherland. ''Tis obvious where

you can find Lord Byron! You must go to the market-place!'

'To the marketplace!' echoed his companions.

Sutherland looked uneasy. 'Why's that? Surely—'

'Because in the marketplace,' he said with an air of increasing triumph, 'You will find many a *buyer on* the cobbles therein!'

'I'm sorry?'

'*Buyer on*,' said the actor, nodding at Sutherland. '*Byron*.'

'I still don't see it.'

'It's a sort of pun,' said the actor, looking crestfallen. 'You see? 'Buyer on' instead of 'Byron'. Thought 'twas quite diverting myself. It isn't easy, this improv business, you know.' His colleagues nodded in agreement. He took off his hat and held it out with a hopeful grin on his face.

'Philistines!' he shouted, as the three of them walked away, ignoring his pleas for money.

'What about her?' said Wickham, pointing to a young bespectacled woman holding a banner that said 'Stop Rotten Boroughs Now!' She was handing out leaflets and had quite a crowd surrounding her.

'What do we want?' she was shouting.

'A Great Reform Act!' came the response.

'When do we want it?'

'1832!'

Colonel Sutherland grimaced. 'Looks like another damned actor,' he said.

'No, wait,' said Elizabeth, her heart pounding. 'I know that voice.' She approached the woman and looked her full in the face.

'Mary?'

The two sisters stared at each other and then embraced.

There was a loud cheer from the crowd of onlookers, interspersed with unnecessarily ribald remarks from some of the men who misunderstood the significance of the embrace.

'What are you doing here?' asked Mary.

'I might ask you the same question,' said Elizabeth.

'In my case, 'tis simple. I moved here to escape the ennui of our *bourgeois* existence.' Twas only a matter of time before I became subservient to the yoke of marital oppression.' She looked at Wickham, who was now standing next to Elizabeth, and raised an eyebrow. 'Speaking of which, I see—'

'Mr Darcy is unwell,' said Elizabeth, a little too hurriedly. There was an awkward pause. 'I mean—what I mean is—Mr Darcy is not with me because he is unwell.'

'I understand,' said Mary with a knowing look. 'Do not be concerned. You will find the people of Glastonbury more sympathetic than the sexually regressive reactionaries that rule the rest of our benighted land!' As she spoke, she raised her voice in a dramatic crescendo, punching the air at the climax of her speech. There was another cheer from her audience, with several cries of 'Tell it like it is, sister!'

Elizabeth was more than a little startled by this. Mary had certainly changed since the last time she had seen her. No wonder Mother was worried. However, time was pressing.

'Mary, I understand little of your struggle. I am, however, pleased you seem to have found something worthwhile and fulfilling with which to occupy your time. But sadly my two companions and I are in need of urgent help. We seek Lord Byron.'

'In Glastonbury, we do not recognise the legitimacy of the aristocracy. I know no one of that name.'

'But surely?'

'And besides, I am not sure I trust your two so-called companions. They appear to be dressed in the uniforms of the global military-industrial complex.'

'Well, they are soldiers. But they're on our side, you know.'

'In which case, I would prefer it if you were to explain to me exactly why you need to locate Mr Byron.'

'Ah, so you do—'

'Maybe I do, maybe I don't.' Mary folded her arms and stared at Elizabeth. This was getting them nowhere.

'Mother is worried about you, you know.'

'Please don't change the subject. It won't help. Just because you're older than me and prettier and cleverer, it doesn't mean you can boss me about.' She turned to the crowd. 'Oh, go away, you lot,' she said with a sigh. 'This is family stuff.' The crowd dispersed, grumbling.

'I'm sorry if that's the way feel.' said Elizabeth.

'Oh, don't. Everything was fine until you turned up. You've always made a mess of things.'

'Mary Bennet, that isn't true,' said Elizabeth, feeling a rising tide of anger welling up inside her.

'Please don't call me that,' said Mary. 'I've changed my name. It's part of my ongoing process of self-reinvention.'

'So what do you call yourself now?'

There was an embarrassed silence.

'Mary Repeal-the-Corn-Laws.'.

'Ah,' said Elizabeth. 'I see.'

'It's a sort of—oh, look, do you want to come in for a cup of tea?' asked Mary with a sad smile. 'It's free trade, you know.'

'Of course we would. Provided that you promise to tell us where Lord—sorry, Mr—Byron can be found.'

'Of course. And you can meet my husband, too.'

'Husband?'

'Well, more my sort of partner really. I would have invited you to the ceremony, but I wasn't sure if you would have felt comfortable around pagans.'

Elizabeth nodded. In this at least, Mary was almost certainly correct.

Chapter Sixteen

H's Preparation — Colonel Sutherland's Embarrassment — When Mary Met Robert — Wiggle Waggle — Agent Lydia

FITZWILLIAM DARCY LAY naked on his stomach in the hotel bedroom, waiting for Sir Humphry Davy's next round of treatment. There was a rustling of curtains and he was convinced for a moment that he heard a spectral voice say 'Nice bum!' followed by an odd tinkling like the sound of far-off girly laughter. Oh, for heaven's sake . . .

'H?' he shouted, 'Are those damned ghosts in here again? It's not right, you know.'

'What?' said H, coming into the room carrying a steaming test tube.

'Look, can you do something? I don't like being regarding as some kind of object. It's unmanly.'

'Ah, I see what you mean,' said H, looking up. 'Do you mind?' he said, addressing the fireplace. 'I really would prefer it if you could leave us alone. Your presence is more than a little off-putting to my subject . . . Yes, but as I've explained before . . . No, please listen, it wasn't him. It was an alien pretending to be him . . . Well, that's what I'm trying to find out . . . No, you can't watch . . . Well, if you're bored, why don't you go and haunt the Baths or something? . . . Good, good.' He paused for a moment. 'Right,' he said to Darcy, 'They're going to leave us alone now. They've decided to go and throw a few cakes around in the Pump Room.'

'I know how they feel,' said Darcy, 'I'm bored, too. Is this going to take much longer?'

'Almost ready for the next procedure. Just stay there for a little longer, old chap.'

Darcy yawned. 'Is there anything to read around here?'

'Nothing unless you count the message that arrived this morning by optical telegraph.'

'Oh, that one.' He picked it up. It was very odd.

SORRY OLD MAN STOP GOT BIT OF PROBLEM STOP LOST ALL OUR MONEY STOP NEED SUB OF FEW QUID SO DONT LOSE NETHERFIELD TOO STOP PLEASE DONT TELL JANE OR LIZZY STOP MADE TOTAL CODS OF THINGS STOP AM BIT OF CHUMP STOP CHARLIE BINGS

Darcy shook his head. No, it still didn't make sense. Maybe when he was feeling a bit better he could have another go at reading it. He cast the paper aside and started humming to himself.

A few minutes later, H returned to the room. Darcy could sense him bending over him, inspecting his body.

'Looks a bit sore, that,' said H.

'You do surprise me,' said Darcy. 'I was about to ask 'Who goes there? Friend or enema?' but I fear I already know the answer.'

'Now, now. We have to make you well again. Anyway, I've made up some cream to sooth you. It's a special formula of mine and I'm going to call it "Prepara-tion—"'

'H, that's all very well, but have you found out what's wrong with me yet?'

'All in good time. The only thing I can say now is those probes must have been used to extract your vital fluids so they could use it to construct some kind of simulacrum.'

'Vital fluids?'

'Well, there's some funny stuff in the body that one of my students is working on. Funny chap, always has a crick in his neck, frankly hasn't a clue what's on most of the time. All he ever says to me is that it's Definitely Not Alcohol. So that's what we call it in the lab, D N—'

'I'm bored now,' said Darcy. 'Just bung it in and let's get on with it.'

He sighed, wondering how his wife was getting on in Glastonbury. He hoped she was making more progress than he was. Right now, he wasn't sure whether he was coming or going.

Mary Repeal-the-Corn-Laws, née Bennet, lived in a small, ramshackle cottage a short walk away from the main square. The floor of the front parlour and most of the furniture were cluttered with revolutionary tracts and sheet music. Mary fussed around, picking them all up and piling them precariously on top of the battered old pianoforte pushed up against one of the walls.

'You still play, then?' said Elizabeth, nodding towards the instrument.

'I most certainly do,' said Mary, with enthusiasm. 'In fact, our love of music is one of the things that brought Robert and myself together.'

At this point, a dark-skinned man entered the room and bowed to the occupants.

'Ah, there you are—' began Mary, but she was interrupted by Colonel Sutherland.

'Splendid! I wasn't aware that you had one of these,' he said. 'Didn't look the sort who could afford one, if you don't mind me saying so.' He turned towards the figure in the doorway. 'Make mine nice and strong, with plenty sugar. Quick quick!' This was accompanied by a peremptory sequence of claps.

The newcomer looked at him with a bemused expression, and Elizabeth was aware the temperature in the room seemed to be dropping unseasonably quickly.

Before Sutherland could say another word, Mary spoke up, her voice filled with emotion.

'May I introduce you to my husband? Robert Somersett.'

Elizabeth and Wickham offered their hands to him in turn, as did Colonel Sutherland, although the latter was unable to meet his eye.

'Oh, Robert,' said Mary, breaking out into sobs. 'Will it always be like this?'

'No, my beloved," said Robert, putting his arm around her shoulders. 'Times will change. As I believe Monsieur Robespierre once said, 'Les hommes naissent et demeurent libres et égaux en droits.''

There was an awkward silence.

'You are no doubt familiar with the *Déclaration des Droits*?' continued Robert, 'Although I must confess I find some of the phraseology a little — shall we say — unsophisticated, and the total lack of any explicit mention of slavery is — to my mind at least — a most unfortunate lacuna. I take it you are also aware of the work of Monsieur Brissot?'

Elizabeth glanced at Wickham, who avoided her eyes and stared intently at a point on the floor.

Sutherland, got up from his chair. 'I think I need some fresh air.'

Once Colonel Sutherland left the room, the tension eased a little.

'Don't be too hard on him,' said Elizabeth.

'I know,' said Mary. 'We may have to wait a long time for attitudes to change.'

'Наше время именно потому великое время,' said Robert 'что оно впервые закладывает основы всемирной истории. На наших глазах оно превращает понятие человечества из гуманитарной фикции в историческую реальность.'

'Exactly,' said Mary.

There was a very long silence.

'So—how did you two—come to—meet?' asked Elizabeth.

She felt as if she were clinging on to a runaway stallion. This was all so far outside her realm of understanding of social norms and conventions, and yet—her sister seemed happy.

Perhaps this was the way things might be between men and women in the future. Maybe one day, too, there would be universal suffrage for both men and women, mankind would travel to the moon and communicate with each other instantly wherever they were on the planet.

And wherever you looked, there would be pictures of cats.

'I had a big argument with Father about the fundamental principles of collectivism,' Mary was saying. 'Mother took his side for once—I don't think she ever liked me much, to be honest—and so I stormed out to seek my fortune in the world.

'As it happened, the Meryton Workers' Revolutionary

Party was organising a coach party to Bristol to protest against the slave trade, so I tagged along.'

'You 'tagged along'?' said Elizabeth. 'Surely a young lady on her own?'

'The MWRP does not hold such chauvinistic attitudes, sister. Am I not just as capable of holding a gun as any man?'

'I don't know,' said Elizabeth, struggling to follow the sudden switch in direction. 'Are you?'

'And is it not written,' said Mary, ignoring her, 'that . . . that . . . oh, what was the phrase?'

'枪杆子里面出政权?' interjected Robert.

'Yes, that was it,'' continued Mary, "Political power grows out of the barrel of a gun.'

Elizabeth was feeling more than a little lost. She did wish that Mary would stick to the point.

'So, Bristol, then?' she said.

'Yes, well, our group arrived earlier than the rest, so we decided to go out for a boat ride around the harbour. But a freak storm blew up whilst we were out, and we capsized. We became trapped underneath the hull of our vessel with very little air, and it seemed certain that we should drown. But then, a saviour appeared, like Poseidon, from the very depths of the ocean.'

'ἀμφὶ Ποσειδάωτα,' said Robert, with a faraway look in his eye, 'μέγαν θεόν, ἄρχομ' ἀείδειν,

γαίης κινητῆρα καὶ ἀτρυγέτοιο θαλάσσης,

πόντιον, ὅσθ' Ἑλικῶνα καὶ εὐρείας ἔχει Αἰγάς.

διχθά τοι—'

Mary coughed loudly, and Robert ceased his oration.

'I do apologise for indulging myself,' he said. 'But Homer's use of language is so . . . so muscular, don't you think? I find him quite irresistible.'

'But wait a moment,' said Elizabeth, 'Are you saying

that he saved your life, Mary?' She was looking at Robert in an entirely new light now. 'But—what—?'

'He was escaping from a slave ship,' said Mary. 'Obviously, I changed my plans then and there. I decided to devote my life to him. Then I heard him sing, and I fell in love.'

'Great heavens,' said Elizabeth, suddenly realising that Mary's life was a whole lot more exciting and romantic than her own, with or without the aliens.

Up until now, Wickham had been completely silent. But now he looked hard at Robert Somersett and spoke in a solemn voice.

'Sir, I salute you,' he said. 'You are an inspiration to us all.'

Robert looked back at him and fixed him with a steely eye.

'Hasta la victoria siempre!' he said.

Elizabeth and Wickham stood up, just as Colonel Sutherland came back into the room. He glanced around.

'Are we off then?' he said.

'Yes!' said Elizabeth. Then she paused. 'Mary, you never did tell us where we could find Byron and Charlotte.'

'Oh, them,' said Mary. 'Two doors down. You can't miss it. It's the one with the terrible mural of the dolphins outside.'

The girl in the dungeon stirred. She sat up and looked at the walls. They were covered in marks—at first sets of seven, crossed through, and then sets of six, four, ten and two and a half. She wasn't even sure what they meant now. She waggled her toes. That felt nice. She tried counting the toes, but they wouldn't stay still. Bad toes. Silly toes.

This is a big house, she thought. I like being in a big house, although it would be nicer if I could explore a bit more of it. I like exploring, she thought. Once upon a time I lived in a much smaller house and there were lots of other people there too. As far as she could remember, they were all a bit annoying though. Perhaps she was annoying too? She seemed to remember that it was quite fun to be annoying.

There used to be a nice man who lived in the room next door, but he went away without saying goodbye. He had a bit of a pompous voice and he seemed sort of familiar, but he must have been a bit of a silly man because he'd lost his name. How could anyone lose their own name, she thought? It's not as if I've lost mine, have I?

It was on the tip of her tongue.

It was definitely on the tip of her tongue.

I'm sure I knew my name yesterday, she thought. I really did know it once, anyway. Oh dear, how bothersome. It might have been a nice name, too. Something like Cholmondeley or Parmesan.

Hello toes. Wiggle waggle. Wiggle waggle.

Still at least the people here had stopped sticking nasty probe things in her. That was good. The funny old lady with the tentacles said they didn't need to do it any more. She also said something about her being expendable now, which was a long word that she didn't really understand. It probably meant that she could go soon. That would be nice.

The lady with the tentacles smelt funny. She didn't like her much. Now that she thought about it, she didn't know any other old ladies who had tentacles, apart from Miss Chancellor who used to run the village school. But maybe those were just whiskers. It was all so long ago and far away. So in fact she probably didn't have any other ladies with tentacles to compare her with.

Actually, Miss Chancellor smelt funny too. But a different type of funny.

I'm glad I'm expendable, she thought. I don't want to stay in this place any longer. But I hope I can explore it a bit before they let me go. I bet there are loads and loads of rooms and paintings and stuff. I like paintings, she thought, drawing a circle in the dust beside her on the floor. She added a smiley face, a stick body, two arms and two legs.

There was a man once: a nice man who looked after her. He didn't have a name, but she used to think of him as the wicket man. He kept watch over her and caught her when she was bowled over. But one day they came for her before she could say bye and she was taken away, beyond their boundaries.

Whatever happened to wicket man? Why hadn't he come to find her? Why was she all on her own? She sighed and slumped back against the wall.

Hello toes, she thought. Wiggle waggle. Wiggle waggle.

When Mary said that Lord Byron was living two doors down, she actually meant the next house but one, a mile down a long, winding country lane. But it was a warm, sunny afternoon and Elizabeth, Wickham and Colonel Sutherland set off with a firm stride.

After a while, however, Wickham turned to Elizabeth.

'You seem pensive, Mrs Darcy,' he said. 'Is there aught that ails you?'

'No, sir,' said Elizabeth. ''Tis just my sister's parting words to me.'

Wickham looked curious. 'Watch out for the horse dung in the road?'

Elizabeth shook her head. 'No, 'twas not that, sage advice though that indeed was.'Twas what she said about poor Lydia. She said 'Do you think we will ever see her again?''

Wickham shook his head. 'Of course we will!' he said. 'I have no doubt of it.'

'Oh, 'tis easy for you to say that, Mr Wickham.'

'No, madam, 'tis not. Please remember that I was—still am—married to her.'

'But I thought you said it was purely to protect her.'

'I did. It was. And yet I cannot deny that—'

'Careful, Wickham,' said Sutherland. 'Remember you are a professional soldier and we are fighting a war here.' He turned to Elizabeth. 'Begging your pardon, Mrs Darcy.'

'I understand,' said Elizabeth. 'And yet, there is still so much that I do not.' She paused. 'I do not wish you to break any confidences that may threaten the safety of our beloved country, but can you tell me any more about how my sister came to be embroiled in this chain of events?'

The three stopped in the middle of the road. Wickham looked at Sutherland. Sutherland gave the slightest of nods.

'Miss Bennet came to me when I was stationed in Meryton,' said Wickham. 'She told me that she had been approached by a tentacled stranger who had asked her certain information about the young ladies of the town.'

'What kind of information?' asked Elizabeth.

'I'm afraid I am not at liberty to reveal that. However, I felt this approach was of such significance we were mandated to respond. Colonel Sutherland and I devised a plan whereby she would feed this person misleading information, whilst at the same time gathering as much intelligence as she could about the nature of their organisation.'

'You turned Lydia into an agent of the Department?' said Elizabeth, scarcely able to believe her ears.

'Yes, we did. We did.' Wickham paused. ''Tis a decision I have come to regret bitterly.'

'So—what happened?'

'She was suspected almost immediately. To be honest, she wasn't a particularly good agent.'

'Bloody useless,' muttered Sutherland, before a look from Wickham silenced him.

'So I had to take her under my protection.' said Wickham.

' Under the guise of eloping with her?'

'Yes. And you know the rest.' They started to walk again in silence. Elizabeth did indeed know the rest; how Wickham had been away on Department business one night and returned home to find her gone, with a trail of slime all over their front doorstep, how he had followed the trail and how the trail had vanished in a pit wherein strange markings were left in the scorched earth.

'Do you think this is it?' asked Sutherland, as they rounded the next corner. Ahead of them lay a large house with a remarkably un-lifelike representation of a pair of cavorting dolphins painted on the front.

'Wickham?' said Elizabeth, touching him on the arm. 'Did you love her?'

'Love?' said Wickham. 'I—well—she was a bit—you know—annoying.'

Elizabeth breathed out. 'Thank heavens for that,' she said. 'I can't stand her, you know. She's horrible. Petulant, childish and downright irritating.' She paused, and then gave a deep sigh. 'But she is my sister. So I suppose we'd better do something about finding her.'

Just then, a naked man covered in blue body paint rushed out of the house, bent over and vomited over Colonel Sutherland's boots.

'And in answer to your question, Colonel, I rather think the answer is yes.'

Chapter Seventeen

Sorted for Ease — Miss Deborah Does
Dahlias — Fluff! — Resistance is Still
Useless — Lord Byron's Stupendous Balls

COLONEL SUTHERLAND STARED at the naked man, then at his boots, and then at the naked man again. Then he sighed and walked towards the house, shaking his feet as he did so.

Elizabeth and Wickham followed at a respectful distance.

As they approached, they could hear sounds of strange, unearthly music issuing from open windows and exotic scents wafted towards them on the summer breeze.

'Had you met Lord Byron before —?' said Elizabeth.

'Rosings?' said Wickham. 'No, 'twas the first time.'

'Perhaps I should warn you then,' said Elizabeth. 'He is not like —'

She was interrupted by the sound of Colonel Sutherland, who had reached the front door and was now alternately ringing the bell and hammering on the front door.

'Hello?' he bellowed. 'Is there anybody there?'

Nothing happened.

He knocked again and all three of them waited.

Still nothing happened.

Wickham stepped forward and pushed gently at

the door. It swung open. He turned to the other two, shrugged and walked in. The hallway was empty.

As they pondered their next move, the door to their right flew open and a young woman wearing nothing but a dishevelled nightgown rushed out screaming, pushing past them.

'Excuse me?' said Elizabeth.

But the woman paid no heed to her and vanished up the stairs. The two men exchanged meaningful glances.

'We'll just take a look in here, I think.' said Wickham.

'Yes, good idea,' said Sutherland.

'In which case, I'll come too,' said Elizabeth.

'That may not be a good idea,' said Wickham.

'And what makes you say that?' she asked.

'It may not be appropriate for a lady of your considerable breeding,' said Sutherland.

Elizabeth pondered this remark, which still made no sense after several seconds thought, and then made her way towards the door. 'I really can't see what there might be to—Great heavens!'

The room was filled with smoke and it was only with extreme difficulty that she was able to make out what was taking place therein. But what she could see was like a vision from hell. Never had she encountered such depravity—not even in Meryton high street on a Friday night at the height of summer.

'Gadzooks!' said Sutherland, staring at the couple writhing on the ground before them. 'Is she? And is he?'

'I fear they are,' replied Wickham.

'But isn't that uncomfortable?' said Sutherland, turning his head on its side to gain a better view.

'I am sure it must be.'

Elizabeth shook her head and pressed on into the room

in search of someone who was in a fit state to be interrogated as to the whereabouts of Lord Byron and Charlotte.

Everywhere she trod, she had to be careful to avoid treading on some vital part of someone's anatomy. A small, long-haired child of indeterminate sex was swinging on the rafters above her, shadowing her every move.

In the far corner of the room, there was a man on his own playing a mandolin and humming a tune to himself. Elizabeth went up to him and shouted above the din.

'Sir?'

The man ignored her and continued humming. She clapped her hands in front of his face.

'Sir, I seek Lord Byron and Mrs Charlotte Collins!'

There was still no reply; the man was clearly in a world of his own. Then she heard a familiar voice behind her.

'May I help you, Mrs Darcy?'

She turned to face the newcomer.

'Lord Byron,' she said, her heart fluttering unaccountably. 'How pleasant to meet you again.'

'The pleasure is all mine,' said Byron, stooping to kiss her hand. Then he looked up at the ceiling. 'Greystoke, get down at once!' he said, admonishing the young boy. The boy leapt down, grinning and ran off. 'Nothing but ill will come of that family, mark my words,' said Byron.

'I have come to speak to Mrs Collins.'

'Ah! The good Charlotte, I will locate her for you. In the meantime —' he waved his hands expansively '—please take your ease. As you can see, Mrs Darcy,' he leered, 'We are completely sorted for ease.'

Fortunately Elizabeth did not have to wait too long before a servant arrived to escort her out of the room into the garden. Here she found Charlotte hard at work with some secateurs.

'Charlotte, dearest!' she said, rushing to greet her friend. 'How lovely to see you once more!'

'It is indeed,' said Charlotte, returning her embrace. 'But what brings you to Glastonbury?'

Elizabeth hesitated. She was not sure how Charlotte would react to the news she had to impart, and felt it might be best to wait until her friend no longer had any sharp implements in her hands.

'I was just passing through,' she said, playing for time. 'Visiting my sister Mary. That kind of thing.' There was an awkward pause. 'So, then, how have you kept yourself occupied during your sojourn in Lord Byron's care?'

'Well, 'tis interesting that you should ask me that question, because I am feeling much better since I have been here. Lord Byron's personal physician is looking after me.'

Elizabeth raised an eyebrow. 'Is he trustworthy? What are his methods?'

'He has a particular treatment he calls method one. When I go to his method one clinic, I no longer have need of my little bottle.'

'But that is wonderful!'

'Not only that, but it seems that I am to become a thespian.'

Elizabeth's eyes widened imperceptibly.

''Tis true. Lord Byron has written a play he intends to have performed on stage here in Glastonbury.'

'How fascinating! And what is the name of this drama?'

''Tis called 'Miss Deborah Does Dahlias.''

'Indeed? Then 'tis a horticultural work?'

'I believe so.'

'Do you have an elegant costume to wear?' said Elizabeth.

'I have petitioned Lord Byron on this very subject,' said Charlotte. 'But he is evasive. All he does is ask me to make sure that my bush is well-trimmed.' Here, she indicated the bay-tree that she had been pruning.

''Tis indeed a very well-trimmed bush,' said Elizabeth.

'I have trimmed it in the Brazilian style.'

'I see that you have.'

'Lord Byron has promised to impart much advice to me on the subject of horticulture. I had no idea he was such an expert.'

'He is indeed a man of many parts, many of which have yet to reveal themselves.'

''Tis so. Only today he was offering to tell me about how to achieve a satisfactory daisy chain.'

'What a remarkable man he is.' Elizabeth paused, taking advantage of their physical closeness to remove the secateurs from the other's hand. 'Charlotte,' she said, 'I have news for you. News of your husband.'

Charlotte's hand shot to her mouth. 'Oh my word! Has something happened to him? Is he unwell? What am I thinking? I must go to him at once!'

'No, my dear,' said Elizabeth, holding up her hand to stay her friend. ''Tis too late. Your husband has gone to a better place.'

'I beg your pardon?'

'Lady Catherine used some kind of alien weapon on him and he vanished. Poof! Just like that.'

'Great heavens! So—I—I am sure I know not what to think, Lizzy. He was—he was—he was a good—was he a good man, Lizzy?'

'I rather think not.'

'No, I feel I must agree with you there. And yet—'

'Charlotte, my dear, these are strange times that we live in. But with your dramatic career and your method one, your life is surely taking a turn for the better at last!'

Charlotte smiled—the first smile that Elizabeth had

seen from her for many a year—and embraced her again, saying, 'I know, Lizzy! I know it to be true!'

Elizabeth remembered she had something important to ask Charlotte.

'Charlotte, my dear,' she said, 'When Mr Collins—'

But she was interrupted by a hearty bellow, which caused both the women to look back towards the house whence Wickham and Sutherland were emerging.

'There you are!' said Sutherland.

'Indeed, sir, here we are,' said Elizabeth. She stared down at their feet. 'You seem to have mislaid your boots, Mr Wickham.'

Wickham turned a bright shade of red before dashing back into the room and returning with his footwear. 'I—excuse me,' he stuttered. 'I—removed—my boots in there in order to avoid—to avoid—'

'Leaving a stain on the carpet perhaps?' said Elizabeth.

'Y-es, that was it, wasn't it, sir?'

'What?' said Colonel Sutherland, distractedly.

'The stain on the carpet.'

'What stain? It wasn't me, you know.'

Elizabeth detected a slightly dubious undertone to their present intercourse, although she did not fully comprehend its meaning. However, she felt it prudent to bring the line of conversation to a halt, so she put her hand on Charlotte's arm and nudged her forward.

'Charlotte? May I introduce you to Colonel Sutherland, who is in charge of our defences against the alien hordes—and of course you have already met Mr Wickham.' Charlotte curtseyed to each in turn, and each of the men bowed low to her. There was a slight pause, and then Charlotte spoke up.

'I trust you find Lord Byron's retreat to your satisfaction?' she said.

Wickham and Sutherland exchanged a glance. 'Most satisfactory,' said Wickham.

'Very satisfactory indeed,' said Sutherland. 'We were having the most fascinating conversation in there with a young lady who helps behind the scenes with Lord Byron's theatrical productions.'

'Oh, how interesting!' said Elizabeth. 'Charlotte was only just telling me that she was hoping to take part in one of these.'

Wickham gave her a curious look.

'Now what was it she said she did?' Sutherland was saying. Wickham looked anxious at this.

'I fear I cannot remember, sir.'

'Ah, that was it! 'Twas all to do with the costumes, was it not?'

'I really cannot——'

'Fluff! That was it. Fluff! It was all to do with fluff. Presumably getting the fluff off the costumes, that sort of thing. Now what was it she called herself?'

'Sir, I think perhaps——'

'Fluffer! That was it. Fluffer! Dashed strange way to make a living, if you ask me, but there you are. If there's fluff, I suppose someone's got to deal with it.'

There was silence for a moment. Wickham was slowly shaking his head from side to side. But before conversation could recommence, they were joined by Lord Byron.

'Ah, Mr Wickham!' he said. 'We meet once more.'Twas good sport, that night at Rosings, was it not?'

'I rather think——'

'I trust you will all be staying here tonight?' continued Byron. 'I am told that we have *Coq au Vin* tonight, and there is more than enough *Coq* for everyone.' Elizabeth found the look that he gave her at this point more than a trifle alarming. 'There will of course be plenty of stuffing to go round as well,' he added, looking at the two men.

'That would be a capital idea!' said Sutherland.

'Um—excuse me?' said Elizabeth. 'But what about my husband?'

Lord Byron looked around. 'Well, I'm sure there will be plenty of *Coq* for him too, if he so desires.'

'No, you misunderstand me. He is not in need of *Coq*. He is ailing.'

'You never told me,' said Charlotte, looking concerned. 'How so?'

'Well, as I understand it,' said Elizabeth, 'He was an alien for a while and then there were two of him, an alien one and a normal one, but now the alien one's gone away so there's just him now, but he's not normal any more. And he's in Bath.'

'Bath? How awful!' said Byron. 'Well, my dear, you most certainly won't want to be going back there tonight.' And before she could protest, Byron took her arm and led her into the dining room, followed by the other three.

Fitzwilliam Darcy woke up to the sound of voices next door. He had fallen asleep after the afternoon's treatment session and was somewhat disoriented to discover the room was now dark. The voices were agitated and one of them was unfamiliar to him. The other voice belonged to Sir Humphry Davy.

'I have no idea what you're talking about,' he was saying.

'Don't lie to me, human,' said the other. 'Resistance is useless. You will soon crack-k-k-k-k!' The voice was harsh and guttural with an undertone of dark threat.

'Your threats mean nothing to me!'

There was a loud crash of china, which sounded curiously like the sound of a teapot being dropped from a great height.

'And you can call off your ghostly friends,' came the alien voice. 'They cannot help you now.'

Great heavens! H was in danger! Darcy rushed to the door of the bedchamber but then heard the alien speak again.

'So one more time, wretched earthling. Where is Mrs Darcy?'

Darcy hesitated. If he revealed himself, there was every chance he could be taken, and in his present frail condition he could very easily betray his wife.

'I tell you, I know nothing,' he heard H saying. There was another smash, followed by a burst of sinister unworldly laughter.

Darcy opened the door the slightest of cracks and peered into the room. H was facing him, tied to a chair. Nearer him was a strange alien creature whose back writhed with tentacles, waving a kind of firearm in the air.

Without warning, a dinner plate whizzed towards them but the alien simply aimed the weapon and brought it down with ease. H caught sight of Darcy and gave a barely imperceptible shake of his head.

'This is getting tiresome,' said the alien. 'Will you please ask them to cease hurling crockery at me? There will be nothing left for supper at this rate.'

H sighed. 'All right, ladies. Do as the man says.' There was a brief soft murmuring in the air, which eventually gave way to a sullen silence.

'Thank you,' said the alien. 'Now, I will try one more time. Where is Mrs Darcy? If you do not choose to cooperate, I will have no choice but to use the probe.'

'Not the probe!'

'Yes! The probe!'

There was a pause.

'Which probe?' said H eventually.

The alien bent down, still aiming the gun at H, and fetched a long pointed object from a bag on the floor.

'Oh, that probe,' said H.

This was too much for Darcy. He burst open the door and launched himself at the alien, causing it to drop both the gun and the probe.

It turned around to face him and he landed a perfectly-placed punch on its head. The alien fell to the floor in a mass of swarming tentacles.

Darcy dived onto it and attempted to continue the fight, despite not knowing precisely which parts of the alien's body were worth hitting.

'Step back,' said H suddenly.

Darcy looked up. H had freed himself from the chair and was brandishing the alien's weapon. He pulled away from the wriggling heap with difficulty and there were still some tentacles wrapped around him when he finally managed to get vertical.

However, when H fired the gun the alien withdrew all the protuberances and shrank into a ball with a ghastly shriek.

Darcy knelt down next to the alien, which now smelt vaguely of Brussels sprouts and was making a revolting gurgling noise.

'Reshishtanshe ish ushleshhhh,' it was saying.

'Ha!' said Darcy. 'Pretty stupid thing to choose to say when all you can do is gurgle. Victory is ours I think.'

'Reshishtanshe—'

Then its eyes glazed over. Darcy looked up at H, who was looking pensive.

'We are no longer safe here,' he said. 'We must leave at once.'

'But what about my treatment?'

H shrugged. 'No idea. Bit of a long shot, to be honest. Gathered a bit more data on a few new enemas, though. Got a paper coming out in a couple of months' time. Feeling any better?'

At the prospect of his treatment being over, Darcy brightened considerably. 'You know, H?' he said, 'I rather think I am.'

Back in Glastonbury, supper was being served. Elizabeth found herself seated near the end of the table, next to Wickham and opposite Charlotte and Sutherland. There were a large number of other guests, most of whom appeared to be of an artistic persuasion.

'Charlotte, my dear, who are all these peculiar people?' she said.

'I know not, dearest Lizzy,' said Charlotte. 'I believe they are a number of renowned painters, sculptors and composers whose names we may yet become familiar with should anyone decided to pay for the provision of a sequel.'

Elizabeth looked at Charlotte with one eyebrow raised. 'My dear, whatever do you mean by your curious turn of phrase?'

'I . . . I know not,' said her friend, looking momentarily distracted.

'I have heard tell of this kind of thing,' said Wickham. 'They say 'tis a tired post-modern authorial device to fill in time when there is little else happening. I believe that it is often referred to as the dissolution of the fourth wall.'

'Ah, 'tis not just me, then,' said Charlotte. 'Oft times do I enter a room and the fourth wall dissolves for an instant whilst I commune with some unseen listener. And then without warning the normal order is restored again.'

Elizabeth stared at Charlotte for a moment. 'Well, I don't like the idea of it,' she said. ''Tis most distracting.' She turned towards the centre of the table where an animated lady opposite Lord Byron was expounding forth.

''Tis true!' she was saying. 'Lord Byron used to have the most stupendous Balls in the South of England!'

Elizabeth was temporarily distracted by the sound of Colonel Sutherland opposite her choking on his *Coq.* Lord Byron gave his guest an indulgent smile. 'Ah, my dear,' he said 'I thank you for your compliment. But my Balls do not deserve to be spoken of in such flattering terms.'

'But they were so flamboyant! So vibrant!'

Byron sighed. 'Ah, do you remember but three Christmases past? The Midwinter Ball?'

'I do. I remember it well.'Twas so cold, we had to wear several layers of clothing.'

'And you had such a pretty muff.' Byron winked at the lady and Elizabeth began to feel a trifle queasy. As always with Lord Byron, there was a peculiar undercurrent to his discourse she did not fully comprehend and which was almost certainly quite distasteful.

However, at that moment, conversation stopped entirely as a pigeon smashed through the window, scattering shards of glass over the table. It flew around the room for a moment or two in an erratic orbit before eventually diving head first into the *Coq* pot.

'Ah!' exclaimed Lord Byron. 'Squab surprise!'

'Great heavens!' said Wickham, leaning over to fish the poor bird out. ''Tis Colin!'

'Colin?' said Elizabeth. 'Colin the bird?'

'Indeed,' said Colonel Sutherland. 'And no braver bird ever lived than Lieutenant Colin.'

'Lieutenant?' said Elizabeth.

''Tis an honorary rank,' said Wickham, holding the bird in one hand and stroking its back with the other. 'He is not really a proper Lieutenant Pigeon.'

Proper Lieutenant or not, Colin looked near to death. He was making all manner of un-pigeon-like gargling and wheezing noises and occasionally spitting out gobs of gravy. Wickham was feeling around the bird's neck trying to find something.

'Ah! Here it is,' he said, handing a piece of paper to Sutherland.

'Great heavens!' said Sutherland, reading it. 'We must leave at once! Darcy and H are in danger. We must go to their aid!'

All three of them stood up and bowed to Lord Byron.

'Some other time?' he said.

'Perhaps,' said Elizabeth, turning to her friend. 'Charlotte,' she said, 'I must take my leave. Although I am sure there was something important I had to ask you first.' She paused for a moment. 'No. It's gone. It probably was not important.' They embraced and then she followed Wickham and Sutherland out of the house.

Halfway back to Glastonbury, she suddenly stopped.

'Excuse me, gentlemen,' she said, turning back. 'But I think I've just remembered what I forgot to remember earlier.'

Chapter Eighteen

Thunder and Lightning—Back-up Plan—Davy's Lamp—The Ghost in the Machine—Locating the Laundry

B Y THE TIME they had retraced their steps back to the artists' dwelling, located Charlotte again and obtained the required information, it was dark and the weather had taken a turn for the worse. It was raining hard and there were occasional flashes of lightning.

'Mrs Darcy,' shouted Wickham as they trudged back towards Glastonbury, their faces set against the gale, 'We cannot get back to Bath in these conditions! We should stay with Lord Byron for the night.'

'No,' cried Elizabeth. 'We must make haste. My husband and Sir Humphry are in mortal peril and we need to locate them.'

'Then we must send Colin to tell them we are on our way,' said Colonel Sutherland.

There was a derelict wooden shelter by the side of the road, and the three of them made for it. Wickham scribbled a note on a scrap of paper, fished Colin out of his pocket and then searched for something to tie the note on with.

'Damn and blast,' he said. 'Pardon my language, but I have run out of string.'

'Maybe I can help,' said Elizabeth.

'But how?'

'In my reticule I have some left-overs that I picked up from the kitchen when cook was making bread for the Midsummer Ball. It's only some mouldy old dough, but I think it may do the trick.'

She handed over a grey lump. Wickham tore off a piece and used it to stick the note to Colin's leg. The pigeon looked at it with disgust.

'Fly, Lieutenant Pigeon!' he said, 'Fly!' Wickham released the bird. It flew off with a noticeable lack of enthusiasm.

'How long before he finds them, do you think?' said Elizabeth.

'Colin is the best bird we have,' said Sutherland. 'There's no one faster.'

They stood in silence for a moment, listening to the rain. Then there was a a flash of lightning, followed almost immediately by loud crack of thunder.

'We'd better get moving,' said Wickham, and the three of them hustled away from the shelter, moments before the next bolt of lightning incinerated it. They continued on their way with even greater urgency, but all the same by the time they reached the town, they were soaked through.

'Now what shall we do?' said Elizabeth. 'We will surely not find any horses at this time.'

'There are still sometimes horses available for hire,' said Wickham. 'Although they do not always travel south of the river at this hour of the night. Not for love nor money, I am told.'

'We are not going south of any river,' said Elizabeth.

'In which case, we may be in luck. But all the same,

perhaps 'twould be best for you to seek shelter with your sister whilst we arrange transport?'

'Perhaps I sh—'

She was interrupted by a loud crack, but it was not thunder. Instead of lightening, a single steady ray suddenly shone down on them from above, trapping all three in its beam. Drops of rain scattered down like diamonds sparkling in the light.

'What now?' cried Elizabeth, thoroughly alarmed by this new arrival.

'I know not,' said Wickham. 'Hey, you there!' he called, tilting his head back. 'What is the meaning of this?'

Something sounding like a foghorn blasted out above them. Wickham drew his sword.

Someone was turning the big clanking key in the big rattling lock. How exciting, thought the girl in the cell! A visitor! I wonder if they will bring cake? I like cake. And pork pies. And little pin-wheel sandwiches with cheese and pickle and . . . and . . .

'Prisoner! Stop salivating and stand up!' said the newcomer, waving a tentacle.

'Oh, it's you. BORING.'

'Cease your impudence, girl!'

'Have you come to expend me, then? I do hope so. I'm tired of this place. It's really awful.'

'Would that it were so.' The nasty octopus lady seemed angry. The girl had no idea why. 'Believe me, young lady,' said the lady, 'I would quite happily terminate you here and now if the choice were up to me. But it seems that you have a small reprieve. Since our agent is missing, presumed dead, and we cannot presently locate our target, we must prepare a back-up in case she is lost to us.'

'A back-up? I haven't got the faintest idea what—'

'My acolyte is on his way here after surviving one of your other fellow human's attempts to kill him.'

'Bet he deserved it.'

'Silence!' A tentacle whizzed out from under her cloak and smacked the girl on the cheek.

'Ow!' she said, trying to grab it and failing. 'I hate you.'

The lady stepped closer to her and leant in so that their noses were almost touching. The girl held her breath to avoid being overcome by the smell. 'You have no idea how much more you will hate me after you have been fertilized.' She stepped back, observing the girl's reaction.

'Well, it can't be worse than that horrible probe.'

'You have no idea, young lady. You have no idea at all.'

The girl considered this for a moment.

'So no cake?' she said.

'Enough of this. At sunrise, you will be prepared for implantation. When the clock strikes six, my acolyte—'

'Has he got a name?' said the girl. 'All this acolyte stuff sounds a bit odd if you ask me.'

'Have you got a name?' snapped back the lady with an evil cackle.

'Of course I have. Everyone's got a name. It would be silly not to have one.' She paused. 'Mine's just gone missing, that's all. I'll find it again some day.'

'So when the clock strikes six, my acolyte—'

'What is an acolyte anyway? Are you sure he hasn't—?'

'Oh, very well. You will know him as Mr Darcy. There, I told you.'

The girl frowned, then shook her head. 'Nope. Don't know anyone with that name.'

'The probe is working better than I thought. Anyway—'

'At six o'clock, blah blah blah!'

A tentacle wrapped itself around her neck and drew her close to the lady once again. This time, she caught a strong whiff of stale cabbage.

'Do not trifle with me child,' hissed the lady. The tentacle released itself, and she made to leave. 'Until tomorrow at dawn, then.'

'Just a moment!' cried the girl.

But the door clanged shut. The girl sat down again.

'You never told me what was going to happen at dawn,' she said out loud. But if the truth were told, she wasn't sure she wanted to know too much about what was going to happen tomorrow morning. She was at least fairly sure now it wouldn't involve cake.

The light in the sky above Glastonbury lowered slowly towards the ground. A small crowd had gathered by now, including several holding placards bearing such legends as 'STOP AND BE FRENDLY ALYEN'S', 'COME IN PEECE' and 'GOLF SALE'.

''Tis the end of days,' said a voice in the crowd. 'Repent ye of your sins!'

'Might take a while,' said another. 'How long have we got?'

As the great light drew nearer, a mechanical noise joined in with the howling wind and the rain, drowning everyone else out. Then Elizabeth realised something.

'Wickham!' she shouted. 'Is that not the sound of a steam engine?'

'Great heavens,' said Wickham. 'I do believe you're right!'

'It's H!' said Colonel Sutherland, waving his arms about. 'In his bloody dirigible! Stand back everyone. This one's friendly.'

The crowd tried to make out what he was saying, but

no one could hear a thing. Eventually, by flapping their arms at the crowd, the three of them managed to clear a space so the great machine could land.

'Ahoy there!' said Sir Humphry, leaning over the side, once the engine had chugged to a stop.

'Great heavens, man,' said Sutherland. 'That's one hell of a powerful lamp you've got there.'

'I know. Couple of hundred candles and a parabolic reflector. Hell of a fire hazard, but it's the only way we could track you down. I'm thinking of adapting it for use down the mines.'

'Why—oh, never mind.'

He was interrupted by Elizabeth pushing to the front. 'Is my husband there? How is he?'

Darcy appeared at H's side, struggling to steady himself against the side of the gondola. He clearly hadn't realised it was no longer moving.

'I was much better until I boarded this infernal machine,' said Darcy. 'Still, 'tis most agreeable to see you once more, my dear. I trust you are in good health?'

'I am tolerably well.'

'I am pleased to hear it. Will you be coming on board?'

'I believe it is our intention to do so, is it not?'

'It is indeed,' said H. 'We must make haste. Our enemies know we are in this vicinity, so we must waste no time in taking the attack to them. I trust you have divined the significance of Mr Collins' last message to his wife?'

'I have indeed.'

'Well then, we had better get moving.' At this, he threw down the rope ladder.

Elizabeth climbed aboard, refusing the assistance of any of the men. Sutherland and Wickham followed afterwards.

'So?' said H to Elizabeth when they were all in the gondola.

Elizabeth reached into her reticule and withdrew a key.

'Aha!' said H.

'Aha!' said Sutherland.

'Aha!' said Wickham.

Darcy, who was still leaning against the side, just groaned. 'Sorry,' he said. 'Still feeling a bit—a bit—whoops, sorry!' He turned to the others. 'I think we'd better get moving, everyone. Fellow down there. Bit annoyed.'

'Right-oh, chaps,' said H. 'Positions for take-off!'

'Splendid,' said Sutherland. 'Time to kick some tentacle!'

'Look out squiddy, here we come!' said Wickham.

'Does nobody want to know what this is the key to?' said Elizabeth. 'Hello? Is anybody listening to me?'

But her words were lost in the wind and the rain.

Once the dirigible was safely aloft, they floated in mid-air for a moment whilst Sir Humphry fiddled with one of his devices.

'What are you doing, H?' asked Wickham.

'I'm priming the navigator,' said H.

'Navigator?' said Sutherland.

'Yes,' said H. ' Had an idea whilst I was twiddling my thumbs in Bath. I thought to myself, why not put one of these ghosts to good use. So I asked her if she minded being placed in one of my machines.' He gestured towards a teak and brass box situated next to the steering wheel. 'Annie?' he said, giving it a gentle tap.

'Turn around when possible,' said Annie Chapman's voice.

'No, Annie, I want to go to Rosings, please.'

'Turn around wh—go left at the cloud, first exit.'

'That's better. Thank you, Annie.' He turned to the

others. 'Y'see? These ghosts have much wider fields of perception than we live chaps have. Comes from being dead, I suppose. Which means—'

'Go left at the cloud, first exit.'

'Which means that she can—'

'Go left at the cloud, first exit.'

'But she can get a little impatient. I'll explain it all later.' H pressed another button and the motor began to chug away, propelling the dirigible forwards.

'I love technology,' said H.

'Well, I don't see what's wrong with using the stars,' said Darcy.

'On a night like this?' asked Elizabeth.

'Maybe we aren't intended to fly on a night like this, then? Maybe we aren't intended to fly, full stop.'

'Oh, come come, my dear. What about our mission to defeat the evil alien hordes?'

'Harrumph,' said Darcy.

The rain had ceased for the moment and the wind had lulled. Only the chug-chug-chug of the steam engine broke the silence on board the dirigible.

'How long until we reach Rosings?' said Elizabeth.

'In half a mile, go straight on,' said Annie Chapman. 'Then go straight on again.'

'If I were you,' said H, 'I'd get some sleep. We will not be there until dawn, and we will need our wits about us then.'

'True.'

'In half a mile, g—'

H threw a blanket over the navigator. Annie's voice continued, muffled and oblivious.

'Do you think she minds?' asked Elizabeth.

'I have no idea,' said H. 'Beats throwing crockery around, I would imagine.'

Elizabeth could think of no sensible response to this, so she took H's advice and located a space for her husband and herself to lie down and sleep.

She slept fitfully with many perplexing dreams. She dreamt of Lydia, all bouncy and childlike and unbelievably irritating. Then she dreamt of Kitty, who for some reason took the form of an oriental cat. 'Hello, Lizzy,' said the cat. 'Hello, Kitty,' said Elizabeth. Then she dreamt of Jane.

She sat up in a cold sweat.

Jane!

She took hold of Darcy's shoulder and shook him awake.

'Fitzy! Wake up!' she said. 'I'm worried about Jane.'

'Ssssalright,' said Darcy. 'Charlie'll look after her. Good egg, Charlie. Had a telegraph from him only th'other day. Good egg, Charlie. Good egg.'

Elizabeth relaxed. Why had she been so worried? Oh, she had to stop panicking like this. She drifted off again, and this time she dreamt of a baptism service where the vicar was startled when a tentacle grabbed him from the font.

Then he looked at her and smiled an ugly smile and his face was the face of Mr Collins and the whole congregation turned at her and stared and began to point and laugh and then they all took off their face masks and every single one had a mass of writhing tentacles where they should have eyes, nose and a mouth and . . .

She sat up again. The engine had stopped.

'You have reached your destination,' said Annie's muffled voice.

It was still dark when the five of them emerged from the dirigible.

'Are you sure no one saw us?' said Sutherland.

'Quite sure,' said H. 'Annie's course has kept us well clear of the house, about half a mile to the south. Look! There it is!'

He pointed ahead, but all the others could see was a vague shape rising out of the pre-dawn gloom.

'So what are our tactics, then?' said Wickham.

'I rather think we need to ask Mrs Darcy here,' said H.

'Mrs Darcy? But she's—'

Elizabeth stepped forward, holding her key aloft once more.

'Aha!' said Wickham.

'Thank you, Mr Wickham,' said Elizabeth. 'I trust you are all going to pay attention to what I have to say this time?'

There was a general mumbling of assent from the men.

'Good. According to Mrs Collins, this key will let us into the house through the laundry. The laundry is unattended up until the hour of eight o'clock, so we may pass through unobserved. From there, it is but a short journey down the corridor to the aliens' control room. In there, we will find their communications device and if we destroy that, the aliens will no longer be able to land on our world.'

'How does she know all this?' said Sutherland with a suspicious air.

'I believe her husband used to talk about it in his sleep. There was much about it that disturbed him.'

'I can imagine that this was so.'

'Indeed. It must have come as something of a shock to find his esteemed patroness was not of this earth.'

'So how do we locate the laundry?'

'Sadly, she was unable to assist me there. As soon as she began to describe the geometry of the rear of Rosings, she became insensible. I believe the place still holds bad memories for her.'

'It holds bad memories for me, I can tell you,' said Wickham.

'Indeed,' said Elizabeth.

'So we still lack one piece of the puzzle,' said H.

'Even so, I suggest we make haste to the house before dawn,' said Elizabeth. 'I am most certain the laundry will make itself apparent when we are closer.'

'I hope you are right,' said Sutherland.

Elizabeth paused, looking at her husband. 'Fitzy dearest? Are you all right? You seem very pensive this morning.'

''Tis nothing, my dear,' said Darcy. 'However, you forget that I was incarcerated here for some weeks. Indeed, incarcerated without any garments to protect my naked flesh from the cold stone.'

Elizabeth put her hand on his shoulder. 'I had not forgotten, my dear.'Tis just that you have not mentioned it, so I thought—'

''Tis nothing, dearest.'Tis nothing.'

'Come, then!' said Sutherland. 'Let us go!'

At this, they all set off towards the house, with Sutherland leading the way. The path was damp with the early morning dew but firm, and they made good progress through the fields. When they were but a short way from their goal, Elizabeth noticed something.

'There's a bustle in the hedgerow!' she cried out.

'Don't be alarmed!' said Wickham.

'No, there really is a bustle in the hedgerow,' said Elizabeth again. 'And look there, ahead of it, a ball gown. They must have blown away from the washing line during last night's storm. Follow the trail of clothes and we shall find our laundry!'

'Great heavens, you are right!' said H. 'Come on!' The five picked up their pace now and within a few more minutes they, by dint of following a path strewn with, respectively, three pairs of breeches, two Spencers, a pelisse and a whole array of assorted gentlemen's hose, located the entrance to the laundry in the west wing of the great house.

Elizabeth produced the key once again and inserted it in the lock. At the exact moment that she did so, the air was rent with a woman's scream.

Chapter Nineteen

Tentacular Caresses — The Control Room — Misunderstandings — More Misunderstandings — The Fertilisation Suite

T HE GIRL STRUGGLED to free herself from the straps holding her to the bed.

'Let me go, you horrible woman!' she cried. 'This isn't fair!'

'Hush, child. Did your father not tell you when you were young that life wasn't fair?'

'I don't know,' said the girl. 'Did he?' A vague memory of someone who might or might not have been her father wafted briefly into her mind. Then it wafted out again.

The nasty lady ignored her, but continued to strap her in. When she finished, she stood up and appraised the girl.

'Hmmm. Bit skinny, but I suppose you'll have to do,' she said. She picked up a bell on the table next to the bed and rang it once.

'What's that for?' said the girl.

'The moment has come.'

'What—oh, I see.'

A man had entered the room. There was something about him that was familiar and yet much that wasn't. The bits that were familiar were mainly the human ones, such as most of the face. He walked with a limp and seemed to have problems breathing.

'Ek—ek—ek—ek,' said the newcomer, his face flapping horribly as he did so. The sound did not appear to come from his mouth.

'This is my acolyte. You may know him as Mr Darcy,' said the lady.

'Ek—ek—ek—ek,' said the one she called Mr Darcy. It was a strange, rasping sound that sounded as if it would be more at home somewhere a long way under water.

The girl felt sick. She tried to twist away but the straps were holding her tight.

'Stay away you horrible man—thing—alien—whatsit!' she cried. 'Don't you dare touch me!'

'Ek—ek—ek!' The creature's eyes lit up with what seemed to be excitement as it continued to lurch slowly towards the bed.

'See what your fellow humans have done to my poor boy,' said the lady. 'He barely knows what species he belongs to these days.'

'It's a pity they didn't finish the job if you ask me,' said the girl.

'I swear you will live to regret that remark.' The lady stepped past the alien Mr Darcy thing, bent over and slapped the girl hard on the cheek. The girl blew a raspberry back at her.

'Nur nur!' she said. 'Didn't hurt.'

The lady was about to slap her again, but the alien put up its right arm and stopped her.

'Ek—ek—ek—ek—ek,' it said.

'Are you sure?' said the lady.

'Ek—ek—ek.'

'As you wish. But on your own head be it.' She backed off, leaving room for the alien to move closer to the bed.

With great effort, it removed its jacket, and then its shirt, revealing a fine, well-toned chest that would have been remarkably handsome if it had not been covered in writhing tentacles.

'Ek—ek—ek—ek—ek!'

'Keep back! Just because you stopped the old bitch from slapping me doesn't mean I'm going to start liking you instead.'

'Ek—ek—ek?' A couple of tentacles were beginning to caress her upper body.

'Yeeeeuch! Stop that! It's slimy and tickly and—and—and just WEIRD.'

'Ekekekekekek!' The tentacles adjusted their positions.

'And that's even worse. No way is that normal.'

The creature withdrew the protuberances altogether. But what followed next was even more alarming. The alien turned to the lady as if it was asking for permission for something.

'Ek—ek—ek?' it said.

'Oh, just get on with it,' she said, turning to go. 'I can't wait any longer. Report back to me when you've finished.'

It gave a kind of alien shrug and then slowly began to remove the rest of its clothing. The girl looked at what was revealed and blinked.

It was at this point that she screamed.

At the sound, Wickham looked at Elizabeth.

'Did you hear that?' he whispered.

'I rather think we all did,' said Elizabeth.

'Well, it sounds like someone's in trouble,' said Sutherland.

'I believe you may be correct in that assertion,' said

Elizabeth. 'I therefore suggest we should split up into two parties at this point.'

'That was exactly what I was about to propose myself,' hissed Sutherland. 'H, take Mrs Darcy and locate the control room. Wickham and Darcy, come with me. Let's see if we can track down the owner of that scream.'

Elizabeth looked at Sir Humphry. 'Come along then,' she said, as the other three scurried away in the direction of the sound. She led the way down the corridor just as Charlotte had told her to.

She was about to give the first door on the left a nudge when it flew open, almost hitting her in the face. She and H immediately backed into the shadows as a servant emerged carrying a large tureen.

After they waited for the servant to disappear around the corner at the end, they continued along the corridor. The next door was on the right and turned out to be a broom cupboard. Almost as soon as she realised this, Elizabeth heard footsteps approaching.

'Quick,' she hissed at H, grabbing him by the arm and pulling him into the cupboard. They waited there in the darkness for a minute whilst the footsteps went past, desperately hoping that the house was not in need of sweeping. Finally, Elizabeth opened the door a fraction and peered out. The corridor was empty once again.

'Come along,' she said, and they resumed their search. At the third door on the left, she found what they were looking for.

At least she assumed it was what they were looking for, because it was full of strange devices, the like of which she had never seen before. Elizabeth and H slipped in and closed the door behind them.

'Great heavens!' said H, rubbing his hands and beaming all over his face. He was like a child with a whole roomful of new toys and set off on a tour of the room, inspecting each one in turn.

'Um, H?' said Elizabeth. 'I think our mission was to locate the homing beacon and destroy it, was it not?'

H looked crestfallen.

'I suppose so,' he said. 'But just think what we could do with all this. For the good of mankind.'

'No, H.'

Just then, a light on a desk on one side of the room started flashing, followed a few moments afterwards by an impatient buzzing sound.

'H?' said Elizabeth. 'How do I stop this noise? Someone's going to hear it. H? H? Help?' She began stabbing at buttons on the desk in turn. 'H? It won't stop! Any ideas?'

'I have no idea!'

'This one?'

'Don't know!'

'Ah, that's better,' said Elizabeth. The dreadful noise stopped. But then she looked up at the wall ahead of her. She now realised it was completely taken up with a sheet of opaque glass, which was now flickering in a most unexpected manner.

'H?'

But before H could say anything, the flickering stopped and a moving picture took its place. It was a moving picture of an alien, waving its tentacles about.

'Ek—ek—ek—ek—ek!' said the alien.

'H?' said Elizabeth.

'I do believe it wants to talk to you,' said H.

'What? Are you telling me that thing's alive?' She looked behind her. H had ducked down out of sight.

'Ek—ek—ek!'

'H? How can a sheet of glass be alive?'

'Ekekekekekekek!'

Elizabeth sank into the chair behind her. Now what?

The thing in the glass seemed to be waiting for Elizabeth to say something. She took a deep breath and leant forward.

'Er . . . ek—ek—ek.' she said. **(My ramparts stretch as far as Canterbury.)**

She could have sworn that it raised an eyebrow—this despite not having anything remotely resembling an eye, let alone a brow.

'Ekekekekekekekek?' came the reply. **(I am very pleased for you. And I do like your new outfit. But how goes the back-up plan?)**

'Um . . . ecky—ecky.' **(The fruitbats are unusually tasty this year.)**

'Ek—ek—ekekekek?' **(Very nice I'm sure. But has the alternative target been fertilised yet?)**

'Ek—ek—ek—ek—ek!' **(To hell with the lifeboats! I'm on skis!)**

'Ek—ek—ek?' **(Are you sure you're all right?)**

'Careful, Mrs Darcy,' whispered H. 'He looks suspicious.'

'How can you tell?' asked Elizabeth.

'Not sure. Something in the way he's waving that tentacle above his head.'

'Hmmm. I see what you mean. I'll try a bit harder, then.'

She cleared her throat and tried once more. 'Ek—ek—ek—ek.' **(There is a family of meerkats nesting in my gazebo.)**

The alien looked startled. 'Ek—ek—ekek!' it said. **(When did you decide to build a gazebo? Have the expenses been cleared? I want a gazebo too!)**

'Careful,' hissed H. 'Although . . . I've just noticed something. See that device next to him?'

'The one with the curious red design on it?' said Elizabeth.

'Yes, that's the one. Now look over there to your right.'

'Great heavens! It's the same!'

'Exactly.'

'Hold on. He's giving me that funny look again.'

'All right. Keep him talking, whilst I try to get a bit closer.'

Elizabeth smiled at the alien. 'Ek—ecky—ecky—ek?' **(Will you have two sugars with that, or do you wish me to sign the release forms for Lord Wilberforce's prosthetics?)**

For a moment the alien seemed lost in thought. Then it seemed to take on a more severe expression.

'Ek—ek—ek—ek—ek—ek—ek—ek—ekekeke kekekekekek?' **(Who are you, anyway?)**

'Ek—ek—ek?' **(Will you join me for a brief mazurka?)**

H had crawled under the desk next to her and was fiddling around with the device he had identified.

'I don't think I can keep this up for much longer,' she said. 'He's bound to work out that I'm not Lady Catherine soon.'

'Just hang in there, Mrs Darcy,' said H. 'If I can just unscrew this—' There was a loud crack and a smell of cordite in the air.

'Ek—ekky—ek.' said the alien. **(What was that? I heard a noise! What's going on down there? I tell you, I'm getting a bit worried here. I may be forced to implement Emergency Protocol B.)**

'Ek—ekekekekekek,' said Elizabeth. **(Let us go into the forest and make sandcastles out of porridge.)**

The alien was standing up now and was waving his tentacles around in a frenzied display.

'Please hurry up,' said Elizabeth.

'I'm trying,' said H. There was another loud bang.

'Ek.' **(Right, that's it. I'm giving you five seconds before I implement the emergency protocol. If you are really who you say you are, I'd advise you to clear the area.)**

'Ek—ek—ek—ek—ek!?' **(Banana fritters, please. With eggs over easy.)**

'Ek!' **(Five!)**

'Ek—ek—ekekekek!' **(Smile, please, for the puffins.)**

'Ek!' **(Four!)**

'Hurry up, please H! I think he's counting down towards something bad happening!'

'Ek!' **(Three!)**

'Ek—ekekekekekekekekek!' **(Red, red, it's always red!)**

'Ek!' **(Two!)**

'Ekekekekekek—ekek—ek!' **(Will it be Kiev or Sparta this time?)**

'Ek!' **(One!)**

And then there was the slightest 'phut' from where H was working and the moving picture disappeared.

'Nice timing, H,' said Elizabeth. Then she smelt burning. Shortly after this, she realised that the room was on fire.

Wickham, Sutherland and Darcy were faced with a dilemma. They had a choice between continuing on down the corridor or taking the branch off to the right.

'Right, chaps,' said Colonel Sutherland. 'We need to split into two groups. Wickham, you carry on ahead. Darcy and I will go this way.'

Darcy hesitated for a moment.

'Come along, man!' said Sutherland. 'No time to argue. This is a military operation now.'

Halfway along the new corridor, the two men heard footsteps coming their way from around the next corner. Both of them froze, desperately looking around for somewhere to take refuge. There was nowhere. The steps came closer and to their horror they saw Lady Catherine de Bourgh heading straight for them.

She stopped, uncertain, some distance away.

'Ek — ek — ek — ek — ek?' said Lady Catherine. **(Well, that was quick! How did the fertilisation procedure go?)**

'Er—' said Darcy.

'Do the ecky ecky stuff! You know, ecky ecky ecky!' hissed Sutherland.

'Ah . . . ekekek.' said Darcy. **(It was entirely satisfactory, madam.)**

'Ek — ek — ek.' said Lady Catherine. **(Excellent. It seems to have done wonders for your complexion, certainly.)**

'Ek — ek — ekek.' Darcy, improvised blindly. **(I am glad you think so. Myself, I would prefer it if my skin tones were slightly darker.)**

'Tell her I'm your prisoner,' whispered Sutherland.

'What do I say?' said Darcy.

'How am I supposed to know?'

'Er . . . ek — ek — ek — ek — ek.' said Darcy. **(I encountered this intruder on my way back from the fertilisation suite. I am taking him to the cells.)**

Darcy blinked, wondering how much longer he could get away with this.

'Ekek—ekek?' said Lady Catherine, frowning. **(I shall accompany you then. I will assist with the interrogation. Is the target still restrained?)**

'Ek.' **(She is. But she keeps asking for cake.)**

'Ek—ek—ek.' **(Greedy little cow. She will be disposed of once the primary target has been located once more.)**

'Ek.' **(Good.)**

'Have you any idea what you're saying?' said Sutherland.

'Not the faintest clue,' said Darcy. 'She looks like she wants to come with us to the cells.'

'That's not so good. Is she armed, do you think?'

'Probably.'

'Ek—ek—ek—ek—ekek.' said Lady Catherine. **(The cells are this way, you idiot.)**

'Ek—ek—ek.' said Darcy. **(Whoops. Silly me.)**

'I think we're going the wrong way,' whispered Darcy.

'Blast the woman! OK, turn me round. Be as rough as you like.'

Darcy manhandled Sutherland and pushed him in the opposite direction.

'Ek—ek—ek—ek!' said Darcy. **(Keep moving, flesh-faced scum whose mother sucked anchovies!)**

'Ouch!' said Sutherland. 'I know I said rough, but that was a bit much!'

Darcy smacked him with the back of his hand.

'Sorry, old man,' he said. 'Need to make this realistic.'

'Fair enough,' said Sutherland, flinching slightly. 'Carry on, then.'

'Ekekekekekekekek!' **(Faster, faster, you grey hairy-eared loon!)**

As they reached another turn in the corridor, they paused for a moment, wondering which way to turn. Darcy stole a glance at Lady Catherine, who appeared to be smiling.

'Ek—ek—ek—ek—ek?' **(Well, then? Which way do you think this time?)**

'Um . . . ek!' **(Er . . . er . . . Prick my balloons, Prime Minister! It's Michaelmas Eve!)**

There was silence.

'What happened there?' hissed Sutherland.

'Don't know,' said Darcy. 'Think I got it a bit wrong.' He turned around. Lady Catherine de Bourgh was holding a firearm.

'Ah,' said Darcy. 'Damn.'

'Tut tut, Mr Darcy,' she said. 'And you were doing so well.'

'Ek—ek?' said Darcy.

Lady Catherine shook her head. 'No, I do not wish to purchase a loincloth.' She sighed. 'Time to bring this little charade to an end, I think.' She narrowed her eye and raised the weapon.

But before she had a chance to fire it, she was distracted by the sound of running feet. A bevy of footmen collided with the three of them, knocking Lady Catherine flying.

'Fire!' screamed one of them. 'Fire!'

Darcy and Sutherland exchanged the briefest of looks and ran.

As Wickham made his way along the passage, he was convinced he could hear the sound of a young woman moaning and complaining. The sound seemed to be coming from a room at the end, on the left hand side. There was a brass plaque on the door, bearing the legend:

FERTILISATION SUITE
ENTER WITH CARE

Wickham took a deep breath and charged, shoulder first, at the door. As it gave way and he lurched into the room, he reflected it might have been a more subtle approach to simply turn the handle.

As he struggled to regain his balance, the sight that met his eyes beggared belief. On the bed against the far wall, a girl was confined with tight leather straps, whilst a ghastly naked alien creature was leaning over her, preparing to undertake some revolting act of unpleasantness.

'You there,' said Wickham. 'Unhand that young lady at once!'

The creature grunted and turned around. Good grief! It was Darcy! And yet not Darcy! Wickham's mind spun frantically back to the Midsummer Ball at Pemberley and that last confrontation on the roof. Surely this thing had been killed?

The alien fanned itself out to its full size, waving a thousand slippery tentacles around in an obscene aerial ballet. Then it opened its mouth and gave a thunderous roar.

Wickham reassessed his earlier assumption. No, the thing clearly hadn't been killed at Pemberley. Oh well, here goes, he said to himself.

He raised his sword and launched himself at the beast, slashing tentacles left, right and centre. The air became thick with flying blubber and sizzling alien blood.

'Die, foul beast!' he cried, aiming a blow at the creature's chest.

'Ek — ek — ek!'

'Try speaking the King's English, you vermin!'

'Thmphth. Shpflugth. Ekekekekekek!'

'Ha! You can't any more, can you? Ha! Take that, failed shape shifter!'

By now, the monster was on the ground, bent over. Wickham squatted down next to it, holding his sword against its gizzard.

'Give me one reason why I shouldn't just kill you now,' he said.

'Thmflth,' said the alien.

'Sorry? Can't hear you.'

'Phfthather.'

'Nope. Try again.'

'Am your phfthather.'

Wickham rolled his eyes. 'Sorry, but if that's the best you can do, you might as well not bother. There is no way in a million years you're my father. I mean, really. Sorry. That's just silly.' Wickham drew back his sword, but he was interrupted by a female voice.

'No!' said the girl on the bed. 'Don't do that!'

'But he was going to—'

'I know. But he still deserves our mercy. Our humanity. And it'll be really really icky.'

Wickham paused for a moment to think about this. Great heavens! He had got carried away there for sure.

If he went any further with this, he would have to make out a report on a form B12/5A, which would be subject to PL19 assessment by the alien liquidation review committee, and if he achieved a score of less then 3.68 he might be sent for anger management training.

How had he allowed this to happen?

'You are right,' he said, standing up. 'I apologise for my unseemly bloodlust.'

'Sawrigth,' said the alien.

'Oh, for God's sake, I wasn't apologising to you. You're still my prisoner.'

'Ek—ek!' said the creature. Wickham deduced from its subsequent leap to its feet and exit from the room this meant 'Oh no, I'm not!'

'Damn,' said Wickham.

'Never mind that,' said the girl on the bed. 'Can you release me? I'm hungry.'

'Of course.' He went over to the bed and began to unhook the leather straps. As he did so, the girl turned over to face him. He looked into her eyes and she looked back at him.

'Lydia!'

Chapter Twenty

*Alien Darcy's Revelation — Freedom! — Lady
Catherine's Revelation — Deus ex Machina —
The End of Rosings*

IN THE WEST wing of Rosings, pandemonium reigned.
The air was thick with billowing black smoke and
servants ran in all directions, some carrying valuable items
to safety and others simply carrying themselves to safety.

At least in the confusion it was simple for Elizabeth and
H to make themselves inconspicuous, but it wasn't easy
to decide who best to follow in order to find the way out
of the inferno.

'Which way?' cried Elizabeth.

'One moment,' said H. He licked a finger and held
it up. One side was quickly covered in black soot. 'This
way!' he said.

'Are you sure?'

'Not in the slightest. Come on.'

They scurried down a long corridor, trying to avoid
attracting too much attention to themselves, behind a
group of footmen struggling with some ornamental candlesticks and a pair of large portraits of Lady Catherine de
Bourgh. Halfway along, one of the footmen gave out a
strangled cry and dropped his end of the portrait he was
carrying.

'Oh, my God!' cried one of them. 'What is it?'

At this, the other three cried out in alarm. They abandoned their valuables altogether and turned back, colliding with Elizabeth and H as they did so.

'Quick,' hissed Elizabeth, grabbing one of the portraits. 'Hide behind these!'

As the footmen disappeared back the way they had come, the two of them crouched behind the two pictures, hoping they looked as if they'd been casually left lying against the wall.

'What is it, anyway?' whispered H.

'I can't see—oh, great heavens! 'Tis Darcy!'

'Darcy?'

'Or, rather, 'tis Alien Darcy. My word, but he has suffered some grievous injuries. There is barely a tentacle left on the poor creature.'

'Save your sympathy for those who need it, Mrs Darcy,' said H. 'Remember what this fiend has done.'

The two withdrew under cover as the alien staggered towards them. As it arrived, it stopped and crouched down. Elizabeth recoiled in alarm as she smelt the ghastly scent of stale brassicas on its breath.

It leant in close to study the portrait, its protuberances tracing the shape of Lady Catherine's image. She watched the back of the picture in fascinated horror as it indented under the beast's touch, knowing that only canvas and a thin layer of paint lay between the two of them.

Then the canvas was torn apart and a tentacle burst through. Elizabeth screamed in terror as the suckers latched on to her neck and pulled her forward.

'Let go of me, you horrible fake!'

'Wifphth of mine,' said the alien.

'I'm not your wife, you revolting beast! Let me go!'

'Yes, let her go!' said H, getting to his feet. But the

alien simply slapped him on the face with the stump of a tentacle and the scientist went down like the opposite of a balloonful of phlogiston.

It pulled Elizabeth close in a revolting parody of a lovers' embrace. She knew she had but one chance.

'Lovfthg you,' said the alien, with a dopey expression on its face.

Elizabeth brought her fist up into the beast's face and connected perfectly. It released her at once, then proceeded to stagger back and forth in a daze.

It fell backwards and impaled itself on one of the ornamental candlesticks.

The alien was trying to say something. She knelt down by it. 'Lookaftfher.' it said.

'Look after? Look after what?'

'Babyfhthgh.'

'Baby? What baby?'

But there came no reply. Alien Darcy was dead.

On the second floor of the *Department of Unusual Affairs* in Whitehall, an infant wailed.

'Hush, my little one,' said the ghost of Mary Ann Nicholls. She looked more closely at the expression on her child's face. Was that a tear trickling down its face? 'Oh, my darling! 'Tis true? Your father? Dead?'

The tiny alien poked a tentacle through the cage and tried to touch her on the arm. This was not entirely successful, and she could tell that once again the poor dear was disappointed at having a spectre for a mother.

'So I am a single mother now,' she said. 'All alone in the world. Alas and alack.'

She sniffed. Oh well, she thought. If Alien Mr Darcy was dead, then maybe they wouldn't need her baby any more. Her hand shot to her mouth! But what if they disposed of it—like horrible Alien Mr Darcy did with all the other alien babies?

There was only one possible course of action. She had to free the little mite—and free it quickly before Captain Maberley came in to work.

Over the last few days she'd tried a few experiments with interacting with physical objects and she'd had a certain amount of success—particularly with teapots, although she failed to divine a reason for this.

But unlocking a cage—that was a different matter altogether. The door to the cage was secured with a padlock. She knew that Maberley kept the key in his desk drawer. Using her teapot-hurling skills, she might just manage to push the drawer onto the floor, but there was no way she could move the key from there into the lock.

Then she had an idea. All she had to do was persuade the occupant of the cage to get the key for her. But how? She couldn't exactly explain what she wanted, could she? The thing seemed quite bright, but there was no way it could understand sentences. Perhaps if she turned it into some kind of game, though?

She started dancing around in front of the cage, waving her arms around and doing the 'Woo woo!' thing that upset Captain Maberley so. Sure enough, her baby started joining in, shooting out tentacles in an attempt to grab her.

'Keep going,' she said, 'Keep going!' She continued dancing, all the time making sure the little alien was tracking her as she moved slowly around to the far side of the desk. It took several attempts to get it to pull the drawer out, but eventually she managed it, and she could see the key fully exposed.

'Look!' she said. 'Shiny key!' But it wasn't in the least bit interested. So she gathered all her energy and started to swirl the contents of the desk drawer around. The alien thought this was terrific fun and joined in.

And then with relief, Mary Ann noticed that the key had fortuitously become stuck to one of the suckers at the end of a tentacle. She immediately stopped what she was doing and danced the tentacle back towards the cage. With some carefully choreographed waving, she managed to get it to locate the key in the padlock.

'Well done!' she said. Then she realised that it had released its grip on the key, leaving it sitting uselessly in the lock.

All she had to do was devise another little game, teasing the creature that she was going to steal its shiny toy.

She soon encouraged it to open the cage.

'Come on! Let's go!' she said, running out of the room with the little alien hopping after her, narrowly avoiding being trodden on by a bleary-eyed Captain Maberley, who was just getting in to work.

Elizabeth knelt down next to Sir Humphry, who was still unconscious.

'Sir H!' she said. 'We need to get moving! This whole building is going to collapse any minute! Oh heavens! What am I to do now?'

'Maybe I can help?' said an arrogant, female voice. Elizabeth knew precisely who the owner was.

'Lady Catherine de Bourgh!' she said, turning around and standing up. 'What a pleasant surprise.'

'The pleasure is all mine,' said Lady Catherine. 'Come,' she said, holding out a hand. 'I know the way out of here.'

'But what about Sir Humphry?'

'We leave him here. He will die.' She nodded towards the body of Alien Darcy. 'What is your problem? You seem to have no compunction in killing my people.'

'That was an accident,' said Elizabeth.

Lady Catherine shrugged. 'I somehow can't imagine all those tentacles all fell off by themselves. Unless you had yet more accomplices?'

Elizabeth shook her head. 'No. 'Twas just me. I acted alone.'

'Curious,' said Lady Catherine. 'For I have already encountered your husband and that bumbling Colonel.'

Elizabeth gasped. 'Are they all right?'

Lady Catherine snickered. 'What do you think?'

Elizabeth let out a wail. 'No!' She held her face in her hands.

'Come, then,' said Lady Catherine. 'As you so correctly observed to your comatose friend, we need to get moving.'

'No! I will not move. Kill me now!'

'Unfortunately, much as your behaviour invites me to do so, I cannot yet proceed with that objective. You are carrying something important to me.'

Elizabeth gaped at her. 'Surely not?'

Lady Catherine pressed her face against her. 'k'Ekkk told you, didn't he, Elizabeth? And you know it to be true.'

'No!' She shook her head violently. Then she thought of something. 'But wait one moment. What if 'tis my Darcy's? 'Tis entirely possible.'

Now it was Lady Catherine's turn to be thunderstruck. 'What?'

'All I am saying is that we have no idea.'

'You two-timing little trollope! I send my acolyte k'Ekkk to you and you dare to have relations with your husband as well!'

'I—sorry?' Elizabeth's head was spinning. It was also

getting hard to concentrate with smoke filling the atmosphere around them.

'Come with me, then,' said Lady Catherine in a softer tone of voice.

'I said no. If I am carrying some kind of horrible half-alien baby thing, I don't want to live. Kill me now.'

'Ah, but if you are carrying Mr Darcy's baby, you would want to live, wouldn't you? More than anything else in the whole wide world.'

'Stop it!'

'Because you want that baby. You want to cradle it in your arms.'

'PLEASE STOP NOW!'

'You want to play with it, nurture it, watch it grow up to be a fine young—'

Elizabeth was sobbing.

'Come, child,' said Lady Catherine, grasping Elizabeth's hand. 'Follow me.'

Out of the corner of her eye she saw H stir at last. She gave his shin a nudge with her foot as she finally allowed Lady Catherine to drag her away. To her relief, she noticed him sit up. With any luck, he would know what to do.

Within minutes they were in the main entrance hall of Rosings, which was mercifully unscathed by the conflagration. As they approached the door, Elizabeth stopped.

'Lady Catherine,' she said. 'Before we go any further, I need to know something.'

'You may ask, but I may not necessarily reply.'

''Tis a simple question, though. Why me?'

Sir Humphry Davy staggered to his feet, coughing. He could hear muffled cries and sounds of people running back and forth but he was completely alone.

'Anybody there?' he shouted. There was no reply. For a moment he thought there was a light at one end of the passage, so he staggered off in that direction, but the heat soon became too intense for him to continue.

'Damnation,' said H, spluttering. He turned and retraced his steps before finding another branch. He only just started down this when he collided with two figures running in the opposite direction.

'Oof!' said one of them.

'Colonel?' said H.

'H?' said Sutherland and Darcy simultaneously.

'So I take it that's not the way out either?' said H.

'I rather think it is not,' said Darcy.

'Blast,' said H. 'What a pretty pickle we find ourselves in.'

'Indeed we do,' said Sutherland.

'Perhaps 'tis this way?' said Darcy.

'No,' said H. 'I've just come from there.'

'In that case,' said Sutherland. 'This must be the way! Come along, men!'

But no sooner had they started along the passage than they ran into another man heading their way. He appeared to be carrying a young girl over his shoulder.

'Wickham!' said Sutherland. 'Great heavens, man—is that who I think it is?'

'It is indeed,' said Wickham.

'Good Lord!' said H. 'Is that really Agent Lydia? Then we are almost complete.'

'Has anyone seen my wife?' asked Darcy.

There was an embarrassed silence. Not far from them, timbers crackled and there was an ominous crashing sound.

'She went off with someone. Lady Catherine de something?' said H. He noticed the expression on their faces. 'Ah, that Lady Catherine. I should have realised.'

'Oh, great heavens, no!' said Darcy. 'We must find her at once.'

'Darcy, old man,' said Sutherland. 'Given that we cannot even find our own way out of here, I fear there is even less chance of us locating your wife in the midst of all this chaos.'

'Well, what are we to do, then?' cried Darcy. 'This is all quite intolerable.'

A few feet away from them, the ceiling suddenly fell down and sent a shower of dust in their direction to add to the smoke. When they all stopped coughing, Sutherland waved his hands for silence.

'Gentlemen, we are at something of an impasse here. The passage to our left—my left, H, your right—is now blocked with rubble. The passage behind me would seem to take us even further into the heart of the house and hence would be a most unwise choice. The passage ahead of us would seem to be a more sensible option if it were not for the fact that I can clearly observe flames licking the walls a little way down'

There was a crash.

'And it appears that the ceiling down there has given way as well.

Gentlemen we are trapped with no apparent escape route.'

'Wait!' cried H. 'Look!'

They all turned. A shimmering, insubstantial apparition was heading their way; a figure of a woman making her way through the smoke towards them. Bits of the ceiling dropped off and fell straight through her, but she kept on walking towards them with a steady pace.

Finally, she arrived and gave all of them a ghostly smile.

'Turn around when possible,' said the ghost of Annie Chapman.

In the great entrance hall of Rosings, Elizabeth and Lady Catherine de Bourgh stood facing each other.

'Why me?' said Elizabeth. 'Surely you can tell me that? What have I got to do with all this?'

There was an ominous crack from above them, and a few chunks of ornamental plaster fell to the floor.

'Come outside before the whole place collapses,' said Lady Catherine, pulling on Elizabeth's sleeve. 'Then I will tell you.'

'No you won't. Tell me now, or I will die here and your spawn—if it is your spawn—will die with me.'

Lady Catherine gave her a look that seemed close to despair. 'All right then. But isn't it obvious? My people have studied your little planet for decades of your earth time. We grew to despise your race—except those of one country: the English! Such ambition! Such single-minded determination! We realised that, if we could but combine our forces, we could rule the galaxy together.'

'You're insane!'

'No. This is our destiny. We searched for one to bear the child—a woman who was intelligent, fierce and brave, who embodied all that was great in your people.'

Elizabeth gasped.

'Yes, you,' said Lady Catherine.

There was another hideous groaning noise from above them and the ceiling bulged slightly.

'It was also convenient that you came from a family of sisters.'

'I'm sorry?'

'In order to ensure that k'Ekkk's seed was not rejected, it needed to be modified in order to make it compatible with your family, so we had to take a sample from your sister.'

'Lydia! You fiend! What have you done with her?' Elizabeth grabbed hold of Lady Catherine now and shook her.

There was another groan from above and Elizabeth glanced up to see a statue toppling towards them. She released Lady Catherine and threw herself backwards.

Lady Catherine turned and looked up. She let out a ghastly alien shriek as the sculpture crushed her.

For an instant, Elizabeth wondered if she should try to help, but masonry was tumbling all around her. She had no choice but to run from the building.

Seconds after she reached the open air, the roof of the entrance hall collapsed.

Elizabeth could see most of the building was now ablaze. Oh great heavens! Was Fitzy still in there? And all the others? And what about poor Lydia?

'Hello, sis,' said a voice. Elizabeth turned and saw—Lydia! Silly, stupid, irritating Lydia.

Tears streaming down her face, she hugged her as if she would never let go.

'Excuse me,' said another voice. 'But may I cut in?'

'Fitzy! You too! You're alive!'

'I do believe we're all alive,' said H. 'Contrary to the laws of probability, the laws of logic and a good deal of the laws of physics if I'm any judge of it.'

'What about Lady Catherine?' asked Wickham.

There was an explosion from the front of the house. Flames billowed from the entrance hall.

'Dead, I think,' said Elizabeth, softly. She turned to Colonel Sutherland. 'Is it over, do you think?'

'I wonder if it will ever be over. Their plans have been badly disrupted and we have scored a decisive victory.

But I have no doubt they will be back one day. We must remain vigilant.'

''Tis wise to be cautious,' said Elizabeth. Then she remembered something. Something important.

She knew instinctively Lady Catherine de Bourgh was wrong. At least, she hoped she was.

'Fitzy dearest?' she said. 'I believe I may have some news for you.'

Epilogue

OUTSIDE THE HUT, a young girl ran barefoot in the mud. A couple of malnourished chickens looked on without interest, from a makeshift coop. Smoke wafted upwards from the remains of a bonfire.

Inside the hut, voices were raised.

'It's no good sitting there, Charlie,' said the woman. 'The traps won't bait themselves.'

'I know, I know,' said the man. 'It's just so demeaning.'

'Yes, well don't start blaming me for that.'

'Please, Jane. I've said I'm sorry.'

'Sorry won't put food on our plates, Charlie.'

'But I really am!'

'I know you are. But that doesn't change anything. If you don't go out and bait those traps, there'll be no rabbits. And no rabbits means we go hungry— again.'

'Actually, Jane, I've been thinking that perhaps a vegetarian diet might be more appropriate in our reduced circumstances.'

'Don't you even so much as mention it, Charlie Bingley. We may be destitute, but we still have standards. We can't allow our daughter to eat that kind of nonsense! What do you think we are? French?'

The man stirred from the box he was sitting on. 'Oh, all right—'

The door to the hut was violently flung open. Charlie

was momentarily dazzled by the light coming through the doorway. Then it was filled by a shadow.

'May I come in?' asked the stranger.

'Of course,' said Jane. 'Of course. Come in, old woman. Make yourself at home.' She waved her arms around in an expansive gesture that was completely wasted on the tiny space inside the hovel.

The newcomer sniffed and then lowered herself with great effort down onto a three-legged stool. Now that his eyes were adapting to the light, Charlie realised the stranger's face was covered with horrific scars.

'Good Lord!' he said. 'Are you all right?'

'I am as well as I can hope to be.'

'Can I get you anything?' asked Jane.

'For the moment, no. And in any case, I understand you are in no position whatsoever to provide me with any sustenance.'

'What do you mean?' said Charlie.

'I know all about you.'

'I beg your pardon? My husband is a simple woodcutter.'

'Oh, do shut up, Red Riding Hood,' said the old woman. 'I know exactly who you are and why you're living in this revolting little shack. I've come to offer you a deal.'

'What sort of deal?' asked Charlie.

'Husband of mine, I fear you've got us into enough trouble already,' said Jane.

The old woman said nothing but opened the bag she was carrying, positioning it so a shaft of light, from a hole in the wall opposite, shone into it. The interior of the bag sparkled and gleamed like a pirate's treasure chest.

'Great heavens!' said Charlie, shielding his eyes.

'Consider it a down payment,' said the old woman.

There was a brief pause.

'So what do you require us to do for you?' said Jane.

THE END

Mrs Darcy will return . . .
in Mrs Darcy versus The Monster!

Acknowledgements

Thanks to my wife Gail for putting up with me whilst I was writing this (in the hope that one day she may forgive me for trampling all over the legacy of her favourite author), to Mark and Rachel for not being too embarrassed by it all, to the best writers' group in the whole wide world, the Verulam Writers' Circle, for their encouragement (especially Toby Frost for that conversation in the Six Bells and Ian Cundell for being really quite annoying and refusing to let me give up on it), and to all the bloggers, facebookers and tweeters who spread the word while it was being serialised. Especial thanks to Steve Haynes at Proxima and everyone at Salt for having faith in the project. Finally, thanks to Miss Austen, without whose earlier efforts none of this would have been possible. Sorry, Jane.